I0653929

SAM GAO

MATTER OF SECONDS

THE TIMEKEEPER'S DAUGHTER
BOOK 4

Cover design by MiblArt.

Edited by Danielle Barthel.

NOTE: This series contains sensitive content, including but not limited to: Child abandonment; Child abuse in a foster care setting; Cult Activity; Eugenics; Forced Sterilization; Graphic violence, death, and murder; Gun violence; Human sacrifice; Kidnapping and torture; Mentions of illicit drugs; Mentions of racism and racial slurs; Mentions of sex/sexual acts; Mentions of sexual abuse against children; Underage drinking; Victim-blaming

E-book ISBN: 978-1-7376930-6-2
Paperback ISBN: 978-1-7376930-7-9

Dear Maria,

Last week, I decided to read several contemporary romance novels in preparation for our reunion. After being employed by Neil, I realize that I have not dedicated any time to learning your modern-day courting rituals.

I asked Allegra for suggestions, and she returned with a stack of well-worn paperbacks, some of which were quite inappropriate. Regardless, I managed to read through them with the digital translator device.

I must say, I find some of these customs odd. For instance, giving your beloved a bouquet seems ridiculous. If we were to exchange gifts, I would bring you a potted aloe plant. Which would you prefer, dead flowers or aloe to soothe your wounds?

And another thing—going to the movies on a date. Why? If you are attempting to form a deeper bond, would you not wish to speak to one another? I have learned that one is not permitted to speak in the theater. Last month, a young boy threw popcorn at my head because I asked Allegra a question.

There were also mentions in the books about the third date. I don't understand the significance, but when I asked Neil, he laughed at me. Allegra merely blushed. I am unsure why.

Yours,
Rhys

Dear Rhys,

If you want to learn about romance, maybe don't use chick lit as a guide. Reddit is much more reliable.

Dating is weird—I won't sugarcoat it. Not that I have a lot of formal experience. I've never received flowers from anyone. Unless you count that one time in eighth grade when Val Shepard told everyone I died, and they stuffed my locker with dead flowers and had a fake vigil.

Anyway, you don't have to get me flowers or aloe. When in doubt, always choose chocolate. Aloe might help with sunburns, but chocolate makes the entire world feel better. And French fries. Chocolate-dipped fries? Maybe.

We don't have to go to a movie on the first date, but I have a lineup of ones we could watch together. Mostly because I want to hear what you think about them.

Sorry you got popcorn thrown at your head. If it makes you feel any better, food at the theater is stupidly expensive. I thought Neil would have a home theater, but I guess not.

The third date rule is about sex, but you don't have to worry about that. It's a stupid expectation. People should be allowed to do that when they're both ready, not depending on the number of dates they've been on.

We can just go at our own pace, okay?

Mar

Chapter One
Mar

Going to therapy is like going to the gym. Instead of working on my muscles, I'll be spending the next hour working on my emotional baggage. Unfortunately for me, that baggage is heavier than any dumbbell.

Dr. Jones' office is in the south building, overlooking the sea. I guess she took inspiration from her location, because everything in the room is ocean themed. The walls are a pale blue, with large black and white prints of dolphins and jellyfish. I've never liked dolphins; their eyes are shifty. Almost like they're hiding something. Seashells and sand fill the glass lamps, and even her desk has a layer of sand dollars pressed under the glass top. I think the theme is supposed to have a calming effect, but the light colors do little to put my mind at ease.

I lean back on the couch while she sits across from me, settled in a velvet armchair with her notepad and pen. She's younger than I expected, probably in her mid-thirties, with ice-blonde hair gathered in a ponytail at the nape of her neck. She's not as polished as I expected her to be, with a few stray strands framing her face unintentionally. A lunchbox with Dory from *Finding Nemo* sits on the desk. If she put it there to lower my guard, it's working.

"So, Miss Rochester," she begins, leaning to one side of her chair. She's studying me, even though she tries to make it seem like she isn't, from behind her thick, black-rimmed glasses. "What brings you to my office today?"

"You can call me Mar. And are you *sure* there are no recording devices in here?" I ask.

"This room has been spelled to prevent listening devices. What you have to say to me is a hundred percent private." She makes a note in her notepad, probably something about me being a paranoid freak. We're off to a great start already. "Are you concerned about someone in particular?"

"Yes. But…I don't even know where to begin." How do you go about telling your new shrink that you think your biological dad is spying on you? We don't have a rapport built up, and I would rather avoid being sent to some shadowborn asylum. I know most of them in the US have shut down—I Googled it in the waiting room—but shadowborn are a bit backward in my experience. I doubt they make mental health a priority. I'm shocked they even offer counseling on campus.

"Why don't we start with your mental health history? Have you ever been to therapy before?"

"Yeah. It sucked," I say bluntly. "I mean, it never helped much. They put me in therapy when I was a kid, but only for a few sessions. Then, as a teenager, I saw a few counselors and three different therapists. Nothing helped."

"Why do you think that is?" she asks, her voice calm.

I shift in my seat. "I moved around a lot. The sessions weren't on a regular basis with the same person. I got tired of having to explain everything to new people. And I thought they were just trying to diagnose me or medicate me."

"Why did you move around so much?"

"Foster care." I used to think that was the root of all my problems. What a joke.

"I see. Do you want to talk more about that?"

"As I said, I wouldn't even know where to begin," I say flatly. "I've been in the system ever since I can remember. I was told my biological father was a drug dealer and was serving time. That's obviously not true, if you've heard the gossip around campus. But we can come back to that. Anyway, I was in the system for a long time. Moved around a lot, though I was able to stay in the same county. Douglas County, Georgia."

"I'm familiar. That's a small area."

"Yeah. Everybody knows everybody." Small towns like that breed rumors faster than you can say "dirty thieving whore." Which was ironically one of my nicknames in high school.

"Why were you originally placed in therapy, Mar?" Dr. Jones asks.

"One of my foster brothers hurt me, so I pushed him down the stairs." I shrug. "I guess I didn't act sorry enough. But I *wasn't* sorry. And neither was he."

"Can you tell me more about it, if you feel comfortable?"

It's never *comfortable* to talk about Max. He's the subject of my nightmares, and when I encountered an *actual* true-blood Nightmare to show me my deepest fears, Max showed up again.

"It's not that complicated. To be honest, I hate talking about it, but I can't deny the impact it made on my life," I explain, trying to keep my voice steady. I will not break down in front of a stranger, therapist or not. "Max—that was my foster brother—used to beat me up. He was ten years older than me, and his parents thought he was God's gift to the world or something. The parents were nice at first, but they let Max's behavior slide. I pushed him down the stairs. He was fine, I was put into a group home, and I felt like even after what he'd done to me was publicized, everyone still blamed me. *I* kind of blame myself, too."

"For getting hurt by him?"

"For not finishing the job." I pause. Maybe that was too harsh. She's writing a *lot* in that little notebook of hers. "Part of me was desperate to be loved. I know it sounds cliché, but it's the truth. I put up with a lot for the sake of love, which is strange because I don't think it was ever reciprocated—it's not like *I* loved these families. I just wanted *them* to love *me*."

"That sounds like a life-changing event." She pushes a box of tissues toward me on the coffee table separating us.

It takes a second for me to realize, to my utter horror, that she thinks I'm going to cry. How mortifying! I shake my head, declining the tissues. God help me. "Anyway, that was the worst experience I had in foster care. There were other unpleasant situations, but not matching that level of violence. Most of the other incidents I experienced were in school."

"What do you mean?"

"I was bullied." I pause again, smiling. "That sounds stupid to say aloud, too. The word 'bullied' is so juvenile."

"But the things done to you weren't childish?"

"No. I was beaten a lot. Sometimes I deserved it. Most of the time, actually," I amend. "And when you live with your bullies, there's no escape. They can attack you at any time. When you're sleeping, when you're in the shower...as long as you're alone and unsuspecting, you're a target. The older I got, the funnier it became to try and catch me when I was naked."

"You mean to say, you grew up feeling unsafe?"

"Isn't that a given?"

"No, Mar. It isn't."

I guess she has a point. "There are normal people, and then there's me."

"You don't feel normal?"

"No. I've seen normal people. People who grow up with families who actually love them. It makes me feel worse about myself. Not that I'm trying to throw a pity party or anything," I rush to say. "A lot of my friends in the system came out just fine. It's just me who's...you know."

"Comparing yourself to others can be a common habit, but it's not always helpful. Instead of focusing on what others are doing or achieving, let's focus on your own strengths and accomplishments, and how you can build upon them to reach your own goals."

"I haven't even explained to you just how fucked up I am yet," I blurt. "Wait, can I curse here?"

"This is a safe space, Mar."

"I've heard that before. But fine. Let's continue. So, after that whole incident with Max, I began...making 'characters.' Alter egos I would pretend to be. This isn't a dissociative identity disorder thing. I've never claimed to have that. But playacting as someone else was how I dealt with challenges. See, I'm the type of person to take things personally. When I'm a character, I don't. It's easier to move on, to stop being so obsessive and just pretend like all the bad things never happened."

"It's a method you use to adapt to new situations," she surmises.

"Exactly."

"Trauma can leave deep scars, and it's normal to deal with it in various ways. Why don't you tell me more about these characters, Mar?" Dr. Jones asks. "Is 'Mar' a persona as well?"

"*Mari* was my first character. A hothead. Pretty aggressive. She stood up for herself, though. I'm rarely ever Mari, anymore. She was always underdeveloped, and frankly, I'd get pummeled here if I pretended to be her." I already get beaten up here enough as it is.

"I see."

"Marilyn was my second character. I created her when I was a little bit older. She's named after Marilyn Munster, not Monroe. And that's just 'cause of her appearance, not based on her characterization in the show." I watch as Dr. Jones scribbles something down on her notepad. "*My* Marilyn is a bit of a slut, to put it kindly. She has no inhibitions. She's bold and not very well liked, but being Marilyn comes easier to me than other characters."

"Why do you think that is?"

"Because I never worry about being liked as Marilyn. I know everyone hates her. There's freedom in that."

"Do your other characters want to be liked?"

"Mary Alice does. She's the character least similar to my true self, I think," I say. "I was Mary Alice when I came to Southeastern. She's not offensive in any way, bland and plain. A girl-next-door type. Don't get me wrong—I don't want to *be* Mary Alice. Not really. But I had the best rate of success as her."

"She sounds quite different from your other characters. What prompted you to create her?"

"I needed someone to be likable. When you're well liked, people are nicer to you, of course. They'll do things for you." I wince. "That sounds pretty manipulative. But it's the truth."

"It's natural to change yourself to some degree based on your audience," Dr. Jones tells me. "I speak to my patients in a different way than, say, my mother. Your case is just more clear-cut. Did you feel that you needed to be manipulative growing up to get what you needed?"

"It would be nice to say that I lied because I wanted attention, or I was trying to avoid getting beaten up. And that's partly true. But there's a third option here that isn't clear to me. I do it without thinking sometimes. It's easier to lie than to explain everything to someone new, like what I'm doing here with you," I say. "I don't like feeling vulnerable. And people are inherently selfish. I learned that lesson over and over again growing up. There are exceptions, but it takes a lot of time for me to trust someone."

"And yet you're telling me this?"

"You're paid to listen to me. Besides, not to use this card, but I'll sue the fuck out of you if anything I say here gets leaked."

"Noted." Dr. Jones smiles. "Thank you for sharing about yourself, Mar. I feel like we've dug into some of the things concerning you. If I may shift the conversation back, I want to ask again if there's anything specific that you want to work on. What brought you into my office today? You mentioned therapy hadn't worked well in the past."

"I was younger. And very frustrated when a therapist didn't immediately understand where I was coming from," I confess. "I guess I thought it would be a good idea to talk to someone. I've always had nightmares, pretty regularly, but they've been so much worse over the past year. My father died. My foster father. He was…murdered. And I don't know how to handle that."

"I'm so sorry to hear that. That must be horrible for you." She says it like she genuinely means it.

"It's rough. And on top of that, my biological father is Neil Abbott. Have you heard the rumors?"

Dr. Jones shakes her head. "I have heard of Neil Abbott, but I'm not very in touch with campus gossip."

"Well, he's my biological father. He thought I was powerless and gave me up. The whole drug dealer thing was a big lie," I say bitterly. "We tried to keep it under wraps, but secrets don't seem to stay secret for long at Southeastern. Neil wants me to attend this school so I can train my powers, and until I do, I'm not allowed to speak to my family again."

I leave out the bits regarding killing Astaroth and Neil holding my family *hostage*. She doesn't need to know that.

"I understand. So you did not know about the shadowborn prior to last summer, and suddenly all this new information is dumped on you." Dr. Jones writes more in her notebook. "On top of it, you lose your father. And this new 'relationship' with Neil Abbott, who is your biological father, is very strained. Do you have a support system here?"

"Not in the least. Allegra, my half sister, hates me since finding out the truth: her father had an affair. She lost her mother, too, not long ago. Neil killed his own wife, because she was trying to kill me. It was a whole thing. My cousin, Nic Woolridge, is a piece of shit, and when he taunted me about my father's death, I broke his leg. There's Marshall, a student who absolutely hates me. He hit me in the face with a rock. And Lilly Hardwicke, who blames me for her sister's death—not my fault, by the way—and made my life considerably worse last semester. Archer Kinsey, who I made out with a few times, hates me because I lied to him about being Mary Alice. Oh, and I fell for a guy who, for certain reasons, can't be seen talking with me. So yeah. I'm on my own. But I prefer it this way."

Dr. Jones nods, taking it all in. "Building a support system takes time and effort, but it's worth it in the long run. I'm here to support you, and you don't have to go through this alone. It's brave of you to reach out for help, and I'm here to listen. Let's work together to identify people in your life who may be able to provide support, or explore ways to build new relationships and connections that can provide a sense of community and belonging."

"Even if I'm a total social pariah here?"

"You are not a social pariah," Dr. Jones says firmly. "Why don't we make a plan? I would recommend we meet once a week and work together."

"Thank you."

"Our time is up for today, but I want to remind you that I'm here to support you throughout your healing journey. If anything comes up between sessions, don't hesitate to reach out."

I didn't cry. Not that I thought I was going to. I know the whole "crying, sobbing breakthrough" won't happen until at least the fourth session. But even after I leave the office and make the long trek back to my dorm, my stomach doesn't settle.

I mentally prepped myself for the meeting beforehand, not wanting to say too much, but the truth ended up spilling out of me easily. I guess that's a good thing. Lying to a therapist, in my experience, doesn't help.

After everything that's happened so far, and my total inability to switch characters anymore, I figured therapy would be a step in the right direction. I already have the herculean task of killing Astaroth—that is, if I can even find him. Aside from Astaroth and Neil, my inner demons are my own worst enemies. Ironically, Astaroth and Neil are also demons, but the literal kind.

It's been a mild winter in Georgia, and Southeastern is just how I remember—a maze of Victorian houses set up like a small town with signs that are difficult to read from a distance. The school map on my phone isn't great, but I still manage to navigate back to the dorm house.

I haven't run into anyone I know yet, thankfully. I thought I'd see Allegra or Nic when I first arrived, since the three of us are staying together. Generally the dorms aren't co-ed, but since we're all related, and Neil donates to the school, they made an exception.

Frankly, I would have preferred they *didn't* make an exception. I hate being around Nic, and Allegra won't be much of a buffer anymore, considering she hates me, too. I know it's probably for the best that we stay together, considering Nic is a sleaze and I should keep an eye on him. Keep your enemies close, or whatever the saying is. But if I had it my way, Nic would be on the next rocket to Pluto.

When I arrived and no one was home, I decided on a whim to do a walk-in therapy session. It eased my anxiety a little, but now I'm back right where I started, standing on the wrap-around porch with my fist raised to the door. The entire house looks like it's been drenched in Pepto Bismol, but at least it's distinguishable from a distance.

This is stupid. I have a key. But with my heart hammering in my chest, I knock anyway.

The lights are on inside, and footsteps quickly approach the door. It swings open, revealing Nic Woolridge.

My cousin looks like a poser from a teen vampire movie. He's got brown hair like me, and bottomless brown eyes that are so dark they're nearly black. In contrast, his skin is pale, almost pasty. He's handsome, sure, but also a total asshole. And unfortunately, his leg has healed completely.

He smiles at me with an almost predatory look. "Well, well, well. Look what the bitch dragged in."

"Technically, I came by boat," I reply, not missing a beat.

Nic responds by punching me straight in the face. He doesn't hold back, using the full force of his fist to knock me right on my ass.

"Welcome back to Southeastern."

Welcome back, indeed.

Dear Maria,

I had the displeasure of meeting your cousin Nicolas today. While you had mentioned him before, I do not recall you detailing what a truly unpleasant individual he is. I find it difficult to be in the same room as him and would rather not even breathe the same air as him, for fear that his stupidity is contagious. He is the type of person who grates on my nerves.

Unfortunately, I cannot bring myself to throw away my pride and shut down my emotions in front of someone whom I so despise. It is a skill you have demonstrated in the past, such as with Prince Gwyn, although I must admit that Gwyn and Nicolas are very similar. They are both sadistic.

Worse, Allegra tolerates his untoward advances, though she does not reciprocate. I wonder about the relationship between them, but both are tight-lipped on the matter. Sometimes, I catch him watching her.

Yours,
Rhys

Dear Rhys,

Nic is a total asshole, isn't he? I'm sorry I didn't warn you about him, but I thought you'd figure it out eventually. And it sounds like you did!

My advice? Whenever he starts talking, just play a song you really like in your head. It'll help drown out his nonsense and make interacting with him a little less painful.

Mar

Chapter Two

"Fuck!" My eye immediately begins to water.

"Watch your mouth," Nic warns.

I knew he would be angry with me, considering I broke his leg the last time I saw him. In my defense, he was practically begging for it. Still, to punch me as soon as he sees me? Pretty uncalled for.

"I just got eyelash extensions," I inform him, raising a hand to my throbbing eye. He got me good. "I had to sit in the stylist's chair for two hours!"

"Do you want to get punched again?"

"Do *you* want me to break your other leg?"

Nic leans down, getting right in my face and shoving me back to the ground, pinning me to the deck. "I should just shoot you. Like how Neil—"

"Don't you *dare* finish that sentence."

"Or what?"

"Nic, calm down," Allegra says, emerging from the kitchen in the back. She's gotten even prettier since I saw her last, if that's possible. Her hair falls in long blonde waves, and her eyes are the same emerald green as our father's.

Allegra has always been beautiful, in a delicate, Disney Princess sort of way. She wears long skirts and turtlenecks no matter the weather to cover up her tattoos, magic seals to keep her powers at bay. When we were still getting along, she explained to me that she has some sort of autoimmune disorder of the magic variety, and the seals on her body are the only things keeping her alive. She gets sick frequently, leaving her bedridden for days at a time.

I don't see any of her previous fragility or kindness. Her eyes narrow to slits when she sees me. "Maria. You're back."

"Just call me Mar. It means 'sea' in Spanish," I say awkwardly. "It's good to see you."

"Is it? Or is that just another lie?"

Okay, I probably deserved that. "I'm being honest. I know a lot has happened between us, but now that we're going to be living together, I was hoping we could try to get along. Or at least *tolerate* each other."

Though, that would mostly be *her* tolerating *me*. I have no ill will toward her, but it's understandable that she's not my number-one fan at the moment.

"I don't care about anything you have to say, or any apologies you're going to make." Allegra puts a hand on Nic's shoulder. "Nothing you say will change what's happened."

She's right—but I don't intend on apologizing.

"Our living arrangement doesn't change anything. Stay out of my sight," she warns.

"Are you serious?" This isn't a large house, from what I can tell. We're going to run into each other—there are sharing living spaces. "We can't just avoid each other forever."

"I'm not avoiding you. You're going to avoid *me*."

"I know I'm pretty bad at problem-solving, but this doesn't sound like the best way to go about things—"

"You're my father's by-blow! I don't even want to *look* at you!" Her voice is raised so high, the birds fly out of the trees to flee the scene. I wish I could do the same.

"What the fuck is a by-blow?"

"Bastard. Mongrel. Illegitimate child. Don't you *read*?"

"Yes, I do!" Comic books, that is. "I think *you're* reading too many fairy tales, because you're acting a lot like an evil stepsister right now!"

"*Me*? You're the evil stepsister, not *me*!" she screams.

This conversation has taken a nosedive. I should backpedal. "Look, Allegra, why don't we—"

"There is no *we*, Maria. There will never be a *we*. There's you, and there's me, two completely different people who have nothing to do with each other."

Except for our blood relation. But sure.

She doesn't wait for a retort, storming upstairs and slamming her bedroom door so hard it shakes the entire house. Real mature. If our situation were reversed, I might have done the same thing. Knowing myself, it probably would have been worse.

I can understand where she's coming from, but it sucks to lose her as a friend. Not that we were extremely close or anything. But we got along, and while I did lie about *some* things, I wasn't trying to hurt her. How would I have even gone about broaching the subject of our blood relationship?

Whatever. There's nothing I can do about it, and frankly, this friendship crap is the least of my problems right now.

Nic stands around, enjoying the show as I stand and dust myself off. He doesn't stop me from going inside, right to the corner of the living room where I wheeled my luggage earlier.

The house is spacious, with an open-concept floorplan. A set of stairs separates the living room from the kitchen and the dining room. Thankfully, Neil didn't have a hand in decorating; there are no creepy statues or terrible artwork on the walls. Much like Dr. Jones' office, the color scheme is airy blue and white, with ocean-themed accents. Very clean.

I grab the handle of my suitcase and begin dragging it upstairs. This will be a challenge due to the impossibly heavy Divinities Sword inside, but hopefully the wheels will—

"Your room isn't upstairs," Nic informs me smugly. "You'll be staying downstairs, away from Allegra."

"In the basement? Again?" Last semester, my room was in the dinky, probably haunted basement of a different dorm house.

"It's where you belong. Unseen and underground."

"That hurts so much. I think I'll have to go downstairs right now and have myself a good cry," I say sarcastically.

Nic doesn't take the bait, leading me to the basement door, through the kitchen. "This won't be like your last semester here, Maria."

"No. It won't be." I know what to expect now. And I'm stronger. Mentally, not physically.

"Everyone here knows you're Neil's bastard," he continues. "That might be worse than everyone thinking you're human."

"What does it matter?" I wasn't well liked last semester,

and this semester won't be any different in that regard. I've spent most of my school days as a social leper. This is nothing new.

"Things are going to be different, Maria," he says again.

"You're right. Things *are* going to be different, because I'm Maria. This is what you wanted, right?"

I yank the door open and roll my suitcase down the stairs, into the darkness. Despite my trepidation, I spin to face Nic, not letting a single emotion show on my face.

"I'm going to tell you this once, Nic. Don't fuck with me. Or next time you'll end up with a broken neck instead of a broken leg."

With that, I slam the door in his face. Is there anything more satisfying than having the last word? I think not.

Turning the light on, I cautiously descend the stairs. The basement is finished, which is a nice surprise, and furnished. It actually looks like it was meant to be a bedroom, instead of just storage space. I take my shoes off before stepping on the plush shag carpet.

Boxes tower by the white desk against the wall, stacked neatly. I'm shocked Nic didn't throw them down here...or decide to snoop. But the boxes are all sealed.

I still feel around the mattress for hidden pins—you don't make that mistake twice—and find none. I guess this isn't summer camp with Shannon Snell all over again, and I'm just being paranoid. Did Neil say something to Allegra and Nic? I can't imagine he'd care if they bothered me.

Either way, it's time to get situated. I unpack the first box, mostly toiletries, and unload the contents into my own private bathroom. Making quick work of putting the room together, I end up with a stack of crushed cardboard boxes and a load of laundry to do. Luckily, the laundry room is right by the stairs.

I walk inside with the bin of clothes and sheets. Opening the top of the washer, I hear the door click open from the kitchen. Heavy footsteps echo on the stairs, and for a second I think it must be Allegra or Nic, here to pick another fight. But it's neither.

It's Rhys.

The moment I see him, relief floods me, and I can scarcely breathe.

It doesn't come as a surprise, seeing him here in one piece. His well-being was one of the first things I asked Neil about after coming back from the past. But hearing he was alive and confirming it with my own eyes are two different feelings.

He meets my eyes, his own a color somewhere between lavender and blue. You could cut the tension in the room with a knife, both of us frozen in place, unsure of how to react.

He moves first, silent as he breaks my gaze and moves to the dryer with a basket. Wordlessly, he begins taking out the clothes and folding them.

They're not *his* clothes, either. They're Allegra's. Jealousy shoots through me before I can clamp it down, and for a moment I wonder if he does *all* her laundry. I want to ask, but all my words get stuck in my throat, and I can't so much as make a sound.

This isn't exactly how I imagined our reunion going. I was picturing that scene from *The Notebook*, the kiss in the rain. I could've settled for a kiss in the laundry room, but Rhys is cold as ice.

My mind spins. His letters were all dated *before* the

Thanksgiving incident, before he got stabbed by Faith and I went back in time. What if his feelings changed, and he *is* in fact angry with me? Or, at the very least, hurt?

His eyes slide over me. "Were you not going to use the machine?"

For a second, I have no idea what he's talking about. I'm so caught up in my own head that I forgot about the task at hand. And even when I do remember, turning to the overflowing basket of fabric, I don't give a damn. All I want to do is stay here with him, even if we're not saying anything at all.

"Yeah," I mutter, opening the top. I begin loading in my sheets first, going slow as molasses while I sneak glances at him.

His hair is short again. Short*er* than when I last saw him, anyway. The pale blonde locks curl at the nape of his neck, unable to conceal the elongated elf ears poking out from either side of his head.

"How is your injury?" I ask finally. "Neil told me you took a few months to recover."

"I am fine." He speaks fluent English now, not Elvish. "You need not worry about me. Though perhaps you should be concerned about yourself, and your inability to take a pulse."

"I missed a lot of first aid class in high school," I admit sheepishly.

"Yes, I imagine you had more pressing things to spend your time on." Rhys bends to grab another armful of clothes from the dryer. I can't tell if he's angry or if he's just joking around, but either way, my stomach is in knots.

He could be uninterested in me after all these years. We spent more time apart than we did together—four years now, for him. But if that were the case, he'd have no reason to work in Neil's household, right? Unless...he's interested in someone else?

As much as it pains me to think about it, I know it's a real possibility that he fell for Allegra while serving her. Yeah, she might have been a bit crotchety earlier, but when we first met she was perfectly pleasant. And she's beautiful, more so than me—even with the hair treatments and eyelash extensions.

I shouldn't have assumed he would just wait around for me. If he's found someone else, I should be happy for him. But I don't *feel* happy for him. I want to cling to him and never let him go, which is either a sign that I'm head over heels for him, or my abandonment issue is rearing its ugly head.

What's *wrong* with me?

Rhys' elbow accidentally knocks a dryer ball over to the floor. As he bends down to get it, he says in a low voice, "We are being watched."

What? I try to discreetly scan the room, looking for any cameras, but I can't see anything. Are they hidden somehow?

"Watched?" I whisper, switching to Elvish. "By who?"

Rhys stands, ignoring me and picking up the basket of Allegra's clothes. He walks out without another word, leaving me all alone with a bottle of detergent in my hand and a thousand questions in my head.

Is that why he acted cold toward me? He knew we were being watched? Or is that just wishful thinking on my part?

Damn it.

I finish putting my sheets in the wash and turn it on. Exiting the laundry room, I do a thorough sweep of the basement, checking every crevice. It takes me hours and several Google searches, but I think I finally found all the cameras.

There are three on either side of the room, and listening devices behind the nightstand. There are none in the laundry room, walk-in closet, or bathroom. I'm not sure *who* set them up—it could have been Nic, Neil, or Allegra—but one thing's for sure: I'm changing in the walk-in.

I don't destroy them, because I know that if I do, they'll just be replaced. And next time, they'll probably be more difficult to find. But it's better that I know, so I can hopefully try to avoid revealing anything. I can also assume my phone and laptop are bugged. Not to mention, living with Nic and Allegra doesn't afford me much privacy, even if Allegra has decided to avoid me.

Well, whatever. A camera isn't going to stop me from doing what needs to be done, and neither will Nic and Allegra.

Chapter Three

I get up at 6 AM the next morning, dragging myself out of bed so I can make my way to Provost Mathers' office. I'm still bleary-eyed (and black-eyed) by the time I get to the main building, and when I open the door, he clearly isn't expecting me. Maybe I should've knocked first.

When he sees me, he lets out a yelp and spills hot coffee all over his shirt. "Shoot!"

"I am *so* sorry!" I frantically look around for paper towels. All I see are piles of books everywhere, and I don't think he'd appreciate me using *those* to clean up the mess.

Mathers pulls some from his desk drawer and dabs at his white button-down. "It's fine. I was just surprised, is all."

"The website said you held office hours from seven to eight, but I can come back."

"No need. Please." He gestures to a leather armchair while he mops up the rest of the spill.

"You got a haircut," I note, taking a seat across from him.

His dark red hair is cropped short, which actually makes

him look much younger than before, when he had a ponytail. He still dresses like a cowboy though, in a bolo tie and boots. It would look like a costume on anyone else, but for Mathers, it looks natural. Maybe he was born in the wrong time period.

"You got a new accent," he drawls, his own accent thick and somewhat comforting to my ears. "Again."

I ignore him, unsure if he's insulting me or simply making a comment. "I'm glad to see you back on both feet. Last time we saw each other, you were being wheeled away into an ambulance."

"No one told me you'd be back," he says, cutting to the chase. He cleans his hands with a wipe and settles in his chair, studying me. "I thought you'd be out for another semester."

"Where did Neil say I was?"

"Mr. Abbott told everyone that you were goin' to train your powers with a private tutor, in order to help you catch up with the other students. I advised against this—you were doin' well in your classes—but he insisted."

Wow, what bullshit. I expect nothing less from Neil. "Is your office spelled?"

"Pardon me?"

"Is it *spelled*? To prevent listening devices and cameras from recording," I clarify. Maybe I'm being paranoid, but you would be, too, if you found spyware in your room! "I want to make sure our conversation remains confidential."

"I do keep the room spelled," he confirms, bewildered. "That's not normally somethin' students ask me, though. Anythin' you tell me can be considered a private matter, as long as you're not a danger to yourself or others."

He says it like I really *am* a danger to myself and others.

I mean, I *am*, but for a different reason than he might assume. My homicidal, demonic biological father enjoys killing people I love.

Mathers could be lying about everything, but based on what I learned about him last semester, I don't think he's working for Neil. I've also done my own research, and beyond that, there's little else I can do to confirm his allegiance.

Mathers is a shadowborn siren, and demons and sirens don't have any sort of political relations in the Veil. Not to mention, since Mathers is shadowborn, aside from money, I don't see what he could gain by associating with Neil. There's always a possibility I'm overlooking something, but I can't deny that Mathers *has* helped me when it didn't always benefit him to do so. And, more importantly, I need some sort of authority figure like him to go to for guidance. Other than my therapist.

"Are you concerned about Mr. Abbott?" Mathers asks in a low voice. "I can assure you that he and I have nothin' to do with one another, Miss Rochester. My loyalty is to the school and its students."

"You can call me Mar, Provost. Everyone does." I take a deep breath. I've been thinking about what to say to Mathers for the past week, but all my mental preparations fly out the window as soon as I begin to speak. "Look, my main goal right now is to kill Astaroth. It's what Neil has tasked me with, and I have to follow through. I think we both want the same thing here. It would be in both of our best interests to stop him."

Astaroth broke free of the time prison on Mathers' watch. He hasn't said anything to me specifically, but I'm guessing he got some heat for that last summer.

"How will you stop him? Astaroth is strong, and last time we spoke, you were..."

"Not strong enough," I finish. "I know. But I didn't have the Divinities Sword."

"You have it?" His brows shoot up. "How?"

"That doesn't matter. What matters is finding allies to help me. I can't do this alone." As much as it pains me to admit, I have to be realistic about this. "Even if I manage to fight Astaroth, he still has his cult to back him. I need help. I don't even know where to begin *looking* for him."

"I see. In that case, what we need to do is twofold: find Astaroth and assemble a team of people to help you defeat him." Mathers catches on quickly. I like that about him.

"I also need more training," I admit sheepishly. "I can't actually lift the sword. It's heavy."

"It's heavy," he repeats incredulously.

"It *is*," I say defensively. Not even a normal shadowborn could lift it. "I can lift it. Maybe. I just need time to refine my strength and technique. Do you know anyone who could tutor me?"

"I will try to find someone." He doesn't sound very convinced, though. "Let's reconvene once a week. I'm glad you came to me about this, Mar."

I didn't have much of a choice, but I'm not going to tell him that and ruin the moment. I just know that I can't continue doing things on my own and expect better results. I'm going to get stronger, and I don't care what I have to do to achieve that. Even if it means going against my instincts and relying on other people for help.

I'm not looking forward to combat class again. Mainly because I know I'm going to get my ass whooped, and who really looks forward to that sort of thing?

Memories of my last semester flood back to me—the humiliation, pain, and frustration all bubbling beneath the surface of my Mary Alice façade. I don't *enjoy* being weak, and at the time, I felt helpless. No matter how much effort I put into training, nothing came of it. But this semester will be different. It *has* to be.

I try my best to ignore the penetrating stares as I step inside, scanning the bleachers for an empty seat. It's no exaggeration to say that at least half of the students are gawking at me, while the other half are stealing furtive glances, pretending they're not staring. Is it because I'm a bastard? Or maybe I have something on my shirt? I glance down, but everything seems fine.

Great. So, it's just because I'm illegitimate. Don't people have better things to do with their time than gossip?

I head to the end of the bleachers, keeping my chin up. Fake it till you make it, right? At least no one is heckling me or throwing stuff at my head, like during the freshman pep rally in high school.

The professor strides in just as I settle into my seat. He's a middle-aged man, balding, in a tracksuit and blindingly white sneakers. He looks like he's dressed for a workout, not for teaching. He starts talking, introducing himself and discussing safety precautions, but I can't seem to focus. Maybe it's because I've been up since six in the morning, or maybe it's his dull tone. Regardless, I find my mind drifting, daydreaming about my bed and a nice, long nap. It's only when he calls my name that I look up, startled.

"Miss Rochester," he says, his voice laced with impatience.

"I'm here," I call, giving a friendly wave.

He gives me a hard stare, on the cusp of a glare. "We're not doing attendance. If you find my class so boring, how about I add some excitement? Come down here. You're going to be the first demonstrator."

Uh oh. I do *not* like the sound of that.

I make my way to the front of the room, feeling like a specimen under a microscope. Every pair of eyes in the room are fixed on me, and I can't shake the feeling that they're judging me.

"Alright, can I have a volunteer?" the professor calls. He didn't write his name on the board, so I'm not sure what it actually is. "Oh, yes. Miss Hardwicke. Why don't you come on down?"

Of course it's Lilly. Because why wouldn't the one person who hates me most at this school get a teacher-sanctioned opportunity to beat me up?

It's not like she even has a valid reason to hate me. She blames me for the death of her sister, which I didn't have *anything* to do with. That was all Faith's fault, trying to pin the blame on me to get me away from Neil and Allegra. Not that her plan even *worked*. Obviously I never wanted Lilly's sister to die, but isn't blaming it on me too harsh? I've already been publicly cleared of suspicion, so it's not like she's unaware.

But apparently crime is thought of differently in the shadowborn world. Lilly looks at me now like I'm the devil, which is ironic since we're both descended from demons.

Last semester, I endured her harassment because I was Mary Alice and didn't know what else to do. I tried not to provoke her, hoping she wouldn't harm me, but now, things have changed. I won't kiss her ass just to make my life easier. Besides, I doubt that's what she wants.

As much as I dislike her, I can't deny that Lilly is different from the other shallow, unimaginative bitches who tormented me in the past. She doesn't demand that I grovel at her feet to humiliate me; she just wants to see me suffer.

Nic is the total opposite. *He* wants me to stroke his ego, like some weird form of validation. Either way, I'd rather scratch my eyes out than indulge him. I've been around the block enough times to understand that giving in to his demands won't make a difference. If anything, it will make the situation worse.

Lilly might be a sadistic bitch, but at least she's straightforward.

"Alright, ladies," the professor declares with a grin. "Let's see how rusty you've gotten over the break. It's time to spar. Two minutes, and the winner gets to enjoy an early exit from class."

Wow, what a bad incentive. Just two minutes?

Lilly doesn't need any convincing. She lunges straight for my throat, shedding any pretense of civility.

It's been a while since I trained regularly, and my fighting skills are probably worse now than they were last summer. To call them abysmal would be a total understatement. Lilly, however, has only improved with time, her movements fluid and graceful in contrast with my clumsy attempts at defense.

She starts our "sparring match," if that's what you want to call this one-sided beat-down, with a punch to my face. I try to keep up, but it's a lost cause. My vision blurs, and I can tell that I'll have two black eyes by the time this is over.

I can only hope that my eyelash extensions survive this brutal beating.

I end up having to curl into a ball on the mat like a pill bug. That doesn't stop her flurry of kicks at my back. Isn't the professor going to stop this? I already lost! Jeez. Maybe I'll just start showing up to this class in full-body bubble wrap.

I try to look on the bright side. At least I *expected* this. It's always much worse when you're ambushed. Getting punched in the face unexpectedly is a bit like a surprise party. Except instead of balloons and cake, you get a black eye and a bruised ego. And let me tell you, I've been to a lot of those parties in the past.

In the end, when the whistle finally blows to signal the end of our sparring match, Lilly wears a huge smile. But when she sees my expression, her face twists in anger.

"What are you laughing about?" she demands.

"I'm actually laughing *at* you," I say pointedly, though it doesn't come out very smoothly with my fat lip.

"Excuse me?"

"What, are you proud of beating up someone weaker than you?" I challenge, the words spilling out without much thought. "Come on. It's like playing a video game on the easiest setting and then bragging about it to your friends. It's a little bit pathetic, don't you think?"

At this point, I'm pretty sure I'm signing my own death warrant. I know this will only piss her off more, but I can't find it in me to care. I guess I'm not the type of heroine who takes the high road when given the opportunity. But I don't want her to be happy, any more than she wants *me* to be happy.

Lilly's face contorts, and she looks about as ugly as I do

right now. But before she can respond, the professor steps between us. Ah, now he steps in. I see how it is. Adults only come to the rescue when the danger has passed and there's no chance they'll get caught in the crossfire.

"Alright, enough," he says sternly. "We're here to learn, not to bicker like children. Let's go back to training. Ladies, take a seat."

We turn away from each other, but Lilly's anger practically radiates throughout the entire room. For the rest of class, I feel her glare on me—and I couldn't be more pleased. Because despite my facial swelling and battered body, I know I have something she doesn't.

I've played this game before, and while I haven't ever *won*, I've never lost, either. I don't plan on losing now—not to Lilly, Nic, or Allegra.

And certainly not to Neil.

Dear Maria,

I have recently started taking part-time culinary lessons on weekends. My instructor, Madame Annalise, imparts her knowledge to me via the video screen, which was arranged for me by Allegra. Admittedly, I am still not quite accustomed to modern technology.

As I settle into my new surroundings, I have come to realize that there are many skills that have eluded me. Due to my previous circumstances, I had little opportunity to learn the basics of homemaking, such as cooking and needlework. Although I have found cleaning to be relatively easy, Allegra has informed me that I am quite the perfectionist in that regard.

During my first culinary lesson, I acquired knowledge on how to create a simple breakfast dish. I must say, it went rather well. I look forward to preparing meals for you. Perhaps we may even work together to bake bread once more, with the hope of avoiding a similar calamity as last time.

Yours,
Rhys

Dear Rhys,

You're an amazing chef, and I'm looking forward to sharing a meal with you again. But this time, I hope we can eat together, instead of you preparing the meal and serving me.

Should we do breakfast in bed? Or is that against the rules of courtship?

Mar

Chapter Four

By the time dinner rolls around, I've got two puffy black eyes, a swollen wrist, and a mess of bruises on my back. All things considered, I'd say I made it through my first day of class pretty successfully. I didn't die, so that's something, right?

After taking a long, hot shower, I get dressed in a fresh set of clothes. A lightweight sweatshirt and leggings hide the injuries on my body, but when I look in the mirror, my face looks pretty bad. Like, monster-under-the-bed bad. I should ice it.

Stepping out of my closet, I head upstairs just in time to see Rhys pull a chicken out of the oven. The rich smell of rosemary and herbs makes my stomach growl.

He looks up, watching me as I approach. His eyes flick to my face, but he doesn't give anything away, even when we're alone.

In the past, Rhys might have been cold, but he didn't hold back his emotions to this extreme. Maybe after these years in the mortal realm, he's developed a talent for repressing his feelings. Or maybe he's not holding back anything right now, and he genuinely doesn't give a damn. But I can't go down that road.

"What are you making?" I ask. When I take a step toward him, he takes a step back. Am I radioactive?

"What does it look like to you?" he returns, his tone even.

"Something delicious?"

"It's not for *you,*" Allegra barks from the dining room. She's set the table for two—presumably for herself and Nic. Rhys never eats with them, being a servant and all. That's never sat well with me, but it's worse now since he's my...

Boyfriend? No. Lover? Nope! Courting...partner? Crush?

You get it.

But what does she mean, it's not for me? That's just childish. There's more than enough for all four of us.

"I'll take a plate and eat it downstairs, so my hideous face doesn't ruin your appetite," I suggest. "Please?"

"Not a chance," she says adamantly. Why does she care? It's just food. A girl needs to eat!

"Pretty please?" I needle.

"I'd rather throw it out than let you have a single morsel."

"That's just wasteful." But I won't press the issue further. I have a food pass; I'll just grab something from the cafeteria.

Why should I let Allegra's little temper tantrum bother me? Sure, it's annoying to be on the receiving end of her immature behavior, but I know it's just because she's struggling to cope with her new reality. After all, she's never had to share her father's attention with anyone else before, and losing her mother must be weighing heavily on her mind. It's not an excuse for her rudeness, but I won't let it get under my skin.

Nic waltzes downstairs, stopping in the kitchen once he spots me. "Wow, you look like shit, Maria. Did you piss someone off?"

"Of course. That's one of my daily goals, I'll have you know," I chirp. "I thought we had that in common, Nic."

He smiles. "I don't think you're fit to eat dinner with us, Maria."

"You mean I can't sit with you? I'm devastated."

"I don't appreciate freeloaders."

"I don't appreciate smarmy assholes, so I guess we're both going to be disappointed this evening." I take a water bottle from the fridge, along with an ice pack for my eyes, purposely moving slowly as I head downstairs.

As I settle into bed with my laptop, I can feel the weight of the day slowly lifting off my shoulders. Speaking with Provost Mathers was a step in the right direction, but I still have a long way to go before I can defeat Astaroth. I need to get stronger, but the traditional methods of training and magical weapons have failed me. That leaves me with the option of blood magic, something I've only dabbled in. It's time to fully commit. Provost Mathers may be on board with stopping Astaroth, but I know he won't approve of my methods. He doesn't strike me as an ends-justify-the-means kind of guy.

Well, I've always wanted to be a villainous heroine.

Okay, maybe that's not true. I've always wanted to be an erotica heroine. But since that's not going to happen, I'll be the villainous heroine instead. I don't care if I have to cross a few lines if it means securing the safety of those I care about.

I've even considered time travel as an option—killing Astaroth as a child—but it's not foolproof. And I definitely don't want to end up like those people who debate whether killing baby Hitler would have made a difference. Not that I'm comparing Astaroth and Hitler. I'm just saying, it's a topic of discussion in online alternate history communities.

But my blood magic skills are pretty limited. The only spells I know are cleaning related, which is not exactly helpful when it comes to defeating a powerful demon like Astaroth. And the worst part is, I can't even research more advanced spells because blood magic is forbidden and there are no dark magic grimoires at the library.

My one advantage right now is my time-traveling ability. I was able to find the Divinities Sword with it, so maybe I can use it to locate Astaroth somehow. However, I'm not sure I'm ready to face him just yet. He's been practicing blood magic for *much* longer than I have, and I doubt I can match his skills at my current level. Despite the odds, blood magic might be the only method I can use against him if the Divinities Sword doesn't work out. Always have a plan B.

Shutting my laptop, I go into my walk-in and close the door. Turning on the lights, I shift the clothes on the rack to my right. Hidden behind skirts and dresses lies a small safe and a wooden cabinet. I ordered both online, along with all the ingredients inside. Opening the cabinet with my key, which I keep in the safe, I lay down a plastic cutting mat and spread my materials.

The marble mortar and pestle are heavy in my palm, despite their small size. I weigh and pour sage, thyme, and eucalyptus together, smashing them with the pestle with a satisfying crunch. Then, after it's ground, I add the mixture to a small bowl.

Now, it's time to add blood.

A few hours later, I'm dizzy and starving. Cleaning up and bandaging my hand, I glance at my phone. It's 10 PM, and everyone is already in their rooms, so the kitchen should be safe to use without another tense encounter. Clutching the railing, I drag myself up the stairs, praying I won't collapse at the top. I think I used too much blood in my spells.

I check the garbage, and to my disappointment, I see half the chicken there, uneaten. She really *did* throw it out just so I couldn't have any. How petty.

And yet, relatable. I guess we're more alike than either of us cares to admit.

Going into the fridge, I scan the contents. Rhys keeps it, like everything else in the house, meticulously organized. My eye catches on something in the back—a Tupperware container of food. Pulling it out, I realize it's leftovers from tonight's dinner. There's a Post-It stuck on top, with handwriting scrawled in Elvish script. It says my name.

THE FOLLOWING WEDNESDAY, I ARRIVE AT PROVOST Mathers' office bright and early. The rest of the week went better than expected. My black eyes have healed, and while I'm still a social pariah, I prefer being alone. Now that I have a phone again, who needs social interaction? I've got access to social media. Plus, I'm on level 130 of Candy Crush.

The staring is getting pretty annoying, but I actually

look okay again. My hair may be a shade of brown that's about as exciting as a plain piece of bread, but thanks to a keratin treatment it's shiny and frizz free.

I'm just trying to stay positive and ignore all my anxiety and guilt by online shopping and scrolling through my feeds. Is that such a bad coping mechanism? Maybe. But I'm also going to therapy now, which means I don't need to psychoanalyze myself outside of Dr. Jones' office.

I make my way into Provost Mathers' office, greeting him with a cheery "Good morning!"

I'm relieved when his coffee doesn't spill this time.

"Good mornin'," he replies. "What happened to your hands?"

"Oh, nothing," I dismiss, shoving my bandaged hands behind my back. They're healing nicely, thanks to my shadowborn genes, but I don't think the scars will disappear for a few days. "Where did all your books go?"

"Spring cleanin'," he responds with a smile. "An organized office leads to an organized mind."

I raise an eyebrow. "So your boss came in, saw the mess, and reprimanded you?"

He nods sheepishly.

"Hmm, I don't think I've ever met the chancellor of this school," I muse, taking a seat.

"He's been on leave for several years doin' research in the Veil," Provost Mathers explains. "You would like him. He's a bit eccentric. Unfortunately, he's been a bit out of pocket these days. But he returned two days ago; he keeps the faculty on their toes."

"What is he researching?"

"Ferals. A few years ago, they started appearin'," Mathers says grimly. "It's an infectious disease that has spread through the beastblood community in the Veil. They didn't use to pose too much of a threat, but in your absence, the number of incidents has been increasin'. Now, we have to send out student huntin' groups every week to go into the Veil and eliminate some ferals."

"Wow."

"Yes, but that isn't what I wanted to talk about." He clears his throat. "I found a student who is willin' to train you. This program will be one hour every weekday. We discussed it, and in your case, we think it's best you focus on workin' out for four days, and learnin' sword techniques for one day. This will supplement your combat classes."

"Will that be enough?" I trained with Rhys for longer periods of time, but we didn't meet every day.

"I hope so," Mathers says. "We considered longer sessions, but there's only so much time in the day. You still need to pass your classes."

That's true. Between the coursework and the whole "kill Astaroth" thing, it's a wonder I have any free time at all. On top of that, I'm thinking of getting a part-time job at the library. I already applied, and I'm waiting to hear back. Considering I lied on my resume, I think I'm going to get the job. I'll be in the library anyway studying, so I might as well make some money while I'm there.

"Your tutor is comin' to meet us. He's on his way," Mathers says, glancing at his phone. "Before he gets here, I must ask—how are you adjustin' to life on campus? Any trouble with other students?"

"I've never been bad at adapting. I'm fine."

"I've heard that Allegra Abbott and Nic Woolridge are livin' with you."

"They live on the second floor, and I live in the basement. It's a good arrangement."

"You don't get along?"

"That's a mild way of putting it. They hate me, more like," I say casually.

"I have a hard time believin' that."

Is that a compliment? He can't imagine anyone hating me? That's sweet—and a little bit deluded. "Provost Mathers, it's not a big deal. I don't mind. I'm used to it. You read my file, right?"

"I realize that you were in foster care."

"This is exactly like that! People here are either completely indifferent, or they hate me. And they have no reason to help me out, so I'm pretty much on my own. I *like* this environment. I'm accustomed to it," I insist. "I'd rather deal with this than have people be nice to my face and talk behind my back."

Provost Mathers looks at me doubtfully. "You will tell me if someone is botherin' you, yes?"

"Oh, I stopped reporting bullying and harassment. It never helps." If anything, it makes the situation worse. The perpetrators learn how to get sneaky. "Don't worry about me, Provost Mathers. Since I've shed all pretenses, I won't take anything lying down. Both in the sense that I won't be a doormat anymore, and also that I've stopped whoring around."

"I must say, you are quite…different than before," he muses. "What incited this change?"

"I have a boyfriend now. I think. It's complicated. I'm not sure what we are, but I wouldn't cheat on him. I've never been a *cheater*, you know?" I pause. "You meant my change in attitude, didn't you?"

"Yes."

"Well, I was Mary Alice because she's the least offensive character I have. I thought that being her would make my social life easier. That didn't work," I explain. "So now, I say 'screw it.' Also, I can't switch characters anymore. I have a major mental block. But without my Mary Alice personality, I can be as vindictive and petty as I want and think about the consequences later."

It's very liberating.

"That sounds like a dangerous game," Mathers tells me.

I shrug. "It is. It's dangerous and it's not fun, but I still play. I don't know any other games."

My words hang between us and the silence is so thick that I can feel it like a heavy coat. Just when I think the awkwardness can't get any worse, a knock on the door echoes through the room like a sledgehammer.

I'm not sure exactly who *you* were expecting, but I wasn't expecting Archer Kinsey. He waltzes in with his perfect blond hair and chiseled jawline that could probably break a few hearts (and rocks) if he wanted to.

Archer takes one look at me and says, "Hell no."

Dear Maria,

I met your former paramour today, Archer Kinsey. From what you told me, I recognized him immediately. He is currently seeing Allegra.

My Maria, you are lovelier than anyone, but you have very poor taste in men. Archer Kinsey? Truly? He is a fool, and he lacks maturity. The mere sight of him incites a deep-seated anger within me. He has even gone so far as to accuse me of being jealous of his involvement with Allegra, which only reinforces my belief that he is a buffoon. I am astounded that you could have ever harbored feelings for such a person.

Perhaps it is only because you and I have not yet met. I assure you, I am still studying methods to woo you once it is appropriate to do so. I suppose you will see the results of my efforts one day.

Yours,
Rhys

Dear Rhys,

First, Archer isn't my paramour. Secondly, that phrase is totally outdated.

To tell you the truth, Archer was a mistake. I make a lot of those, especially when I'm desperately trying to make myself feel better about the situations I have to face.

I know I have terrible taste in guys. Aside from you, I don't have the best record with men. But it's kind of cute you're jealous.

On another note, what the heck kind of study materials are you using? Not more romance novels, I hope!

Mar

Chapter Five

I don't exactly expect a *warm* welcome when I see him, and I guess I deserve his somewhat harsh reaction. Still, it kind of stings.

"Archer is the only one you could find?" I exclaim, spinning toward Mathers.

"I didn't realize *you* would be the student in need of tutoring," Archer says icily. He's almost as good as Rhys at icing me out. At least I know for certain that this isn't an act. "I wouldn't have accepted, had I known."

"I figured as much. That is why I didn't mention it," Mathers replies calmly. "Unfortunately, Mar, Archer is your best chance if you want to improve quickly. Archer, I won't demand you tutor her, but at least consider it."

"With all due respect, Provost, she is a liar," Archer accuses. "She's a class-A manipulator. I don't even like being in the same room as her right now."

Okay, I get that he doesn't like me, and I won't dispute the fact that I'm a liar. But isn't he being a *little* dramatic? I lied about my name, and a bit about my past, but I don't think I crossed any lines when it came to Archer.

If anything, *I* should be angry with *him*! He didn't want to be seen with me in public, but he had no problem sneaking around with me in private. And when push came to shove, he didn't even have the decency to defend me *or* Allegra when we were being attacked by our classmates. He just stood there like a bump on a log.

To my surprise, Mathers defends me. "Mar has her quirks, but she's not a bad person. I believe her cause is noble, and she has matured over the past year. Just give her the opportunity to prove herself."

He has more faith in me than I have in myself.

Archer snorts. "I can't. She hasn't even apologized for what she's done. She just disappeared without any notice."

"There were other circumstances," I say. "Look, I know we don't have the best track record here, but—"

"But nothing. I don't want anything to do with you."

Anger floods me. *He* doesn't want anything to do with *me*?

"Fine," I snap. "I don't need you. I'll find someone else to tutor me. Someone who doesn't hold grudges like a *child*."

Yeah, yeah, I know. Pot, meet kettle.

"You're not going to find anyone else who can help you like I can," he says, sneering.

I put my hands on my hips. "What, are you going to change your mind now?"

"No," he says, his voice low. "But you're going to apologize for what you did to me."

"Well, people generally apologize when they're sorry. And I'm not sorry," I lie, the twinge of guilt in my gut intensifying. But I plow ahead anyway. "I had my reasons for lying, not that you give a shit about them. Don't even pretend to be Mr. Holier-Than-Thou, because you're not. I could grovel on the ground and start apologizing right now, and you'd still refuse me. You're just like everyone else. Nothing I say or do will ever be good enough for you."

Wow, where the hell did that last part come from?

Both men turn to look at me, and I can feel their disapproval like a physical weight.

Archer opens his mouth to respond, but Mathers cuts him off. "Alright, let's just calm down and talk this out. There has to be a compromise we can all agree on."

I'm not convinced, but I hold my tongue and wait to hear what they have to say. Maybe there is a way to salvage this mess. But I'm not holding my breath.

"There's no compromising," Archer says. "I'm out of here."

As he storms out, slamming the door behind him, I can feel my frustration mounting. "Well, that could've gone better," I mutter to myself.

Provost Mathers gives me a withering look. "Are you serious right now, Mar? 'I'm not sorry.' Why'd you have to say that?"

I know he's right, but I bristle at his criticism. "Archer is mad because I lied to him. But apologizing when I don't mean it…what good would that do? It's like putting a Band-Aid on a broken arm. It's not going to fix anything. It would be disingenuous."

Not that I have a leg to stand on, as far as that's concerned.

"Mar, I hate to break it to you, but you can't defeat Astaroth with just your powers and a snarky attitude," Mathers chides me. "You also need to work on your social skills and figure out how to communicate effectively with others. This is a lesson you have to learn if you want to become stronger."

I roll my eyes, but inside, I know he's right.

SPELLCRAFT SHOULD BE INTERESTING, RIGHT? THAT'S what I thought before I realized I'm a mere observer in this class. I can't cast spells without blood, so I'm stuck watching everyone else have all the fun. And let me tell you, observing other students is worse than watching paint dry. On top of that, my lack of sleep is starting to catch up with me. I thought therapy would help with my nightmares, but it's not like I'm magically cured or anything.

I'm still dragging myself to therapy, though. Dr. Jones says that building habits are important, and I assume she meant building good habits like drinking lots of water and taking your vitamins every day. Not the bad habit of practicing blood magic in your closet at 3 AM when you can't sleep. At least that's one aspect I'm improving in, even if the improvements are incremental.

By the end of spellcraft class, I'm barely conscious. It isn't until the teacher gives me a poke that I jolt upright and sluggishly walk to the door.

Maybe it's the sleepless nights or the horrible eating schedule I'm on due to being unofficially banished from the first floor of the house, but my head is spinning like a blender.

I make my way toward the girls' bathroom, holding onto the wall until I'm safely inside. Heading to the window, I take a seat—not by choice—and dig into my bag for a granola bar. My head still pounds against my skull, but at least with some food in me, the wave of dizziness passes and is replaced by nausea. If I didn't know any better, I'd think I'm pregnant or something.

But let's be real, to get pregnant, I'd have to have sex. It's been a dry few months, and I don't even know what Rhys is to me anymore. I want to believe, based on his letters, that he's in love with me. But what if that's just wishful thinking? I initially thought that he was acting cold because he didn't want Neil, Nic, and Allegra to figure out our connection. The thing is, Rhys is a good actor. He even has me convinced.

It's not that I *need* him by my side or anything, but it would be nice to have someone in my corner, someone who doesn't actively avoid me or glare at me in the hallways. I mean, I don't need a parade or anything, just a friendly face. Is that too much to ask for?

But I know better than to try and force someone to like me. You can't control other people's emotions, no matter how much you wish you could. Love, like empathy and regret, is something that needs to come naturally. And the fact that I'm even worrying about this is pretty pathetic on my part.

I take a deep breath and mentally slap myself to shake off the negative thoughts. As much as I'd like to collapse into a teary, sorrowful mess, I know better than to give in to that impulse. It just makes things worse.

Instead, I head to the nurse's office. I should grab some more bandages and painkillers before the start of my shift at the library. I'm working there part-time now as a shelver, which isn't the most exciting job, but at least I'm getting paid minimum wage for it.

The nurse's office is upstairs, but when I walk inside, she's not there. Instead, Allegra lies down on the single bed inside. She sits up when she sees me, her lips twisted into a frown.

"What are you doing here?" she asks, though her voice lacks venom. She just sounds exhausted, like she doesn't want to be bothered by me. The feeling is mutual.

"Just picking up Advil and bandages," I reply, going into one of the cabinets.

"You aren't allowed to do that."

"Are you gonna tell on me?" I pluck a few packages of gauze from the shelf and stuff them into my bag. "Hey, do you remember when we first met?"

Allegra stares at me for a long minute, her lips pressed into a thin line. Finally, she says, "No, not at all."

A laugh escapes my lips. "Now who's the liar?"

"Still you."

I shrug. "Well, if you choose to selectively forget, let me enlighten you. We were on the ship, and I had been injured. You were in the infirmary at that time, and you helped me."

"I wouldn't have, if I'd known who you were," she snaps.

"Are you pissed because I lied to you? Or are you pissed because your dad cheated on your mom?" I ask her. "You can't get mad at him, so you're redirecting your anger toward me?"

Maybe therapy is paying off, after all.

But I'm sick of fighting, sick of these social politics. Maybe Dr. Jones is right, and my mental health is taking a blow due to my lack of a support system.

"You wouldn't understand."

I shouldn't be pressing my luck, especially not when it

comes to her. But I just can't help myself. "What wouldn't I understand?"

"You wouldn't understand what it's like to lose a father!" she snarls.

My body locks in place, sheer rage settling into my bones. "You're kidding me, right?"

The contempt is clear in her eyes. "I don't want to talk to you anymore."

I could tear her apart with my bare hands right now. Fuck civility.

At the moment, I don't care that she's hurting. She just crossed a major line, and while arguing with her won't solve anything, I can't let her walk away after saying that. I'm seeing red, and my instinct is to use whatever words I can to make her feel as awful as I do.

I don't understand what it's like to lose a father? How exactly has she "lost" Neil?

She's the one who doesn't understand. And I can't force her to.

But when I see her face, *really* look into her eyes, she seems like she's holding back tears. And immediately all the fight drains out of me.

I take a deep breath. "Ignoring me won't make me go away. You *know* I'm not here to take your place. I don't even *want* to be here. I want to go home. *My* home. Neil is forcing me to stay because—"

"Stop *lying*," she seethes. "You're lapping up being special and having a rich real father, aren't you? You enjoy it more than being some plain Jane. Or should I say, plain Mary Alice?"

"You're delusional!" I explode, unable to control my volume or my words. My body trembles with undulating fury. "Do you honestly think that? If you do, you don't know *anything* about me."

"And whose fault is that?"

"Neil's! What do you think I could have told you about my past without revealing the fact that we're siblings?"

"We are *not* siblings!" she screams. "You are not one of us! You are illegitimate and nothing you ever do will change that!"

"Do you think that hurts, Allegra? Do you think I haven't heard some variation of that all my life? I have no control over who my parents are, any more than you do. Pointing it out doesn't change anything. It just makes you look pathetic. Can't you come up with a better insult?"

Her eyes narrow. "I am *not* pathetic, Maria."

"Sure, whatever you say. But the fact remains that we're both pawns in Neil's game. Whether you like it or not."

Allegra's jaw clenches, but she doesn't respond. For a moment, we stand there in silence, the tension between us palpable.

I've let her involvement in Luke's death slide, because it wasn't her fault or intention. But then she brings him up, and it's like a knife twisting in my gut.

"Whatever happens between us, I hope you know that it's your fault," she finally says, her voice low and angry. "You betrayed my trust first. You lied to me. You were just laughing at me behind my back."

"When did I laugh? When Neil killed my father? When he took my family hostage and erased their memories? When your mother tried to kill me? I was never *laughing* at you, Allegra. And while I did lie to you, how in the world do you think I could have told you the truth? Even without my family's lives hanging over my head, how would I have told you that your father cheated on your mother? Is that even something you would've wanted to hear from me?"

As she storms out of the room, I can't help but feel a small sense of satisfaction mixed with guilt. Maybe I should have just apologized and made things easier, but the stubborn part of me couldn't bring myself to do it. Especially not to Allegra, who always seems to have the upper hand in our family dynamic.

But I don't have time to dwell on it. I need to focus on my job at the library for now. As a part-timer, I don't have any time to waste on family drama. And let's be real, there's always plenty of that to go around.

Dear Maria,

I had yet another unpleasant encounter with Archer Kinsey today. He again accused me of harboring feelings for Allegra, and has warned me to stay away from her. To make matters worse, he did so while I was serving him food. Should I have added chili flakes to his sweet tea?

I cannot fathom the inability of this society to comprehend that members of the opposite sex can be friends without romantic involvement. I am not even Allegra's friend. I am her father's employee.

Despite my vehement denials, Archer refused to listen to reason. That is not uncharacteristic of him. But his opinion does not sway me as much as yours does.

I miss you.

There is simply no other way to express it. I find no enjoyment in watching television or movies, listening to music, or reading novels without you by my side to discuss them with.

This separation is unbearable. We should not be kept apart in this manner. My heart yearns for the day when we may once again be reunited.

Yours,
Rhys

Dear Rhys,

That's funny. I'm having trouble with Archer right now, too! He hates me, and I'm pretty sure it's because he's jealous of my awesome hair. (Just kidding, he hates me because I'm a liar and kind of a bitch. Valid.)

Anyway, I need him to do me a favor, but I have no idea how to make him un-hate me. I mean, I'm not exactly the most convincing person, unless I'm lying, which is what got me in trouble in the first place.

I really miss our tutoring sessions, even though you were pretty tough on me. Who knew running laps in the scorching Georgia heat could be so fun? And by fun, I mean I almost passed out a few times.

But seriously, I wish you were still here to help me out with Archer. You always knew how to deal with difficult people, whether it was with kindness or a well-timed sarcastic comment.

Mar

Chapter Six

"So, should I stalk him or what?"

Dr. Jones looks at me, completely unamused. She can't take a joke, I've learned. "Mar, let me see if I'm getting this right. You want to befriend your ex-boyfriend?"

"He wasn't my boyfriend," I correct. "We just kissed a few times. That doesn't count."

"I thought you said you went on a date?"

"Yeah, like once." He took me to a state fair on the mainland, which was admittedly sweet. "Just because you kiss someone and they take you out doesn't mean you're their girlfriend."

She writes that down. "And now, you need his help, which is the only reason why you are approaching him again."

I snap my fingers. "Bingo."

Dr. Jones hums. I hate it when she does that. It means she disapproves.

We sit in her office, surrounded by shells. I scheduled appointments every Thursday, between my classes and my shift at the library. Unfortunately, the sessions aren't in the main building, so it's a bit of a trek back and forth. But I can use the exercise.

"And you aren't apologetic at all for lying to him?" Dr. Jones asks.

"I lied about my name and my family situation. And about being human. I was honest about the important things. I didn't lead him on."

Trust me, I thought about this a lot. I tried to remember every interaction we've had so far, and while my memory isn't perfect, I communicated my feelings to him pretty clearly when it came to our relationship.

But instead of explaining this in a calm, rational manner, I say, "I'm not sorry at all. He watched as his *friend* hit me in the face with a rock and tossed me into a Nightmare den. Didn't lift a finger to help or say anything in my defense. And did I tell you he lied about getting me help?"

"Are you angry because he did not rush to your aid?"

"He didn't help Allegra when she was pushed into a pool, even though he *knew* she couldn't swim. It's not just about me—it's about seeing someone in danger and not doing anything about it, all for the sake of his vanity," I say, getting angrier as I continue. "He never wanted to see me in public, and the only time he invited me to a place where we could be seen by other people, it was a masquerade."

Dr. Jones scribbles furiously in her notebook, her pen moving so fast it's a wonder it doesn't catch on fire. I swear, if I blinked I would miss an entire paragraph of analysis. I wonder if she's ever considered taking up a career in stenography, or if her hand gets a permanent cramp from all the notetaking during our sessions. "Have you stopped to consider if you misinterpreted some of his actions?"

"Yes." No.

"Really?" She tilts her head to the side. "From what you told me last week, he would hardly have had time to bring you around to his friends. Maybe he wasn't ashamed, but rather, he had other reasons for not associating with you."

"And letting Allegra almost drown?"

"As much as it pains us to admit, some people *do* panic and freeze in the face of danger," Dr. Jones says. "Just because you might not necessarily do that, doesn't mean other people won't. You say he's a coward, but it's possible he is just ill-equipped to deal with confrontation and doesn't know how to act. On top of that, he might have lied because he was afraid to admit it to you, a girl he was trying to impress."

Damn. "Does that make me a bitch?"

"No. It just means you might not understand each other well." Dr. Jones folds her hands in her lap and sets her notebook down. "I've noticed that you don't seem to be a naturally inquisitive person. You tend to take people and their actions at face value. That's not to say you're incorrect —the people in your life have certainly given you cause to do so. Did you feel like, growing up, you had to make snap judgments of your foster families every time you entered a different home?"

"Well, I needed to know whether to unpack or not."

"What would make you not unpack?"

"Bruises on the other kids. Empty alcohol bottles. Locks on the pantry and cabinet doors. I wasn't usually wrong about those things. And I'd rather be wrong than…you know."

"I don't."

"You do," I insist.

"Do you find it difficult to say, Mar?"

I shake my head. "No. Not at all."

"Is that so? Because you seem to be unable to admit to it now," Dr. Jones points out. "You told me during one of our early sessions that you had a lot of 'neutral' homes—neither good nor bad. But every home you've spoken about has been physically or emotionally abusive in some way."

"That's not true," I say in a small voice.

"Really?" She picks up her notebook again and flips backward. "The Robinsons—neglect. The Moores—food restriction."

"They locked *all* the cabinets," I remind her. "Not just the ones containing food."

"You told me you went to bed hungry because if you weren't home at five o'clock sharp every day, you missed dinner and had to go without food until breakfast."

"It was just a rule of the household. It doesn't count as abuse," I say warily. "It wasn't personal. They made all the kids do it."

"The Browns—physical abuse."

"Of their other children. They didn't hit the girls. They didn't lay a hand on *me*."

"But you thought they could. You didn't feel safe."

"They didn't hit me."

"The Andersons—verbal abuse. The Harrises—neglect. The Martins—overprotection and slut-shaming. The Jacksons—isolation. The Millers—obscenity." She pauses, stopping entirely when she sees my expression. She moves the box of tissues over, but I refuse like I always do.

"I'm not crying," I say defensively, my heart hammering in my chest. "Those things…they weren't always the parents."

"But you didn't feel safe or loved in any of those households, did you?" she asks softly. "I need you to understand that abuse is *never* okay, no matter what form it takes or who is involved. You deserve to feel safe and respected in all your relationships."

"That kind of stuff happened to everyone," I explain. "All the foster kids I know dealt with it, and worse. And I was *glad* when the Harris family and the Robinson family left me alone. The Anderson kids said some hurtful things, but they were just words. Nothing I hadn't heard in school. The Martins, too. At least they cared enough to ask me about what I liked to do. And the Millers were just careless. Their daughter hadn't known I was in the room, otherwise she would have never watched that movie. The Baker family was the worst, followed by the Smiths. And the group home wasn't so great either. But everything else..."

"It's common for survivors of abuse to compare themselves to others and minimize their own experiences. But I want you to know that your feelings and experiences are valid and important, regardless of what other people have gone through. What happened to you was wrong, and it's important to acknowledge the impact it's had on your life."

"I *wasn't* abused," I insist. "Max was the worst offender, but that's it!"

"Mar—"

"My childhood was fine, for what it was. It sucked sometimes, but there were good times, too. We don't talk about that here, do we?" I ask. "The Andersons took Tash and me to the park once, during the weekday. We got to skip school for the family outing. We got to eat ice cream and play on the swings all day."

"And what did they call you after you threw up in the car due to motion sickness?"

My mouth dries. I didn't realize I had already told that story. "It doesn't matter. Tash and I had fun that day. *That's* what I remember."

"Mar, you have a difficult time admitting to these events. Do you feel ashamed of what happened?"

"I..." I struggle to come up with the right words. It's like a frog is caught in my throat. "Do you know what it will cost me?"

"I know it's difficult. I don't mean to force you," Dr. Jones says gently. "Healing is a process, and it can take time. We can work together to help you develop coping skills and self-care strategies to manage any difficult emotions that come up. When you're ready, we can start to explore your experiences more deeply and help you work through any trauma that you may be carrying with you."

"I'm not carrying *trauma,*" I say. "I'm fine. I'm...I'm perfectly fine."

If she says "It's okay not to be okay," I swear I'm running out the door. But to my relief, she doesn't. She doesn't say anything at all.

Being honest with myself isn't easy. Being honest with Archer *is,* but it won't yield the results I want. There's a line between "brutal honesty" and "honesty" and I can never tell when I'm crossing it. To me it's an all-or-nothing game.

Maybe that's why I can't think of ways to make up with Archer. Aside from my complete lack of social skills. I've practiced what I could say to him in the mirror, asked for advice online, and then practiced some more. Nothing seems good enough.

I'm not being honest because I *want* to be. I need something from him. We both know that.

When I can't come up with a plan, I do what I've always done: wing it and hope for the best.

Standing outside his dormitory isn't the most productive use of my time, but it's necessary. It's not like I have any better options, and at least the students on campus have gotten over staring at me like I'm a three-headed ogre. So I wait, shifting my weight from one foot to the other and trying to ignore the grumbling of my empty stomach. Finally, he shows up around dinnertime.

Understandably, he's not happy to see me. "What are you doing here?"

"Waiting for you," I say cutely. Or, *I* think it's cute. He doesn't, judging by the expression on his face. Yikes, tough crowd. "Can we talk?"

"There's nothing to say."

"I don't think that's true."

"I'm not interested in training you, Maria," he says firmly, adjusting the bag on his shoulder. He must have had a busy day, if he's just getting back from class now.

"Mar," I insist. "No one calls me Maria, unless they're trying to get under my skin. Like Nic. And, more recently, Allegra."

"So what? You're here because you have nowhere else to turn? Because you think you can manipulate me further?"

I know we're arguing semantics now, which is never a good thing. "I didn't manipulate you. I lied about my background, but—"

"Your background *is* important. You misrepresented who you are," he insists. "You even put on a fake accent."

"My accent isn't *fake*. I've just learned to temper it based on who I'm speaking to." In truth, I used to have a very thick drawl. But one family I stayed with told me I had to fix the way I spoke, because I sounded like a hick. So I did, imitating movies and television shows I saw. Now, the drawl only comes out naturally when I'm angry. "Don't you change the way you talk depending on the audience?"

"No, I don't. That would be dishonest," he says pointedly. What bullshit!

"Oh, so you talk to your friends the same way you would talk to a teacher?" I press. "Did you talk to *me* the same way you spoke to Allegra when you dated her?"

"That's not the point."

This isn't going how I thought it would. "What would have been the dealbreaker for you, Archer? The fact that I'm a demon? That I'm a bastard—which I only *just* found out, by the way?"

"You're a bitch."

My cheeks burn, and it feels like he just slapped me. I *know* I'm a bitch, but hearing him say it…

It doesn't hurt, I tell myself. *He can't hurt me.*

But I can't deny it's unpleasant all the same. "I didn't lie because I wanted to *trick* you."

"No. You did it because that's just who you are, isn't it? A liar."

"Exactly! It wasn't about you at all," I snap, my frustration bubbling. I hate this situation, and I hate even more that I can't explain myself properly to him. Or anyone else, for that matter.

"Then can't you understand that I don't want to deal with a liar like you in any capacity?"

"I'm a liar," I admit slowly. "But you're a coward. You can call me whatever you want. That won't change who *you* are, too."

He shakes his head, turning on his heel. And, for the life of me, I can't think of anything to say to get him to stay.

Whatever. This was a stupid idea in the first place. Archer isn't the only one who can train me—I don't care what Provost Mathers thinks. I can find someone else and work things out on my own.

And I know just where to start.

Returning to the dorm, I sneak in the back door and head straight to the basement. Locking the door behind me, I make a beeline for the closet and turn on the light.

"Jenna?" I call, breathless. "Jenna, where are you?"

I *know* she can hear me.

Jenna Cooper is a Time Agent. When we first met, she tried to kill me. Now, she's tasked with helping me...I think. I don't actually know what her goal is, but it involves protecting me.

The door to the closet opens, and Jenna steps out. Behind her, the light from the sterile, all-white Infinity Hallway is blinding.

Jenna shoves her hands in her pockets. She's in her 50s now, with streaks of grey in her bun. Every time I see her, she seems to be a different age. Time travel gets *weird*.

Unlike me, Jenna needs to use the Infinity Hallway to time travel. She doesn't seem to have much of a say in where she can go, outside of her mission to protect me. Still, she seems to be in a good mood. It's a nice change of pace, since the last time we spoke, she wasn't very happy with me. No one seems to be, these days.

She smiles, her dark eyes curving. "Long time no see, Mar."

"Hey, Jenna. I need your help," I say, cutting to the chase.

"Oh." She looks around the closet, rifling through a few of the hangers. "Well, I wouldn't say you need *help*. I would say you need a total revamp. Like, dump all these clothes and just start from scratch."

"Not with my *wardrobe*."

"Seriously?" She holds up a dress. "Did you buy this from Ugly Clothes 'R' Us?"

I need a minute to pick my jaw off the floor before responding. "That's not even clever! What's wrong with that dress? Wait—don't answer that. I don't care. I need your help with *blood magic*."

The hanger dangles on two fingers as she shoves it in my face again. "Are you positive?"

Yes, I'm positive I'm going to smack her in a few seconds. "Do you think you can help or not? I need training."

I'm not getting that far on my own. There are only so many cleaning spells I can master, and there aren't any spare blood magic grimoires just lying around.

"I mean, I *could* help," Jenna muses, leaning against the doorway. "I trained those humans who infiltrated the cruise ship. You remember that?"

"You mean, when you tried to sacrifice me?"

"No, that's not fair," she says, wagging a finger at me. "I only tried to kill you. Penny Bennett is the one who wanted to sacrifice you. And you're not allowed to get mad about that anymore, because you slit her throat."

"Technically, I stabbed her in the neck." Because she chased after me with a knife, trying to kill me. She literally stabbed Archer in the back.

Jenna plops down on the carpet, folding her legs in a pretzel. "Fine. I can help. I'm just surprised you'd even ask me. But I guess you don't have anyone else to turn to."

Sadly, she's right. I can't tell anyone I'm practicing blood magic, seeing as it's illegal in the shadowborn world. I know very little about its usage and limits, particularly compared to regular magic.

I kneel by my wooden cabinet behind my clothes, brushing them aside to show Jenna my supplies. She picks up a few baggies of ingredients, nodding in approval.

"Not bad," she comments, "but none of this is going to kill Astaroth."

"I don't know any spells. I've only been using the regular cleaning spells I've learned in class to practice," I admit. "Where can I start?"

"You're not going to *clean* him to death. There are plenty of other magic spells. Has anyone explained to you the difference between blood magic and regular magic?"

"Nope." It's never come up, even in my remedial classes. All I know is that you need blood for blood magic, and it's more powerful.

"With regular spells, you can only do a certain set of things," she explains. "Cleaning is one of them. Elemental spells, flash bombs, temporary memory potions. But magic can't create something from nothing. I can't snap my fingers and make a plant grow, or start a fire. Truebloods barely even use spells, because they have built-in magic."

I think back to Rhys, and his ability to transform plants into weapons or other tools. "So there's not a killing spell I can use?"

"No. Regular magic spells are generally not great for combat. But with blood magic, you can do more. Illusion casting, temporary glamours, binding spells, poisons…you name it. And you know that spell bags can be created with blood magic, too."

Yes, there were spell bags on the ship with *teeth* in them. I remember. "What is the purpose of spell bags?"

"They make spells last longer, and sometimes become more powerful. Or they can create a delayed effect. They're very useful for combat, if you don't have time or ingredients to prepare a spell on the fly," Jenna explains. "You know blood magic is outlawed because it encourages users to hurt themselves or others."

She looks at my hands, still bandaged.

"You're lucky you have shadowborn healing. My human compatriots were not as lucky," Jenna says. "Humans can do blood magic, too, but it requires much more blood. But with shadowborn and truebloods, the amount of blood needed for the spell is roughly the same. That's another reason why truebloods don't like blood magic—it levels the playing field between us."

"So I could potentially use magic just as powerful as Astaroth?" There may be hope for me yet.

But Jenna's smile falters. "There's always a price to pay, Mar. It's not a fix-all solution. You're going to need to put in the *blood*, sweat, and tears to improve. But yes, theoretically you can become as powerful as him."

"And what is the price?" Not that I'm unwilling to pay it.

"Regular magic is safe. There's no usage limitation, though it's mentally exhausting. Even if you don't complete a spell, nothing bad will happen," she says. "But blood magic is wild. Unpredictable. And inexplicably tied to you. If you don't complete a spell, or safely disarm it, the magic will go wild and you could get hurt. The magic could bounce back in your face and kill you."

"Only if you do something wrong?"

"Not only that, blood magic has hard limits. It's not just mental exhaustion you have to worry about. If you push yourself too hard, your body will pay the price. It's more than blood loss; you could get severely sick. Is that a risk you're willing to take?"

I picture my family. Isabelle, Tasha, David…and *Luke*. I picture Rhys. Hell, I even think about Allegra. God knows why her face pops up in my head. But it does.

"Yes," I say without hesitation. "Teach me everything you know."

"Alright." She hands me my mortar and pestle. "Let's begin."

Dear Maria,

I saw you for the first time today. You were lost on the ship. You still have a horrific sense of direction, I see.

But you were radiant all the same. I forgot how strongly my heart reacts to your presence, how quickly it beats when you are near.

I wanted so badly to approach you, but in the end, decided against it. It is too soon, and I cannot do anything to jeopardize the timeline.

Still, knowing what is in store for you here, I am tempted to warn you away now.

You told me only vaguely about your time on the ship, and now that we are here, I can only dread what is to come and hope others will step in to lend you a hand.

It is not easy, waiting for danger to strike. Perhaps I understand your previous anxieties a bit more, now that I am in a similar situation.

Yours,
Rhys

Dear Rhys,

I'd kindly ask you not to insult my sense of direction. That ship was a maze and I will fight anyone who says otherwise. The interior designer should be put on trial for inducing mental stress.

That being said…wow. I was sweating like a pig in that Florida summer heat, and probably looked pissed off. Your rose-colored lenses are too strong. But…you also have a huge effect on me.

Oh jeez, that sounds so corny when I write it. Ignore me.

Mar

Chapter Seven

Thank God it's Friday. I've been getting antsy for the weekend—not because I have any fun plans. Between classes, studying, working at the library, and practicing blood magic with Jenna, I'm exhausted. Even if that weren't the case, I'm still not very popular here. The staring has lessened, and I'm not a sideshow freak anymore, but my attempts to make friends hasn't been off to a great start.

For one, I have no clue what to talk about with my peers. I have people I'm friendly with in class, but I don't even know their names. For attendance, the teachers pass around a sheet. And it's far too late in the game to ask.

In short, I'm still a friendless loser with no weekend plans. But sign-up sheets for hunting in the Veil are posted on the main bulletin board, so that's something.

I end up putting my name down, arriving at the main building a few minutes before class. Thanks to Jenna's tutoring sessions, I have a few spells up my sleeve in case of emergencies. Am I confident they'll save me from a beastblood? No. But I'm not *that* intimidated by the Veil anymore.

Granted, in the past I had Rhys to help me. And by "help," I mean "fully protect me with his magic." But I've gone through three books now relying on other people to protect me. Isn't it due time for a strength boost?

As soon as I write my name on the list, someone behind me snickers. I spin around, only to see my stupid cousin smirking at me.

"What?" I demand.

"You're signing up to go on a hunt?" he asks, dressed in jeans so tight they might as well be leggings. Is he a masochist or something? Does he enjoy having the circulation cut off down there? "Do you have a death wish?"

"Some would say yes, based on recent behavior. Others would call me surprisingly adventurous."

"You're unsurprisingly *stupid*."

"And you're unsurprisingly an ass."

"I guess it runs in the family," he says lazily. "I'm just looking out for you, Maria. I don't want you to get killed by someone else. Not when I'm ready to do the deed myself."

"Then why haven't you?" I challenge, probably proving his earlier point about having a death wish. "We live in the same house. Come downstairs tonight and smother me with a pillow, if you have the balls for it."

"As tempting as that sounds, I have other plans for you. But I won't spoil the surprise for you just yet."

"I'm anticipating it," I reply sarcastically, breezing past him.

But walking to my history seminar, his words replay in my head. He has other plans for me? What the hell does that mean?

Is it possible he's not working with Neil anymore? I assumed Nic was Neil's lackey, but maybe not. Maybe he's planning a mutiny. I don't have proof, so I can't run to Neil with this. That would be great—let them battle it out by themselves.

I enter the classroom and take a seat in the second row from the front beside Ava. I wouldn't say we're friends, exactly, but so far she's been the nicest classmate I've worked with. Next to her is a long black bag laying across two seats, which I learned recently is for her compound bow. She is cute in a girl-next-door kind of way, with platinum blonde hair in loose curls down her back.

"Hi," she greets, flipping open her laptop, the front covered in glittery pink stickers. Her bow is, too. She showed me last week. "Are you ready for the quiz?"

"Yeah." We've been covering elves and fae. Specifically, the war between them. You'd think I would know a thing or two about that, having lived through it. But I was a little busy trying to find the Divinities Sword; I wasn't too concerned with the political aspect.

"I can't believe that stuff happened three centuries ago," Ava murmurs. "I wonder what it was like back then."

"Well, there was no plumbing or Wi-Fi, so I can't imagine it was fun." I don't have to imagine anything. I *know* it wasn't fun.

She laughs. "That's true. My older trueblood relatives are always amazed by how far tech has come."

"They see it as a positive thing?"

"Mostly. They still get on my case when I use my phone too much." She wrinkles her nose. "Parents, right?"

"Yeah. So do you think it's going to be an essay or multiple choice?"

Professor Lewis arrives before Ava responds, and class begins. Luckily, the quiz *is* multiple choice, and I breeze through it. After handing it in, I head out and a feeling of nausea hits me. It's so sudden and intense, I have to brace against the wall for a moment.

Rushing toward the nearest bathroom, I barely make it into a stall before throwing up. I'll spare you the details on that. When I can finally stand, my head swims and I stumble toward the sink. Rinsing my mouth and face, my body feels heavy, and I could fall asleep right now on the cold tile floor.

This has never happened to me before, even while drunk. I'm not sure what spurred it—maybe I caught a stomach virus? That would be typical. As much as I'd love to go home and sleep off whatever this is, there's too much to be done. And, as if on cue, I get a text from Mathers asking me to meet him in his office when I get a chance. Since I'm already in the main building, I touch up my makeup and drag myself to Mathers' office, picking up a water bottle from a vending machine along the way.

"What happened?" Provost Mathers asks as I walk in.

"What do you mean?" I croak.

His eyes flit over my face. "You look pale."

"I'm fine." I shrug, trying to ignore the throbbing at my temples. "What did you want to talk about?"

"I saw you signed up for the hunt in the Veil," he says. That was fast—I only put my name down this morning. "I don't think that is a good idea, Mar."

"I'm not known for having great ideas," I say.

"And yet you persist." His lips press together in a thin line. "You do realize that pointin' out your own stupidity does not make it any less stupid."

"It? Or me?"

"You are not stupid," he assures me. "Your actions, however, are debatable."

Yeah, no argument there. But I'm pretty desperate right now, and I need some real-life fighting experience. Combat class isn't enough. I also figure that, if I go on a hunt and am assigned a team, I can meet more people and befriend them.

"I will not send you to your death. I know we talked a bit about ferals, but are you sure you understand what a hunt would really entail?" Mathers asks. "Once the beastbloods are infected, they become crazed and go on rampages, killin' and infectin' every creature they come in contact with. The frenzied beasts are dangerous, and infection is fatal."

Well, that's nothing short of terrifying. You'd think they would include this very important information on the sign-up sheet. "And you're sending college kids out to fight them? What a great plan."

He ignores my sarcasm. "Last spring, a student at Northeastern thought it would be a good idea to use blood magic on the ferals. To what end, we're not entirely sure, but it caused a horde of them to come through the Veil into the mortal realm. They've been comin' in droves ever since, threatenin' the lives of mortals. Thankfully mortals can't *see* beastbloods' true forms—they have a naturalized glamour over them."

"What does that mean?" I ask. "Like, they're invisible?"

"Not quite. But mortal brains replace the magical with the ordinary. For example, a human could look at a mermaid's tail and only see a pair of legs. Or they could look at an elf and see a normal set of ears. You *do* know elves have elongated ears, correct?"

"Oh, I'm aware," I mutter. "So the infection is the real threat, not exposure to mortals?"

"The ferals will attack and kill anythin' they lay their eyes on. Luckily, most aren't intelligent. We've been sendin' groups to hunt them, but their numbers seem endless," he says. "Since there is a chance that infection could spread to you, and there is no cure, I cannot allow you to risk going to the Veil. Especially not alone."

Wow, I guess I *did* miss out on a lot when I went back in time. This just goes to show how little I know about the shadowborn world, no matter how many classes I'm taking and how much studying I'm doing.

"You just said you send *groups* out to hunt," I say. "If I were with other people, could I go?"

"We do, but you need a bodyguard, not a teammate."

"If I get someone to protect me," I say slowly, "will you let me go?"

"If you get Archer Kinsey and a group of people to go, I would *consider* it," he relents. "But from what I can tell, you and Archer are not seein' eye to eye on this matter."

"No," I agree. "We're not."

But I have other plans. I don't need Archer, I just need someone strong. And I think I know who I can ask.

Dear Maria,

Yesterday was quite busy. I did not have a chance to write to you.

Masked men and women attacked the ship. You were injured, and I volunteered to bring you to the infirmary. It was a hasty decision on my part.

What I had not anticipated was how much our interaction would affect me. It was strange to meet a version of you who did not remember me.

Yours,
Rhys

Dear Rhys,

It feels like so long ago when we met in that stupid sickbay. I didn't even see your face, because you were covering it up. If you hadn't, who knows what would have happened?

Mar

Chapter Eight

After speaking with a few students around campus, I find myself standing in front of Georgia Kyle's mustard-colored residence, patiently waiting for her to finish her class.

As I keep watch, I spot her making her way toward me from the walkway. Her distinctive white-blonde buzz cut stands out in stark contrast to her dark and warm complexion. At first, she seems to look past me, her gaze scanning the area before eventually settling on my face. It takes her a moment to recognize me, the confusion written on her face. Understandable; it's been a while since we spoke, and I'm not exactly memorable.

"Georgia." I stand up from the porch swing. "I'm Mar. Do you remember me? From the cruise ship?"

"Hmm." She meets my dark eyes with her own. "Oh, you're Allegra Abbott's long-lost sister, right?"

"Not exactly how I'd like to be remembered, but sure. Allegra is my half sister."

"Wow, that sucks."

Tell me about it. "Anyway, I was hoping we could talk."

She thinks about it before responding. If I remember correctly, she's not exactly Allegra's number-one fan. I'm not sure if something personal went down between them or not. Finally, she says, "Sure. I guess. What's up?"

"I was wondering if you're planning a Veil hunt soon," I blurt. No need to beat around the bush, right? I'm not saying I'm suddenly a paragon of honesty or anything. It's just that I've got enough complications in my life already, thank you kindly.

"Unfortunately, no. I went on a bunch of summer hunts, but now that we're back in school, I'm overloaded with work. I'm on track to graduate this semester," Georgia says, her tone apologetic. "No spare time."

"Well, it was worth a shot," I say with a half smile. "Don't worry about it."

"Don't take this the wrong way, but we're not friends. I'm surprised you'd even consider asking me."

I nod, feeling a little embarrassed. It's true, we barely know each other, but I wanted to ask on the off chance she'd agree.

"I've heard you're the best swordswoman at school," I tell her. "I figured I might as well ask you. The most probable worst-case scenario is that you'd say no."

"And the least probable?" she asks, slightly amused.

"You'd get so angry you'd chase me around with your sword and turn me into sashimi."

"Well, I'm not a raging psycho, so that's not going to happen. Sorry. You might have better luck asking Ophelia Blackwood."

I try not to groan out loud. If there's anyone I'd rather not ask for help, it's Ophelia Blackwood—not just because she hates me, but also because she's been nothing but unkind and condescending ever since we met.

"Thanks, Georgia," I say. "I'll see you around."

"Hope it works out for you, Mar."

Well, where there's a will, there's a way. Or so I tell myself.

Working at the library is about as dull as watching grass grow, especially on weekends when no one comes in. But at least it gives me time to hit the books, even though my hands are bandaged again from practicing blood magic with Jenna.

Today, I'm slowly shelving returns on the second floor, near the balcony where I once pushed Nic off. Good times—*not*.

When the bell rings downstairs, I don't rush down immediately. They can wait a few seconds while I finish up. But the sound of loud voices carries upstairs, and soon a young woman's screeching fills the air.

"You're supposed to be my *boyfriend*. What do you mean you're too busy?" the girl demands.

"I have a class. I'm not going to skip it."

I glance downstairs and spot Archer Kinsey running a hand through his admittedly perfect blonde hair. The girl beside him is a petite blonde, probably shorter than me, but about ten times more intimidating.

"You think you can just ignore me like this?" she accuses, taking a threatening step toward him. "You're not going to fail because you miss one class."

"I have an assignment due, and if I don't get good grades, my father is going to freak out," Archer complains.

The girl isn't sympathetic in the least. "You can make time for fun with your friends, but when it comes to me, you can't spare a second! I *won't* be ignored!"

"I'm not ignoring you, for the last time," he grits out.

I'm not *trying* to eavesdrop, but they're speaking pretty loudly. And this is juicy gossip, not that I have anyone to share it with.

"Don't you have any self-respect? Or time-management skills?" she harps. "You're a goddamn Kinsey. And you committed to me."

"I didn't know I would be getting this assignment when I agreed. I asked the professor for an extension and he said no! What am I supposed to do?"

"You're supposed to be my boyfriend!"

"Why?" he explodes. "Because our dads agreed on it?"

"Because *I* allowed you to sow your wild oats with two sluts, both of whom were coincidentally from the same seed—"

"Uh, can you *not* bring Neil Abbott and his...*stuff*...into this?" I ask from above, leaning over the railing. "It's kind of gross. Also, you're in a library. How about y'all lower your voices?"

The lovely couple glares at me, none too happy about being interrupted.

"If you're gonna argue, take it somewhere else," I say dryly, descending the stairs. "You're disturbing the other patrons."

"What other patrons?" Archer asks icily, sounding more upset at *me* than he is at his girlfriend. Need I remind him that she was digging into him a few seconds ago?

"Sorry 'bout that," the girl says, sizing me up. At least she has the decency to be polite to strangers. "You're Mary Alice, aren't you?"

"Maria," Archer corrects.

"Actually, it's Mar. But Mary Alice *was* my nickname. Because my full name is Maria Alison," I explain. "Now, how can I help you today? Are you looking for something in particular?"

"Fake accent again?" Archer scoffs.

"Excuse you. The accent is real, as I said before. It just fluctuates sometimes, depending on my mood." Which is quickly souring. "Didn't you grow up in Georgia, too? Where's your drawl?"

"I had a speech coach growing up."

"I'm sorry for interrupting your work," Archer's girlfriend tells me, and I think she actually *means* it. But just because she's being polite now doesn't mean I've forgotten about how she yelled at Archer. Not that I care about him—she was just being a bit harsh, in my opinion. "You and Archer dated, didn't you?"

"I wouldn't call it that. But it's all in the past." Now that he hates my guts, that is.

I can practically feel the anger still radiating off him, along with the frustration. I can't imagine it's *all* for me.

"She's right. None of it meant anything to her," Archer says.

"It didn't mean anything to you, either, Archer," I remind him, unwilling to let him pin everything on me. If I'm being totally honest with myself, neither of us acted very maturely in our short-lived relationship.

"You can't have a relationship with a liar."

"No, you can't," I agree, just trying to end the conversation. "If you're not looking for something specific, I'll let you peruse at your leisure—"

"I'm still waiting for that apology."

An apology? Do I truly owe him one? He looks utterly convinced, though I maintain my previous position. He doesn't *really* want an apology; he wants to feel superior to me. Nothing I do will make him forgive me, and at this point I don't care about his forgiveness. Even if it would mean using him as a tool for my mission.

"Don't hold your breath," I say finally, breezing past the couple. "If you're not going to check out a book, then I suggest you find somewhere else to argue."

ARRIVING BACK AT THE HOUSE AFTER FINISHING MY SHIFT at the library, I'm relieved to find Allegra and Nic are out for the weekend. I don't have to worry about them hassling me or my already exhausted mind.

Stepping into the kitchen for an early dinner, I find Rhys sitting at the counter, his blonde hair tucked behind his ears as he focuses on a book. I can't tell if he's completely engrossed in it or simply ignoring my presence.

I follow suit. If someone put cameras in my bedroom, I'm going to assume someone is watching us in every part of the house.

I try to cram my feelings down as best I can as I pass by him, but it's like cramming trash down an overflowing garbage bin. It doesn't work too well.

I head to the fridge, opening the door to reveal its fully-stocked interior. I quickly gather the ingredients for a chicken rice bowl, feeling like a culinary mastermind. I mean, who needs formal training when you can learn everything from cooking shows, right?

As I start to prepare the chicken, I can sense Rhys' gaze on me. He sets aside his book and observes me closely, but I suspect he's less interested in me and more interested in what I'm cooking. I season the chicken and start to cut it up, but he shakes his head disapprovingly.

"You are not skilled with a blade," he informs me in a very matter-of-fact tone.

"Would you call my cooking skills 'abysmal'?" I tease.

He doesn't take the bait, not that I expected he would. "You lack even basic knowledge of spices."

"I've barely done anything. I've added salt and pepper."

"You have done plenty," he says solemnly, "and it is all wrong."

"Oh really, Mr. MasterChef? You think you can do it better than me?"

"That is a given." He comes closer, peering over my shoulder. Even though we're not touching, his proximity is enough to send my heart into palpitations. "The pieces are not cut well. They will have differing cook times and you will inevitably burn some."

"They look pretty even to me."

"Is something wrong with your eyes?"

"Yeah, I can't take them off you." I crack a smile, but his frown only deepens. "What?"

"Do not make this more difficult," he warns sharply. "Charred food is not healthy for you. If you continue to cook like this, that is precisely what you will end up with. You might as well discard it and start over."

"I'm not going to waste the food. I can handle some

overcooked chicken. Besides, all the bad food I've eaten hasn't killed me yet," I retort.

"Are you a fan of tempting fate?"

"I'd rather tempt you."

"That is not funny."

"I thought it was cute, in a cringy way."

He shakes his head. "Move over. You are taking up too much room. Wash your hands and sit at the counter."

"Fine, fine." I do as he says, washing my hands thoroughly after touching the raw chicken. Meanwhile, Chef Boyardee over here rolls up his sleeves and gets cooking.

You know, if I delude myself enough, this is kind of like a date!

Not wanting to sit still and just watch him cook, however aesthetically pleasing it might be, I decide to help by making the rice. I grab a bag from the pantry—all in Japanese, how fancy—and a pot from the cabinet.

"What are you doing?" Rhys asks, his voice cutting into me.

"Boiling some rice." Duh.

"We have a rice cooker." He points to the white monstrosity of an appliance on the counter.

"It's in Japanese. I think," I add. I'm not the best at recognizing non-romanized alphabets.

"It's the best rice cooker on the market right now," he says.

"Can it cook rice in five minutes?"

"That is not five-minute bagged rice, and I have downloaded the instruction manual for the rice cooker in English. It works perfectly well. If you boil the rice, you will ruin the entire dish. Allow me to cook it for you."

"And what am I going to do?"

"Sit," he commands, as if I'm a dog.

As I drop the bag of rice on the counter and kneel on the floor, a grin spreads across my face. It's comforting to fall back into this familiar rhythm with Rhys, even if we're not making grand declarations of love. I just hope I'm not the only one who feels this way.

"Happy?" I ask.

"Ecstatic. Can you not tell?"

"Can't you tell I was just joking with you?"

"You were not flirting?"

"Oh, I like to be extra careful around guys I nearly killed. No flirting until I determine whether or not they're pissed off," I say, choosing my words carefully for the cameras. "Which, of course, they would have a right to be."

"And if he is not angry?" he asks me in Elvish.

"Then I'd be relieved. And sad," I admit.

"Sad?"

"Because we have to talk in code instead—"

The front door swings open and I stop mid-sentence. Allegra and Nic walk in, earlier than I expected. Damn, I shouldn't have assumed they were on the mainland again. They went last weekend. Why didn't they go *this* weekend?

"What are you doing?" Allegra asks, her eyes narrowing when she sees us. "Why are you sitting on the ground, Maria?"

"She is being punished," Rhys replies easily. "She nearly burned down my kitchen with her incompetence."

"Are you cooking for her?" Allegra accuses. "There's a cafeteria. She can get food there. Or, better yet, a pet store on the mainland."

"Well, I would need a recommendation. Which kibble keeps *your* fur nice and shiny?" I ask sarcastically, standing up and dusting my knees off. Not that there's even a single crumb to dust off; Rhys keeps the house immaculate.

"Do you only know how to speak in sarcasm?"

"It's a defense mechanism."

"Whatever." Allegra turns from me. "Rhys, I'm starving. I'd like dinner now, too."

"As you wish."

I want to vomit, hearing Rhys quote *The Princess Bride,* however unintentionally, for Allegra. It wouldn't be so bad if she weren't my sister, but the way she touches his shoulder sparks insane jealousy in me.

Yes, yes, I know it's irrational. But the green-eyed monster is a hard beast to tackle, possibly even more difficult than Astaroth.

Dear Maria,

I nearly killed Nic today. I know it would displease you, but I must get it off my chest, so to speak.

I'm still trying to discern why you were brought to the plantation last night, but you did not look happy. I caught a glimpse of you exiting Neil's limousine. And Nic antagonizing you.

But to beat you the very next morning? You were in a horrid state. It took all my self-control not to kill him. Though the more I think about it, the angrier I become.

I am going to take a cold shower and hopefully regain my composure for tomorrow. At least tonight, when Neil sees you, he will punish Nic in my stead.

Yours,
Rhys

Dear Rhys,

You can't kill Nic. That's my job. I'm dead serious.

Get it? Dead? Because I'm gonna kill him?

Hahahaha. I crack myself up.

In all seriousness, I'm not that mad about Nic. That's just who he is, I guess. And in retrospect, it didn't hurt as much as other beatings I've received. He's just not that creative.

Mar

Chapter Nine

The doorbell interrupts my jealous thoughts, and Rhys quickly washes his hands before answering it. However, the visitor doesn't wait for an invitation, as Archer Kinsey storms into the kitchen, his anger palpable. Smoke might as well be coming out of his ears.

"Archer?" Allegra asks, but he completely ignores her. It would have been a little bit satisfying, had he not come to yell at me.

"What gives you the right to be mad at me?" he demands.

"I'm not angry." I'm surprised. I thought he wanted nothing to do with me. So why show up here unannounced? Why continue the argument, if you can even call it that, from the library? Doesn't Archer have better things to do? "Rhys, is the rice almost done?"

Rhys pauses, taking a moment to collect himself before closing the door and checking on the fancy rice cooker. "No, it does not seem to be."

"I'm not mad," I repeat, "I'm just hungry. And maybe a little impatient. But *you* seem to be hangry."

The sound of his voice booms through the house. "Not everything is a goddamn joke! Do you have any idea how frustrating it is to constantly feel like I'm being played by you? That every word out of your mouth is just some lie you use to manipulate me? To make me feel like an *idiot*?"

"I don't think you need my help with that!" I snap.

To make matters worse, Nic chooses this exact time to chime in, wearing a huge grin that would make the Cheshire Cat jealous. "Well, well, well. Look who's having a little tiff," he says with a playful tone. "What's the topic of discussion? Relationship troubles? Exposed secrets? Do tell."

"We're talking about how I'm a lying, manipulative bitch. Nothing new here," I supply.

"Did he bring up how you're just a lowborn bastard?"

"Not yet, but thanks for adding to the conversation. Super helpful, Nic."

"No problem." He shrugs, sitting at the counter. "I'm just here for the show."

"It's a rerun," I say, rolling my eyes. "Maybe you and Allegra should rekindle your romance, Archer. Then you can both hate me together."

By this point, I'm exhausted from it all. The constant repetition of the same arguments, the constant yelling…it's all just too much. It's not like it hurts me or anything, but it's a reminder that nobody here truly gets me. I feel like some angsty teenager, which I guess I still am at nineteen.

"Hey, Maria. I've been wondering this for a while now," Nic says, "but how did you get the Blood Chalice to say you were human on the ship?"

"What?"

"The Blood Chalice. We got it from Northeastern to test your blood," Nic explains. "Remember? It feels like eons ago, but it was just last summer."

"Oh, that." I sigh, turning toward Archer. "I got your cousin, Ethan, to switch out the real chalice for a fake one. I also kissed him to convince him."

"*What?*"

"We weren't dating. You didn't even like me at the time," I remind him. Rhys says nothing, but I can feel his eyes on me. Is he angry? Shit. Even *I* know that you don't talk about your history in front of your…whatever Rhys is to me. Boyfriend? I still haven't worked out the terminology, and now is *not* the time. "I didn't even remember doing that."

"What the hell?" Archer sputters.

I could try to lighten the mood with a joke or some sarcasm, but Archer looks truly upset. What I did wasn't exactly the most admirable thing, even if it wasn't *technically* wrong. In hindsight, I realize it wasn't the best way to handle the situation. "That was a crappy thing to do. I was desperate to leave at that point, and I made a mistake. I just wanted to go home."

"But you can't go home now, can you?" Nic says quietly. "It wouldn't be the same."

My jaw tightens, and I can feel the anger building up inside me, like a fire igniting. "No. It wouldn't. Because of you, Nic. You and Neil have destroyed everything. Are you happy with yourself?"

"Not yet."

I can't bear the thought of continuing this conversation. Because I know that all the hatred and pain I feel toward

Nic, all the anger, is right at the surface, threatening to overtake me.

I turn away from him and the rest of them. My stomach churns, and suddenly, I've lost my appetite. I just want to crawl into bed and shut out the world, even if it means enduring another night of nightmares. At least those are something I can wake up from.

Without another word, I head downstairs. I shut the door behind me, but Archer follows me anyway, grabbing my arm.

"Hey. We aren't done talking," he says roughly, but his voice lacks the fight and rage it had a few minutes ago. Now, he sounds as tired as I am.

I shake off his hand. "What more is there to say? I won't bother you anymore. We're done with each other. Let's just let it die and move on with our lives."

"I don't *want* to be done with each other."

For a moment, I'm stunned. He's not coming onto me—I know *that* much—but I didn't think he wanted anything to do with me. Understandably so. I thought he'd be happy to be rid of me.

"There's no closure," he insists.

Closure? What a joke. Only naive people expect it, especially when it comes to relationships. I learned long ago to never count on it, to never even let myself think about it, because the truth is, it never comes. You'll never know why you weren't enough for someone, why they left, why they hurt you. It's better to just accept it and move on, no matter how much it stings. And as for those childhood scars that still linger, the ones that make me feel like a burden, like damaged goods? There's no closure for *that* either. It's just something I have to live with, something I've learned to push to the back of my mind and ignore as best I can.

"You know why I did what I did," I say slowly. "You know it wasn't personal."

That should be enough for him. It would be for me, if our roles were reversed.

But Archer isn't like me. That's something I need to accept. He asks, "So why do I feel so confused?"

"Only you know the answer to that." I take a step back, creating some much-needed distance between us on the stairs. I can see the hurt and anger in his eyes, but there's something else there, too. Something that I can't quite place.

"Why did you do it?" he asks finally. "Why did you even pursue me?"

"You're handsome. I was attracted to you."

Archer scoffs. "That's it?"

"What else do you want me to say? That I fell madly in love with you from the moment I saw you?" I roll my eyes. "I'm sorry, but that's just not true. The first time we met, you flashed me. You know Ophelia spilled Coke all over my head because of that? I should've sent you a dry-cleaning bill!"

Archer chuckles, the sound deep and warm. It startles me. "Back when you were pretending to be nice, were you secretly cursing me out in your head?"

"I don't remember. All I recall from the ship is trying not to get killed by cultists."

"Fair enough."

It was simpler when Archer was just angry at me, when his animosity was easy to understand. But now, seeing this raw and vulnerable side of him, I'm thrown off-kilter. It stirs up my own discomfort with emotional conversations. Being honest is one thing, but heart-to-hearts never seem to end well. It's like opening yourself up for more hurt than necessary.

"I fucked up," I admit. "I probably shouldn't have kissed you while I was a character. I'm sorry about that. And I shouldn't have kissed your cousin. I could have handled things better."

"I could have, too. I'm sorry. I guess…we're wrong for each other."

"Most romantic relationships fail," I note. "Are you still mad at me?"

"That depends. Are you going to be honest with me from now on?" he asks. "Can I trust you?"

"I'm not sure," I admit. "I want to go home, Archer. That's pretty much always been my end goal. Going home and ensuring the safety of my family. And in order to do that, right now I need to play by the rules and follow Neil's orders. If he wants me to kill Astaroth, I'm going to do it."

"Where is your home? Your *real* home," Archer asks. We move further into the basement, and I take a seat on the bed, gesturing for him to take the desk chair. It's strange how quickly our dynamic shifted from anger to a more peaceful state. Despite everything, I don't mind having him here and talking like this.

"Georgia." Thinking about my house brings a smile to my face. "I grew up in foster care, but I live with my old social worker, Isabelle. She ended up quitting and taking me and my foster sister, Tasha, with her."

It takes a moment for the information to settle in. "Foster care?"

"Yeah. Oh, don't make that face. It wasn't—" I catch myself before I say "that bad." Dr. Jones told me that downplaying my experiences in a dismissive manner is not helpful for my emotional well-being. It's hard to talk about my past experiences without feeling like I'm being too dramatic or throwing a pity party. But I know that downplaying them isn't healthy either. It's a work in progress, I guess. "It was a tough experience, but I've learned to appreciate what I have now. My foster family may not be related to me by blood, but they mean the world to me. Tasha, my sister, is more like family than Allegra, Nic, and Neil could ever be."

"You have a sister?" He sounds genuinely surprised.

"Yeah, and a little brother, too. David. He's probably not so little anymore, though," I say with a laugh. "He's twelve now. I've missed his birthday twice."

I can't help but feel a twinge of guilt at the thought of missing his birthday. It's not just David's, but also Tasha's birthday in January, and I missed hers as well.

Archer's expression softens. "I'm sorry you can't be with them right now."

"Me too. But I'll get back to them, one way or another." My stomach growls, breaking the moment. "Are you hungry?" I ask, trying to shift the focus.

A small smile tugs at the corners of his mouth. "Starving."

"Do you want to grab dinner in the cafeteria with me?"

Archer considers my offer for a moment. "Sure, why not?"

"Once more, with *feeling*."

I cast a glare at Jenna, who seems all too pleased with

herself. "How the hell am I supposed to do blood magic 'with feeling'?"

"I don't know. I just thought it would help," she says with a shrug. "I've never trained anyone in blood magic before, except for cultists who respond better to sadistic punishments and yelling. You seem like you'd hit me if I tried that."

"Your assessment would be correct."

Frustrated, I look down at the bowl of my blood mixed with herbs and attempt the spell—for the fifth time. It's supposed to ward off evil, but at this point, it seems like it's more likely to summon a demon than banish one.

I mean, how hard can it be? Spells are supposed to be all about intention, an anchor (in this case, my blood), and magic, right? But apparently, I missed the memo on visualizations, because my spell is as effective as a marshmallow sword in a battle with a dragon.

"You look exhausted," Jenna observes. "I don't think your spell is going to work unless you visualize it better and call on the magic."

"I don't understand."

"Are you focusing on summoning the magic around you?"

"No," I say. "I thought I was supposed to be visualizing my intent."

"*And* attracting magic," Jenna supplies.

The frustration builds within me like a pressure cooker, threatening to boil over at any moment. "You didn't think to tell me that earlier?" I demand. "I've never had to draw magic to me before. It comes by itself, like a magnet."

"You've been doing it subconsciously. But now, you have to focus." She snaps her fingers. "Maybe you have to go through a traumatic incident to unlock your powers. Why don't I try sawing off your arm and see if you can do a spell?"

Sometimes I think Jenna secretly hates me. "Um, no. That's stupid. And I've had plenty of low moments at Southeastern—why haven't my powers been unlocked before?"

"Hell if I know. I'm given very limited information," she replies. "I'm just as irritated as you are."

Somehow I doubt that.

We've been in my closet for hours now, practicing the same protection spell over and over again. It's well past midnight, though time for Jenna doesn't mean much.

Jenna's eyes narrow as she studies me. "Look, I get it. You're determined to take on Astaroth and save the world. But you're not doing anyone any favors by pushing yourself too hard. If you burn out, what good will you be to anyone?"

"No way, I'm fine. I can handle it," I protest.

"I'm not saying you have to take a long break. Just a few hours to rest and recharge. You'll come back stronger and more focused."

"But I don't have time for that. I need to defeat Astaroth."

"Newsflash: you don't even know where Astaroth is yet. Maybe you should slow your roll and take it one step at a time," Jenna advises. "Your hands are already beyond saving. I don't think those scars are ever going to go away."

I try to argue with Jenna, insisting that I'm fine and that we need to keep going. But then a wave of sickness hits me, and suddenly I don't feel fine at all.

"Maybe you're right," I grumble. I can't fight Astaroth if

I'm not even able to stand up straight. "It's getting late, anyway. We should take a break until tomorrow."

Jenna nods, satisfied with my answer. "Good call. Now get some rest and we can pick up where we left off in *a few days*. Tomorrow is way too soon; you're looking positively *green*, my dear. Don't call me again until your scabs fall off your palms."

"Gross."

She stands up and stretches her arms over her head before walking out of the closet without another word, leaving me alone with my thoughts—and my growing feeling of nausea.

I'm not sure what it is, but something about this spell has me feeling more than a little off. I try to stand up, only to find that my balance is completely gone. I stumble and collapse onto the floor, heaving and retching until I can feel the acidic bile rising in my throat. Suddenly, a wave of dizziness comes over me and I rush to the bathroom, barely making it before I start vomiting. The pain is unbearable and all I want to do is curl up in a ball and wait for it all to be over. But as soon as the nausea passes, reality sets in and I realize that something is very wrong.

My reflection is almost unrecognizable. My skin is the color of chalk, slick with sweat. My eyes are bloodshot to hell, and it looks like a vessel burst.

"What the fuck?" I mutter to myself.

I bend down and peer into the toilet bowl, feeling a sickening dread churn in my stomach. The water is a deep crimson, a shocking contrast against the porcelain. I can't look away, even though the sight makes me want to puke again.

My throat feels raw and scratchy, as if I've been

screaming for hours. This has to be the blood magic rebounding—there's no other explanation.

I know Jenna warned me about the dangers of blood magic, but I didn't think it would be this bad. I can't shake the feeling that I'm being consumed from the inside out.

I pull myself up and rinse my face off in the sink. The water is icy cold, but it does little to quell the heat that's building inside me.

As I stumble back to my room, I can feel the energy shifting around me. I stagger to my bed and collapse onto it, feeling the sweat soaking through my sheets. The room spins around me, and I can barely stay awake.

My eyes drift closed, and I can feel exhaustion take me in its grasp. I don't fight it, hoping tomorrow will be different—that something, *anything*, will change.

Dear Maria,

You were ravenous this morning. I only learned just now that you had not been fed. Nic is truly a scoundrel. And yet, you looked undefeated.

I wanted to tell you right then how I feel about you. But from your perspective, I am a stranger. As hard as it was to be without you, it's even more difficult to be with a version of you who feels nothing for me.

When it is appropriate, I promise I will sweep you off your feet.

Yours,
Rhys

Chapter Ten

I can't even get out of bed the next morning. My limbs feel like lead, and my head pulses with pain right behind my eyes. I stay in bed for another few hours before finally mustering the strength to rise on shaky legs.

I don't think I've ever been *this* sick before. I'm definitely dehydrated, too, which is making things worse. I stumble to the kitchen, holding onto the railing for dear life, and grab a water bottle from the fridge. Tearing the lid off, I sit on the cold tile floor and chug it. The water burns as it slides down my throat.

Rhys and Allegra come into the room as I'm slumped against the cabinets, neither of them looking very happy to see me. I can't imagine I look great—they probably think I'm on drugs or something.

"You look pale," Allegra comments, which is great coming from someone with chronic health issues. There's not a note of concern in her voice, and I guess there wouldn't be, given our current relationship. "What are you doing?"

"I'm just hungover," I explain, which isn't *technically* a lie. Hangovers happen when you drink too much, and this happened because I did too much blood magic. So, it's a blood magic hangover.

I grasp the water bottle with both hands, hoping they won't notice the cuts on my palms. I forgot to bandage them last night, but they've already begun to scab over.

"I will remove her," Rhys tells Allegra.

He reaches under me, helping me up by the elbow. I don't know whether I want to jerk away or lean into his touch, but I will myself to remain frozen, my expression giving little away. Slowly, we make our way downstairs again. But instead of going to my bed, I hobble to the bathroom. No cameras in there, at least. If we speak softly, I don't think the voice recorder will be able to pick up our audio.

I lower myself to the ground, wedged in a corner where the tub meets the wall. The ceramic is ice against my skin, and I press my forehead to it hoping it will soothe the throbbing of my head. It doesn't.

Rhys closes the door behind him firmly and reaches for the first aid kit in the medicine cabinet. Kneeling beside me, he gingerly takes my hands and begins wiping them down. He doesn't seem at all aware of how dangerous the situation is. And not because of the blood magic.

I've had a lot on my mind lately, with school and Astaroth and everything else. The therapy sessions opened a gateway I've spent years locking up tight, making sure nothing escapes. And still, the first thing I think about when I wake up is Rhys.

I don't know how to control it, or even if I *want* to control it. I was never the type of person who expected "good morning" and "good night" texts from their significant other; I didn't understand how some of my peers could be so obsessive and needy. But now I kind of get it. It's like all those songs about love suddenly make sense.

Gross.

Rhys occupies a significant portion of my mind. Admittedly equal to how much I think about my family.

In Elvish, Rhys whispers, "Ask me to stay."

He has no idea how much I want him to. As pathetic as it makes me, I would love to hurl myself into his arms and pretend like all my problems are gone. But the world doesn't work that way.

"Allegra is waiting for you," I reply, the words ripped from my throat.

"She can wait."

"Rhys…there is so much I want to say to you. But there's no time." And I'm certainly not going to make a grand declaration of love in a *bathroom*. One I threw up in last night. "If Neil discovers us, he'll kill you."

I thought I lost him once; I can't do it again.

Rhys wraps my hands, covering the ugly gashes in each palm. "Have you received my letters?"

"Yes." I hesitate. I don't tell him I've written replies—it's too embarrassing. "Has anything changed?"

"Everything changes," he says, "but not how I feel about you."

There it is. The answer I had been waiting for, as plainly as he can say it.

"I just need more time," I promise. "I won't put you in jeopardy again."

He nods, a ghost of a smile on his lips. "I will find a way for us to meet again. There is much we need to discuss, but we can't do it here. Not while Nic is watching you."

Nic? Does that mean he's the one who put the cameras in my room?

Somehow that's worse than Neil being the culprit.

Rhys stands, lingering for a moment just to look at my face before leaving.

Allegra waits for him at the top of the stairs, her slim figure casting a long shadow on the wall. I close the bathroom door again, shutting my eyes tight so I don't have to see Rhys return to his place in the light, beside my sister.

It takes me another three days to recover, despite the numerous bottles of water I drink.

Rhys doesn't come downstairs again, not even to check on me, but he leaves food out for me a few times every day when Allegra and Nic aren't home. He's still a servant of the Abbotts, and since I'm now "recognized" by Neil, I guess it wouldn't be too far of a stretch to say he's in charge of making sure I don't starve to death, at the bare minimum.

Avoiding the one person who makes my heart skip a beat is just the icing on top of my crap cake. I've never had *this* much difficulty hiding my emotions. Then again, I've never felt this strongly for anyone, in a romantic sense. It's like a wave that looks unassuming from a distance, but when it crashes against you, the tide is enough to pull you under.

God I hate ocean analogies. But there's no other way I can describe it, and even that doesn't do it justice. It's terrifying and consuming and *lovely*, all at once. As forces of nature tend to be.

In a lame attempt to get my mind off my love life, I've thrown myself into my studies. Not blood magic—obviously I need a break from that—but my other work. I think I'm becoming a nerd, because for once I'm caught up with all my assignments. I even read *ahead* in the textbook. *Me*, Mar.

No, I have not been body-snatched.

After class, I have a jammed schedule. Lunch, studying, a shift at the library, and then my first training session with Archer. That's either going to go really well or totally shitty.

I haven't spoken to him much since we made up, on account of being sick and all. But we've exchanged texts. I still feel like I'm walking on ice when it comes to him. We don't have any classes together, so I can't stealthily observe him, either.

Admittedly, I'm curious how he's going to treat me in public now. Will it be like before, when he wouldn't acknowledge me?

Frankly, now that we're not making out and there's no romantic tension between us, I don't care if he ignores me. That hit a nerve because in the past, guys would hook up with me and not want to be seen with me the next day. But, since we're sort of friends now, or at least acquaintances, I don't give a damn if he's too self-conscious to be seen with me in broad daylight.

Maybe this is something I should talk to Dr. Jones about. I've got a session tomorrow, and last week I kind of had a meltdown. Not my finest moment.

As I walk out of class on my way to the cafeteria, I run into a familiar blonde. I recognize her immediately as Archer's new girlfriend, the one from the library.

Before you say anything, I'm not jealous. But it's admittedly weird to see him with someone else—mostly because he looked miserable when I last saw them together. Archer mentioned that his parents are strict, and I got the feeling this relationship might have been arranged.

The girl approaches me with a frown, books held tightly to her chest. I think her name is Celeste.

I've noticed a lot of Southeastern students are wealthy, but Celeste looks wealthy with a capital W. Maybe it's the scarf tied around her neck, or the sunglasses balanced perfectly atop her strawberry blonde hair, or the high red-bottomed shoes that clack on the ground as she walks. Any way you put it, she gives off an aura of money.

I wonder what kind of aura I give off. Desperation? Possibly.

"Hi," I greet awkwardly as she steps in front of me, blocking my path.

"Are you going to be training with my boyfriend today?" she asks, cutting to the point.

"Yeah. I'm out of shape."

She looks me up and down. "I guess you are."

Hey. "You're his girlfriend Celeste, right?"

"You dated Archer last year." It's not a question.

"I wouldn't call it *dating*. We went on, like, *one* official date," I say. I thought we already established this. "Anyway, there's nothing between us. He's just doing me a favor."

She sizes me up again, not even being subtle about it. "Well, I guess so. It's not like you're his type anyway."

Yeah, I'm not a blonde bitch.

I'm a *brunette* bitch. There's...not much difference.

"You're going to be in the gym, right?" Celeste asks.

"No. I'm actually going to be screwing him in my dorm," I say sarcastically.

She must have never encountered sarcasm before, because her entire body tenses. "*What?*"

Suddenly, she drops her books and slams me against the wall. One of her heels digs into my sneaker, and I swear she could stab me with it if she pressed hard enough.

"I was *kidding*, goddamn it," I choke out.

Her arm presses my neck against the bricks. "Do *not* joke about having sex with my boyfriend."

"Got it." If I'd known she was going to Hulk out about it, I wouldn't have.

She releases me with a glare, bending down to pick up her books. "If you touch my boyfriend, I'm going to make your life a living hell."

Get in line.

I don't have the guts to say that out loud, of course. Not after the way she slammed me into the wall. It's good to know I still have some form of self-preservation instinct.

After the odd encounter with Celeste, the rest of my day passes rather uneventfully. I head to the library, where I manage to buckle down and get some assignments done, and even squeeze in some studying with my trusty flashcards. It's amazing how a little peace and quiet can work wonders for productivity.

Archer and I had planned to meet at the gym at six. Fortunately, most students are busy having dinner, so the place is pretty much deserted. As I step into the gym, I immediately spot Archer by the weight racks. He's stretching on the mat, bending over to touch his toes, looking like a human pretzel. When he finally straightens up, he notices me and waves.

"Mar, I'm glad you made it. I wasn't sure if you would," he greets me with a smile.

"Why not?"

He shrugs. "Let's get started. Do you have any specific goals you want to work on?"

"Um, everything. Strength, speed, overall physicality," I say. "I just don't want to die within ten seconds of seeing Astaroth again."

Though even with all the training in the world, I'm not sure how much of a chance I stand against a giant demon.

"Okay, so it looks like we'll be starting from square one. That's fine. I make no promises, but we'll see what we can do."

That sounds promising.

He then proceeds to force me to stretch first, which I'm pretty sure is some sort of torture technique. After that, he gives me a short tour of the gym and explains all the machines. But, to my surprise, we start with free weights. He shows me how to properly curl a dumbbell and, of course, I've been doing it wrong all this time.

"I ran into your girlfriend earlier," I tell him, struggling to keep proper form with even a ten-pound weight. "She sends her regards."

Archer looks at me, puzzled. "Who?"

"Celeste. She's your girlfriend, right?"

"I guess."

My eyebrows shoot up. "*Wow*."

"What?" he asks, confused.

"How do you not know if she's your girlfriend?" I ask incredulously.

Archer shrugs. "I don't even know if *you* were my girlfriend."

"No, I wasn't! I told you, we went out once. That doesn't count for anything."

"Romeo and Juliet went out once, too," he says defensively.

I can't help but roll my eyes. "That's a play, and you're delusional. No offense." I pause for a moment before adding, "Celeste says she's your girlfriend."

Archer puts down his weights, moving over to the pull-up bar. "Watch my form. And I haven't even kissed Celeste. I kissed *you* several times."

"Ugh, can we not make a big deal out of a little kiss? If I dated every guy I locked lips with, I'd have a long list of ex-boyfriends," I retort.

He raises an eyebrow, sweat dripping down his forehead as he performs five pull-ups effortlessly. "So the whole shy, innocent act was just that…an act?" he asks, his muscles bulging with each lift. There's no way I'm going to be able to do that. Not even once.

I can barely do one push-up, let alone a pull-up. "Hey, it worked on you, didn't it?"

"Not particularly."

Now who's the liar?

"I've known what sex was since I was, like, seven or eight," I explain. "I had an older foster sister who was a bit of a slut. We shared a room." She didn't care if I was there or not. "It doesn't matter."

He drops from the bar, landing safely on his feet. "Your turn."

I jump up to reach the bar, but once I get a good grip on the metal, all I can do is hang there like a sack of potatoes. "I don't think I can pull myself up."

"Try," he insists.

I attempt to pull myself up, but my body seems to have a mind of its own. My arms shake uncontrollably, and my strength gives out before I can even lift my head above the bar. I grimace. "See? I told you it wasn't going to happen."

"We'll come back to that," Archer relents, moving to a different machine. Thankfully, I get to sit down for this. He adjusts the weight and situates me in the leg press before continuing. "Why did you pretend like you've never dated before?"

"It's part of the character. And I never *did* date before. It was just hooking up." The leg press is easier than any arm exercises I did earlier, and I'm able to complete a set of fifteen reps before continuing. "It didn't matter much. Growing up, everyone knew about the characters—and about how much of a slut I was. But guys liked that whole virgin role-play stuff."

"But you can only do that once."

"No. With Mary Alice, with *any* of my characters, I just...reset them." I continue with another set, adjusting the weight to be a little higher. "It's like a clean slate. I just pretended that things didn't happen."

"And you're calling *me* delusional?"

"Hey. I said I *pretended*. It doesn't mean I didn't realize the difference between make believe and reality."

Archer takes a moment to think it over. "That sounds like a lot of work."

"Yeah. But as much work as it was play-acting as someone else, it was much harder to be myself," I say, my cheeks immediately heating. "Oh my God. Forget I said that. Erase it from your memory *immediately*!"

"Why?"

"Because. It's embarrassing." Do I have to spell it out for

him? "Anyway, enough about that. What's the deal with Celeste? She said she'd make my life miserable if I touch you. But it seems like you're the miserable one."

He shrugs again, and for a moment, I wonder if he finds it difficult to talk about. "It's an arranged marriage," he explains. "We're both angel shadowborn from prominent families, and our fathers want to seal a business deal. I was always supposed to marry Celeste, even when I was dating Allegra. But I never took it seriously until last winter."

"Why last winter?" I ask, genuinely curious.

"My father threatened to cut me off unless I started officially dating her," he admits, his voice tinged with resignation. "Which means attending social functions with her like an accessory, taking her on dates, and that sort of thing."

The way he explains this makes it sound like he's being held hostage. Except, in his situation, his father isn't holding his loved ones above his head. This is a monetary exchange, a business transaction dressed up in the guise of marriage.

But hey, who am I to judge? Money makes the world go round, after all.

"Celeste isn't a bad person," he concludes.

I beg to differ. "She slammed my neck into a wall."

"She's not a good person, either," he adds. "She can just be...intense."

Intensely psychotic?

"She doesn't actually like me, anyway. This is a territorial thing, guaranteed. She doesn't want anyone to think I cheated on her. That would be humiliating. I know it's taboo in the human world, but I think it's worse in the shadowborn world." He looks at me pointedly. "To Allegra, knowing that her father was unfaithful was probably the end of her world."

I know. I'm sure sucks for her—especially since when I first met Allegra, she was fighting against the very thing that is now happening to her. Her entire goal in helping me was to protect her family, but through no fault of her own, it ended up getting destroyed.

"Learning Neil was my father shattered my world, too," I say. It's funny how one shared experience can either bring people together or tear them apart. In this case, instead of bonding with Allegra over what happened, we're completely divided. It's not exactly my ideal scenario, but there isn't much I can do about it. As much as I'd like to mend things between us, I wouldn't even know where to start. I mean, everything she's angry at me for is so out of my control that it's like trying to fight gravity.

Archer pauses. "Hey, Mar? Can I ask you something personal?"

"Go for it." It's not like I have anything to hide anymore. Aside from the whole time-travel thing. And the blood magic. And my relationship with Rhys.

"You just seem like a different person right now," Archer admits. "Calm. Cooler. It's strange for me. But…I think I would have been attracted to you anyway, even without your Mary Alice persona. So I guess what I'm trying to ask is, why do you still need the characters?"

It's an interesting admission, coming from him. There are a million ways I could answer his question, but to narrow it down into a more digestible answer, I tell him, "I got my first suitcase when I was a teenager. My mom, who was my social worker at the time, gave it to me."

"A suitcase?"

"Yes. I moved around constantly, but no one ever gave me a suitcase before that," I continue. "I hated moving. It was always a gamble—you never knew if the next house would be better or worse. I used to throw up because of the nerves, so at one point they just stopped telling me in advance that I would be moving. I would just come home and see the trash bags by the curb, and someone from the agency would be waiting to pick me up. They would load the trash bags of my belongings into the car and escort me away, always afraid I'd make a scene. And I used to think to myself that I was like trash, too, you know? Like a piece of garbage. Easily disposed of. So to answer your question, my characters are like gloves. I need them to interact with the world around me, because without gloves... Well, no one wants to touch trash."

Dear Maria,

Forgive me. I told myself I would not interfere with your relationship with Archer. You deserve to have your experiences. But tonight, you looked stunning. You might have been concerned about receiving a hand-me-down, but your beauty is very different from Allegra's.

And then he put his hands on you. He doesn't even know your name.

No, I apologize. I am trying to temper my jealousy. But seeing you smile at him, kiss him, is not easy.

Yours,
Rhys

Dear Rhys,

Oh man. I forgot about that. I'm sorry. If it makes you feel any better, you're a much better kisser.

Archer has no idea how to lead up to a kiss. He'll just do it, even if the mood doesn't call for it. With you, it was different.

Oh jeez. What are you making me write?

Mar

Chapter Eleven

After the workout session with Archer, I swear my condition worsened because, as soon as I come home and shower, my headache returns with a vengeance. It's like my body just can't catch a break, and I'm still not feeling 100%.

I decide to wait until midnight before sneaking upstairs for some much-needed hydration. I'm extra cautious, trying my best to avoid running into anyone. Allegra usually hits the sack early, and Nic has been MIA lately, so I should be in the clear. However, as I enter the kitchen, I'm startled to find Rhys still awake, leisurely sipping on tea at the counter.

Damn it, I wish I had seen him from around the corner so I could have made a quick getaway. But now that he's staring at me, his eyes completely inscrutable, I realize I can't just crawl back downstairs without making things awkward.

"Uh, hi," I say awkwardly.

"What are you doing up so late?" he questions, his voice sharp but quiet.

"I'm a college student," I answer. "We're not exactly known for having good sleep schedules."

"Yet you wake up early."

"To avoid Nic and Allegra." It also gives me some extra time to study. My grades have never been higher. Maybe that's the secret to doing well in school—being a morning person.

I grab water bottles from the fridge, sneaking a glance at Rhys from the corner of my eye. He's wearing pajamas. I think this is my first time seeing him like this, in just a T-shirt and cotton pants. He's thinner now than he was in the past—*leaner*, I'll say. His muscles aren't as big; I imagine he doesn't have much time to work out. And he's not in the midst of war, having to live in forts and camps and survive the wilderness.

"Are you stocking up for winter?" he asks, a hint of amusement in his voice.

"Winter is almost over," I reply.

"Is that so?"

"Yeah." I unscrew the cap to one of the bottles and take a sip. "Spring is just around the corner."

"It feels as though this winter has lasted eons," Rhys says.

"I—" I stop abruptly when I hear the front door open.

Nic strolls in, whistling. He stops when he sees Rhys and me in the kitchen. "I didn't think you two would be awake."

"I'm just getting water bottles. Don't worry. I'll be out of your sight in a minute," I tell him.

Before Nic can respond, I grab the armful of bottles and scurry back downstairs to the basement, alone. I unload the bottles on my desk and head to my closet, closing the door behind me. In the safe, on top of my magic supplies, are Rhys' letters.

I've already read them all, but sometimes I like to go back and re-read my favorite ones. They make me feel better, in a strange way. Even if we can't be seen together, his words on paper are a reminder of the connection we share. It's a connection that I can't explain, but I know it's there.

"DIDN'T ANYONE EVER TELL YOU TO STOP PLAYING WITH your food?" Archer asks.

"Didn't anyone ever tell *you* that life is about having fun?" I counter, which yes, I realize is hypocritical of me.

"Having fun, or clogging your arteries?"

"Oh, lighten up." I place the final fry on my volcano of French fries and pour ketchup in the center. "There! I hereby dub thee...Spudcano!"

Archer casts a furtive glance around the cafeteria, as if to make sure no one caught what I just said. I guess he's still self-conscious, even if he's willing to be seen with me in public. "Maybe now that we're training, you should eat some food that isn't fried. Or potato based."

"Neil's holding my family hostage, someone planted spy cameras in my bedroom, Allegra and Nic are constantly checking up on me, I'm barely holding it together in therapy, and I'm on a hopeless mission to take down a monster that I'm not sure I'll survive," I list off. "Are you suggesting I stop the one joy I have left in the world?"

He looks away. "No."

"I thought so." I swipe a fry from the volcano. "Are you sure you don't want any?"

"I'm fine with my quinoa salad."

"Suit yourself." From my observations, Archer actually *enjoys* eating healthy food. We've been having dinner together after our training sessions, and he goes to the salad bar every time. Worse, he eats *kale*. He told me it was his favorite snack growing up. Kale. Raw kale.

And I thought *I* had a rough childhood.

"Valentine's Day is coming up. Are you doing anything special?" I ask.

Archer side-eyes me. "Are you asking me out?"

"Oh, please." Hell will have to freeze over first.

"It's an honest question."

"I'm not interested. I know enough about you now to understand we'd make a horrible couple. We would never decide on a place to eat or what movie to watch. Besides, I already have plans." Mainly, listening to sad songs on repeat and replying to more of Rhys' letters. Yes, it's as pathetic as it sounds, especially considering I'm not going to give him my replies. But I'm allowed to be a little pitiful, given the circumstances. "I was just making conversation."

"Fishing for gossip, more like."

"Aw, see? We're getting to know each other so much better!"

"Yes, it's amazing how much I've learned about you now that you're not lying to me."

"So, your plans?" I prompt. "Are you going on a date with your girlfriend?"

"Yes." He sounds thrilled. *Not*. "She booked dinner and a hotel on the mainland. It's a Thursday night, so I asked her to postpone to the weekend…but she said no."

"And you're going anyway," I conclude. Sounds about right.

If there were two paths in front of him, a safe route and a risky one, Archer would turn around and go home. He doesn't have any fight in him, which is ironic since he's teaching me how to fight. Maybe I should reconsider that.

"Celeste isn't a bad person. I think she's under a lot of pressure, too. Her parents are more intense than mine."

"Not a bad person? She choked me right in the hallway! But sure, she's 'not bad,'" I say sarcastically. "Have you hashed things out with her? About how you don't like her?"

To my surprise, he says, "Yes. But she wants to go through with this anyway. What can I say? *No*? Twice?"

As much as I want to give him some tough love and tell him to refuse, to "man up" and take control, I've come to realize that I may have underestimated these shadowborn. During my session this week, I learned that their experiences are vastly different from my own, and their fears and insecurities are valid, even if I don't fully understand them.

Growing up, I never had a stable home. I was constantly being shuffled from one temporary living situation to the next. Being kicked out, often for reasons that were beyond my control, was just a normal part of my life. It's a stark contrast to Archer and Celeste, who may have never been kicked out, but the constant threat of it looms over them.

Archer is a man of routine. He wakes up at the same time every day, meticulously plans out his schedule, and follows it to the letter. It's his way of controlling what little he can in a world that is often unpredictable and scary. And while it would be easy for me to give him crap about it and tell him to just suck it up, I realize that he doesn't need me, or anyone else, to invalidate his fears.

"Hypothetically, if you could spend Valentine's Day *any* way you wanted, what would you do?" I ask.

He pokes at his salad. "Study. It's just a regular day. I don't see anything special about it."

"Because you're with someone you don't like? Or because you don't have a romantic bone in your body?"

"I can be romantic," he says roughly. "I won you over, didn't I?"

I burst into laughter. "You're joking, right? You won me over? *Please*! When you kissed me, there was *no* romantic build-up whatsoever!"

"Are you criticizing my kissing skills?"

"No. You're good at kissing. Just not what happens before. Do you even know what fore—"

"What are you two doing together?" Ophelia asks dubiously, putting her tray down beside Archer.

Ophelia Blackwood hasn't changed a bit—still a bombshell blonde, with a stunning spray tan. She's pretty, but certainly not the nicest person you'll ever meet. Although, to her credit, she's not as cruel as Lilly. Ophelia is just very confrontational. I still remember the time she spilled Coke over my head shortly after we met, making it abundantly clear how little she thought of me.

But the feeling isn't mutual. Sure, she was rude to me when I was Mary Alice, but as Mar, I'm able to brush that off. It's all water under the bridge now. I'm effectively indifferent to her, and that's probably the best way to deal with someone like Ophelia.

"We're talking about how Archer is a good kisser, but he needs to watch more rom-coms and stop the true crime documentaries," I reply. "He doesn't know a thing about romantic tension. Building anticipation."

"You two kissed?" she asks, her eyes wide. She turns to him, swatting his arm. "Archer!"

Archer shakes his head. "Seriously, Mar?"

"Hey, you should count yourself lucky," I say. "I'm a *great* kisser. It comes with the experience."

"I thought you weren't speaking with her," Ophelia says, ignoring me entirely.

"Well, now I'm training her. Also, we're friends."

I gasp. "You mean that?"

"Shut up." He reddens. "You're making it more difficult than it should be."

"Now that we're *friends*, get used to it," I tease.

"The secondhand embarrassment?"

"Yes."

"But she's a liar!" Ophelia points to me, still in a state of shock. "She peeped at you while you took a shower. You should have her thrown in jail!"

"Hey, *he* flashed *me*," I say. "It's not like I asked to see his privates!"

"*What*?"

As if the situation couldn't get any more awkward, Allegra and Rhys choose the perfect time to walk by. I can see Rhys carrying a parfait on his tray, and I assume he's carrying it for Allegra. But his expression tells me that he might have heard everything we just said.

"Good Lord," I mutter under my breath. I glance over at Archer, and his face is as red as a tomato. On the other hand, Rhys glares daggers at him. I wonder if I should just blend into the wall or make a quick getaway before things get any more uncomfortable. "And it looks like that's my cue to—"

"Sit down," Archer growls, pulling my arm. "If I have to suffer, so do you."

"I blame you," I hiss.

"You two had sex?" Allegra asks dully, looking between us.

"Gross. No," Archer says.

Wait, *gross*? He would *be* so lucky! But one look at Rhys, and I know I should keep my mouth shut. I shrug off Archer's hand for good measure.

"We're done," I say. "I was just explaining that there was a misunderstanding when we first met. But why do you care? You're not dating him. Neither are you, Ophelia."

Her jaw drops. "Obviously not. I'm sapphic."

"Sapphire?"

"I'm a lesbian," she clarifies, rolling her eyes. "Wait. You didn't think I was jealous, did you?"

"Uh, no..." Yes.

"That's so typical," she scoffs. "Archer is my childhood friend. We grew up together, and he's like a brother to me. Even if I wasn't gay, I'd never date him."

"Thanks," he says dryly. "Now that we've established that no one at this table is dating me or interested in me—great for my self-esteem, by the way—can we move on?"

Allegra frowns, pushing her hair behind her ears. "What are you even doing here?"

It takes me a moment to realize she's speaking to me. "Eating dinner."

"Dinner? A pile of fries?"

"It's Spudcano."

"I thought you hated her," she says, shifting her gaze to Archer. "She lied to you. To *us*."

Since when were they "us"? They broke up years ago.

"We talked it out," he replies. They stare at each other for a few seconds, unspoken words flying between them. I can't hope to decipher it. Did something happen while I was gone? I'll have to ask him about it later. "Allegra—"

"You must really enjoy my hand-me-downs," she spits, her voice dripping with intense resentment. It's hard to tell if it's directed at me or the whole situation. I doubt *she* even knows where her emotions are coming from at this point.

"That's not fair," I say. "*They* like *me*."

Archer groans. "Seriously, Mar?"

Ophelia's already disappeared, having probably slipped away while we were distracted. Damn, I'm jealous. I want to leave, too.

Because now, it's just us four. Archer, me, Allegra, and Rhys. Allegra and I both dated Archer. I'm sort of involved with Rhys. Allegra might be in love with him—the jury's still out on that one.

It's like I'm in hell. I'm certainly sweating like it.

"Archer is just working out with me," I explain, mostly for Rhys' benefit. "He has a girlfriend. Who isn't me."

"Come on, Mar. You don't have to explain yourself to her," Archer says. "Let's go."

Leaving Spudcano behind, I follow Archer outside. Honestly, I'm grateful to be out of there; I don't think I could have handled a confrontation with Allegra. She's like a ticking time bomb waiting to explode, and I don't want things to be so rough between us. Unfortunately, our situation has put us at odds, and I'm not sure how to fix it.

As Archer and I step out of the main building, the cool night air hits us like a refreshing wave. It's a welcome change from the heated atmosphere inside moments ago. I turn to Archer, trying to gauge his mood.

"So what happened between you?" I probe. "While I was gone, I mean."

We begin walking down the street, not sure of where we're headed. Not toward my dorm, that's for sure. Not toward his, either.

"We slept together," Archer admits. "After you disappeared, and her mom died, and everything was just chaotic… She came over one night and we slept together."

"Wow." And I thought I was self-destructive. That just seems like a bad idea. "Y'all aren't back together, though."

"No. It was just a one-time thing. We didn't speak about it after, but it's been awkward," he says. "We don't have *feelings* for each other or anything. But…I can tell she's still upset with you. Very upset."

"I know that."

"I'm serious, Mar. Be careful," he warns. "I wouldn't cross her if I were you. Her behavior has been erratic and unpredictable. It's like she's a completely different person now. She wants to hurt you."

"She wants to hurt *Neil*. He killed her mom. But she can't hurt him. She loves him; he's her dad. And until she can reconcile her feelings toward him, she'll push all her anger and pain toward me," I say quietly. "I'm an easier target. I get it."

"And you're not mad?"

"At Neil? Yeah. But Allegra…for some reason, I'm not mad."

Not about this.

Maybe it's because I've grown as a person, or maybe it's because I can see myself in her. We're both walking on thin ice here, and I understand that. However, as long as she doesn't cross the line, I'm willing to forgive her occasional outbursts. I'd like to reconcile with her and move forward in a positive direction.

After a moment of silence, Archer nods. "I see what you mean. It's a complicated situation, but it sounds like you're managing."

"Well, I don't know about that. It's not like there's a manual for dealing with your half sister who hates you because her dad killed her mom."

"Yeah, that's not exactly a common problem."

We both laugh, and the tension eases a bit. It's nice to have someone to talk to about this, someone who doesn't judge me for being in this situation.

"I just hope that eventually, Allegra can come to terms with everything and we can all move forward," I say.

"I'm sure she will. It might take some time."

I'm not sure we have that. I may be a time traveler, but even I can't escape the precious nature of time—it's always slipping away, no matter how hard I try to hold onto it.

Dear Rhys,

It's Valentine's Day. I can't believe we're living together, and yet I can't so much as look at you without worrying about Nic and Allegra ratting us out to Neil. Maybe being constantly monitored has made me paranoid.

I've been getting sick a lot lately. The blood magic is starting to take a toll on me, and the stress isn't helping either. I'm frustrated with my lack of progress in every aspect of my life. The fight against Astaroth isn't going well, and I haven't even faced him yet. Despite Archer's help, my preparations are moving at a snail's pace, and I'm not sure how I'm going to outsmart him with my blood magic. Therapy isn't going any better either. We keep circling the same topics, and it's hard to talk about without completely breaking down.

I miss you. When we meet in passing, it feels even worse because you're always with Allegra. I know I shouldn't be jealous, and that it's not your fault, or even hers. But something sinister churns inside my stomach when I see you two together. She can be seen in public with you, but I can't. I see your death in my nightmares, on rotation with Max and the Bakers, and…

I miss you. I miss you. I miss you.

Mar

Chapter Twelve

February comes and goes, and when March arrives, Archer thinks I've finally shown improvement.

"I don't think you'll die within ten seconds of facing a beastblood," he clarifies, pointing a fry at me. Yes, a fry—I've turned him into one of my junk food minions. Well, he usually gets a small plate of fries and throws them in his salad. But that's *progress*, at least.

"I'd give her thirty seconds," Ophelia replies. It's not a glowing endorsement by any means, but it's about as much as I can expect from her. We're not friends, though she eats dinner with us most days of the week. We're not enemies, either.

"Thanks for worrying about me," I say, putting a hand to my heart. "It means a lot."

"I'm *not* worried." But she is. And, on top of that, I think she's socially awkward. Hard to tell, though. I'm still trying to figure her out.

Ophelia isn't one to open up. So far, all I know about her is that she eats more or less the same healthy food that

Archer does, she's a werewolf shadowborn, and she's a lesbian. Not that she ever talks about any of those things. She mostly just observes, and if she *does* have something to say, it's usually an insult aimed at me.

"So does this mean you'll take me on a hunt?" I ask him.

"I guess." He dips a fry in ranch dressing. That's another thing I've done for him—coerced him into using dressing. I like to think I'm making his life better by encouraging him to try different foods, but in reality, I'm probably just making his diet unhealthy. At least he throws me a smile once in a while.

Ophelia perks up immediately. "A hunt in the Veil? With *her*? She's going to be mincemeat."

"Mar-meat," Archer supplies unhelpfully.

"Fighting against ferals is a whole different ballpark," Ophelia warns. "You're going to be dead weight."

"That's why I want you to come along, too, Ophelia," Archer says. "Ask Georgia or someone else to join us."

"What, Celeste doesn't want to come?"

"Is she giving you the cold shoulder?" I ask.

"I don't want to talk about it."

Celeste is still a touchy subject, it seems. From what I've gathered, their Valentine's Day date ended in a huge fight.

"There's been an uptick in ferals near the borderlands. They're kind of like canyons, Mar," Archer explains. "It used to be filled with people and beastbloods, but after the rivers dried, it became a barren wasteland."

"So, pretty much in line with the rest of the Veil," I conclude.

"There are still some nice areas. But the rest of the realm is a disaster. No wonder they want to come here," Ophelia mutters. "Most of the shifters have already relocated. A huge group of them live in communities in Canada and the northern states."

"And you're from the South."

"My maternal grandmother lives here." She doesn't elaborate.

"It's dangerous," Archer tells me. "But I think you can handle it. You've been training for a while now, and you understand the risks. We just have to stay alert and be prepared. And hopefully we won't run into any nasty surprises."

Ophelia raises an eyebrow, but I can tell that she's excited by the prospect of a hunt in the Veil—even if she won't say it aloud. "What type of beastblood is on the menu? Not a flying one, I hope."

"No. Feral mountain lions and hyenas. We'll try to take on the hyenas; they're smaller."

"What makes these animals different from the ones here in the mortal realm?" I interject. "Can they talk or something?"

The Veil *does* have creatures like that. I remember the creatures guarding the Wisdom Tree, and doing a poor job of it.

But Archer shakes his head. "These borderland creatures are different. They're bigger than mortal animals, and much more intelligent. They used to be able to speak, but with the feral illness infecting their brains, they've been stripped down to animal instinct."

In other words, they're larger and more ferocious than mortal animals. Fantastic—I'm looking forward to cowering while Archer and Ophelia do all the work.

"What's the plan of attack? How do these things usually work?" I ask.

"We'll meet in the field on Saturday, the one near the Hopkins building. You know, the one with the hideous purple color and the weathervane shaped like a clown?" Archer explains. "Provost Mathers will be there to oversee everything and open a rift. Then, groups will head inside and take a bus to the borderlands. But the most important thing is that we stick together. We don't want anyone getting separated and lost in the Veil. So, please, be careful and keep an eye on each other. And if, by chance, you do get lost, don't wander around aimlessly looking for us—just head back home, got it?"

As he looks at me intently, his gaze serious and unyielding, I can tell that he means every word. He doesn't want anything bad to happen to me on this hunt. Bless his heart, but he doesn't know that I've been honing my blood magic skills on the side. I'm ready to show him just how much I've grown since we last trained together. It's time to put my skills to the test and see what I'm capable of.

I HAVE NEVER BEEN TO THE GRAND CANYON, BUT I HAVE seen enough pictures to know what to expect. The way Archer described the borderlands, I thought they would be just as grand, daunting, and barren. Boy, was I wrong! It's much worse than I could have ever imagined.

The air is filled with smog, and every time I take a breath it feels like I'm breathing in something I shouldn't. It smells like burning tires and rotten food. Wind whistles through the canyon, playing an eerie song that sounds like someone blowing air over an empty glass bottle.

I can't even see the sun. The world looks mottled, grey,

and dead. The ground is cracked and parched, with charred debris strewn across the barren landscape. The canyon itself is an abyss, seemingly stretching on forever with its steep walls of jagged black rocks.

Archer leads the way, our weapons at the ready. I have a few spell bags tied to my belt, just in case we come across any ferals. Ophelia walks behind him, her sword drawn and ready. I bring up the rear, my senses heightened and on full alert.

As we move deeper into the canyon, Archer's eyes scan the surroundings for any signs of danger. Ophelia and I remain on high alert, constantly looking out for any lurking ferals.

My heart races as I keep my eyes darting from left to right, searching for any sign of danger. My palms grow clammy with each passing second, and I can feel the adrenaline coursing through my veins. Suddenly, Archer stops in his tracks, holding up a hand to signal us to be quiet. My muscles tense as I prepare for an attack, but nothing comes. Instead, Archer points to a small crevice in the canyon wall.

"Look," he whispers. "There's something in there."

A deep growl reverberates through the darkness. Archer motions for me to stay back as he and Ophelia inch toward the crevice. I stand frozen as they ready their swords, not daring to move a muscle until they get a closer look. My heart races with dread as I anticipate whatever lies ahead.

Suddenly, a hyena lunges forward, its jaws snapping dangerously close to Archer and Ophelia. They jump back, avoiding the attack, and I see Archer's sword glint in the dim light as he swings it at the creature.

I've never seen a feral, but I can tell that this hyena-like creature is, in fact, infected. Its skin sags, almost like it's slipping off the bone, rotted with patches of matted fur over its back. Black goo drips from wounds on its side and from its mouth. Its eyes are black as night, sunken into its skull.

I know I should stay back and let the more experienced hunters take care of it, but I can't help feeling a surge of adrenaline coursing through my veins. I take a step forward, my hand hovering over my spell bags.

Before I can do anything, a chorus of howls echoes through the canyon. A moment later, a pack of twenty feral hyenas appears from the shadows, their eyes blazing.

Despite their zombie-like appearance, the ferals are fast. They attack all at once, quickly overwhelming us. Archer and Ophelia fight bravely, each stroke of their blades sending a shower of black blood into the air. But the ferals circle them like sharks, pressing in closer with each attack.

I barely manage to lift my sword in time to block one of the ferals from flinging itself at me, my reflexes lagging. Another feral lunges at me, its jaws snapping. The feral desperately tries to bite me, but I twist away in time, my arm burning from just holding the sword.

"Run!" I yell. Grasping one of the spell bags, I cut my finger on my sword, activating the spell and throwing it in the air. A blinding light engulfs us, and I take the chance to run.

My feet pound against the dirt, and the wind rushes around me as I run. I risk a glance over my shoulder, hoping desperately to catch sight of Archer and Ophelia, but they are gone. Damn it. I guess I'll just need to find a place to open a rift, and we can regroup in the mortal realm. Or, if need be, I can get help from Provost Mathers.

I drive myself forward, only to find the hard ground crumbling beneath me like sand. Adrenaline rushes through me as I freefall into the abyss. The ground below rushes toward me and I brace myself for impact. The next thing I know, I'm tumbling down a rocky slope in total darkness, bouncing painfully against the rocks.

At last, I come to a sudden stop, my body aching from the fall. Groaning in pain, I roll onto my back and take stock of the situation. I squint into the darkness, my eyes barely adjusting. I try to move my leg and yelp at a blinding spike of pain that shoots up through my body. Oh God, it's probably broken. I guess this is karma for breaking Nic's leg, huh? My other limbs feel flabby, like they're made of rubber.

As the eerie silence surrounding me is broken by a low hiss, I freeze in place, the hairs on my arms standing on end. Inch by inch, something slithers across my body…a lot of "somethings." They crawl on me like a living blanket, their cool skin sending shivers down my spine. Snakes. Just my luck.

On pure instinct, I reach for my sword, but it's gone, lost somewhere during my fall. I guess I'm lucky I didn't immediately impale myself with it. Then again, that would have been a quicker death than the one I'm facing now.

In a flash, the first snake strikes, its fangs sinking into my neck like daggers. The venom courses through me like icy fire, numbing my body as the snakes begin to constrict around me. Another one bites my hand, reopening the wounds on my palms.

I'm slipping away, a wave of dizziness engulfing me, and I'm frozen in fear, unable to move or even scream as death creeps ever closer.

I'm not sure how much time passes in that suspended

state between life and death, but when I finally regain my senses, I can hear Ophelia's voice calling out to me.

"Damn it. I found her!" Ophelia screams, peering over the ledge of the cliff.

I pry my eyes open to see the shine of her blonde hair. The canyon is brighter than before, as if dawn broke through in the middle of the night. The cliff felt much steeper as I fell, but now that I can see, I realize it's only a two-story drop.

"Mar, are you dead?" Ophelia calls.

I can only respond with a pitiful moan.

There are no snakes around, but my skin still burns where they bit me. The bite marks and blood are the only ways I can tell I didn't just imagine the whole thing.

Ophelia and Archer scale down the rocky cliff face, careful not to slip like I had. When they reach the bottom, they immediately come over to me and assess the damage. Their own clothes are worse for wear, covered in dirt and stains. Their hair is mussed, but both seem unharmed.

"We need to get her back to campus," Archer murmurs, his eyes sweeping over me. I can't imagine I look camera-ready at the moment. "Her leg is busted."

"What the hell?" Ophelia kneels beside me, peering into my face. When she sees it, her eyes widen and she scrambles back, nearly losing her footing. "What the *hell*?"

Archer carries the same look of shock on his face, backing up in disbelief.

"What?" I croak.

"Your eyes," he says finally. "Mar, your eyes are yellow."

Dear Maria,

Today, while we were training, I nearly smiled at the absurd words coming out of your mouth. It amazes me how effortlessly you are able to lift my spirits. Your power over me is dangerous, particularly considering the limitations of our situation.

I wanted so badly to tell you how I feel.

However, the timing is not yet suitable for such actions. I fear that I may allow my anxieties to get the better of me and jeopardize our chances of seeing one another in the past. You once mentioned that you perceived me as cold, and that our bond was one of mere friendship. Therefore, I shall maintain the necessary distance to avoid misunderstandings.

Please do not misunderstand. If given the opportunity, I would have already begun courting you in earnest.

Yours,
Rhys

Dear Rhys,

I think you might be reading a few too many romance novels. Not that I'm judging, mind you. It's just that every time you write to me, I feel like I'm in one of those bodice-ripper historical romance novels. Minus the smut, unfortunately.

It's funny, when you originally wrote these letters, you were hiding your true feelings from me. Now I have to do the same. I don't know how you managed. This is killing me. (Not literally, obviously.)

Every time I see you, my heart skips a beat and my brain turns to mush. It's like you're doing weird things to my head. Ew, listen to me. I'm turning into some romantic sap, and I blame you entirely.

Mar

Chapter Thirteen

My eyes aren't just any shade of yellow. Oh no, they had to be the *least* pleasant color on the spectrum. Ophelia, who is ever-so-observant, wastes no time pointing that out, even as I lie in bed with a broken leg. Apparently, on this island, doctors make house calls and nurses aren't afraid to take on broken bones. Once my leg is set and I'm showered and all settled in, the trio—Archer, Ophelia, and Provost Mathers—decide to grace me with their presence.

"You passed the twenty-four-hour threshold of infection, so thankfully you weren't bitten by *feral* snakes," Provost Mathers offers. It's a small comfort. "How are you feelin', Mar?"

"Like I got bitten by a bunch of snakes and broke my leg," I reply dryly. "And my eyes hurt."

"What did the doctor say?" Archer asks.

"That they look like lemon rinds. And also, they don't know what's causing it."

"They look like they're filled with bile," Ophelia adds.

"Thanks for the observation, Ophelia. That's super helpful," I reply sarcastically. But she's right. My eyes look freaky and unnatural, which suits me, I guess. However, the excruciating pain and the sudden shift in eye color aren't even the worst part about coming back from the Veil.

In the face of danger, I panicked. I thought I had gotten used to people trying to kill me, as much as one person *can* get used to that sort of thing, but no. I threw a flash bomb and ran. What's wrong with me?

I didn't even have the presence of mind to warn Ophelia and Archer before taking off. My rash actions could have gotten us all killed. Even though they say it's fine, the guilt still weighs on my chest like a ton of bricks.

Why couldn't I have handled it better? Was I just not prepared enough?

I can only imagine how disappointed Provost Mathers must be in me for not being able to keep a level head and think clearly under pressure. He trusted me enough to let me go on the hunt, and here I am, unable to even protect myself from danger. Ugh, I'm such a disappointment.

"I've never seen a trueblood with that color iris," Archer says, turning to the provost. "What do you think caused it? The snake venom?"

"No, Mar was cleared for venom. I'm not sure what caused the shift, but you're correct. I've only seen that eye color in animals and beastbloods," Mathers says.

It's definitely the blood magic. I can't come out and say it, but it's the only thing that makes sense.

"We shouldn't make any assumptions about her condition," Mathers continues. "I'll run some blood tests and find out more. Until then, why don't you rest, Mar? I'll excuse you from classes for the week while you're recoverin'."

As soon as he finishes, the basement door creaks open. Rhys descends the stairs, holding a tray of soup in his hands.

"Mr. Abbott has instructed me to ensure you are well fed," he says in a monotone, speaking directly to me.

Mathers gives him a nod of acknowledgment and then turns back to me. "I'll be in touch with you shortly. Just ring if you need me."

Archer's green eyes narrow as he runs his gaze over Rhys. His lips are pursed in a thin line as he tilts his head. "Are you sure you'll be okay, Mar?"

"Probably. I'll text you later."

"Let's head out now," Mathers cajoles. "We don't want to tire her out any further."

The three of them file out of the room, leaving me alone with Rhys. And the cameras.

He waits until they're gone before coming closer. "Neil is not concerned about your eye color and considers this a trivial matter."

"And he sent you to make sure I'm okay?" I guess.

Rhys nods once and sets the tray of soup down on my lap. "He has also ordered colored contacts, in case you would like to conceal them."

"I'll be fine."

"I believe you should wear them."

That's an order. I study Rhys, searching his face for something, *anything*, that could indicate his inner thoughts. But he gives nothing away. Instead, he leaves as abruptly as he came, his words echoing in my mind.

He thinks I should wear the contacts? But why would Neil care? It's just an eye color; it's not like this school isn't filled with magic. I can't imagine that having a rare eye color is unheard of. Neil, himself, has a shade of emerald eyes so bright they look almost unnatural. And Rhys' eyes dance the line between blue and purple, which is also a very rare shade. Not to mention, he has *elf ears* sticking out of his head.

But what if there's another meaning to it all? Maybe it's an indication that I'm a time traveler, and Neil doesn't want anyone else to know? It brings me back to the question of how I got my abilities in the first place. Despite researching in the school's library and on my own, I've found nothing. Jenna hasn't been any help, either. It looks like I'm going to have to launch my own investigation.

I SLIP THE COLORED CONTACTS INTO MY EYES, WINCING slightly at the unfamiliar sensation before adjusting them until they fit comfortably. They're a dark brown and look almost too natural, which is exactly what I need to avoid any unwanted attention. No one will be able to tell that my eye color has changed unless they look closely.

What do you think is my one class on my first day back? Yeah, Combat. Just my luck. I still have to attend the class and take notes, but at least I'm excused from sparring, on account of having a broken leg.

After finishing in the bathroom and getting ready, Rhys has to carry me up the stairs to my wheelchair, making a scene in front of Allegra who's watching like a hawk. It would have been romantic if not for the discomfort of being jostled around.

Well, at least the pain is finally gone. I've been hopped up on painkillers for the past week.

Rhys sets me down in the chair, placing my bag on my lap. It's the first time I'll be getting out since the incident in the Veil, so he's made up the excuse to Allegra that he's accompanying me to class to ensure my safety, as Neil requested. She bought it, but she doesn't like it.

Rhys hands me a pair of sunglasses and walks behind me, wheeling me down the side ramp and out of the house. He has to push me across the lawn—not the most comfortable experience—and onto the street.

"Is it safe to talk?" I murmur, putting on the sunglasses. It's way too bright outside; I guess being a basement dweller is getting to me now. "Or is she still watching?"

"We must be careful," he replies, switching to Elvish. "Allegra has discovered something. She sent away for test results, stealing hair from the hairbrush you left behind. I could not stop her due to my injuries, but she received a letter several months ago."

"Hair? Like, for a spell?"

"Perhaps. She is being quite secretive, particularly with Nic. They have never been this close before. I believe they are working together."

Well, that can't be good.

"And Neil?" I probe.

"I have only been able to uncover a few documents. But I have reason to believe his mission for you and Astaroth is all strategic. That, somehow, Astaroth is only *part* of his plan," Rhys explains. "There is something under his house, which he often disappears to. A secret level I am not permitted to enter."

Which means that there's something down there. Or some*one*.

As the main building comes into view, there's so much

more I want to talk about. Not about Neil, but about Rhys. I wonder how he's holding up, being caught in the middle of this cold war. I haven't even gotten a chance to ask him how he's adjusting to modern-day Earth. While some of his initial letters hinted at a bit of culture shock, he hasn't expressed any significant complaints or shown any signs of grief.

There's something else that still lingers between us. That strong undercurrent of desire that I feel every time he's near.

"Be careful," he warns in English, leaving me at the front door. He leaves, just like that, and I'm left feeling this empty void inside myself. But, like with all painful things, I shove it down.

I wheel myself to the gymnasium just in time for class to start. Technically, I'm supposed to be here taking notes, but my mind is consumed with Rhys' words. How can Neil be so secretive and careful that even someone as intelligent as Rhys, who's also a trueblood like Neil, could only gather a little bit of information in three years?

Still, this is a start. I suspected Neil had bigger plans for me. What if he knows about my fate, like the Wisdom Tree foretold?

The girl who should not exist. The timekeeper's daughter.

If *Neil* is the timekeeper, then wouldn't that make Allegra a timekeeper's daughter, too? Or is the title of "time-keeper" someone else? It's related to the Time Agents, like Jenna and Todd. Maybe being a timekeeper's daughter isn't about biology but more about the role they play in time travel. Regardless, I assume Neil has some insight into my supposed fate.

I don't remember everything that the Wisdom Tree said;

it was all quite shocking. I probably should have taken notes, but at that moment, my mind was too preoccupied with trying to process everything. Now, I'm regretting not being more diligent.

I can't help but feel like I'm in the middle of some sort of grand scheme, a chessboard where I'm the pawn being moved around for *their* purposes. And I hate it.

As class begins, I try to focus on the lecture, but it's no use. My mind is wandering too much, thinking about what Rhys said. Aside from Neil's secret basement underneath Foley-Hill, what goal are Nic and Allegra working toward? Because it sounds like it's a separate mission from Neil's. What the hell was in that letter?

If she took my hair, it could have been some sort of genealogy report. But why would she need—

A memory comes to me suddenly, or a snippet of one. Something I completely forgot about, with everything else I'd learned from the Wisdom Tree.

Jenna pretty much spelled it out for me, didn't she?

You're going to kill my dad.

And I get to watch, knowing I did whatever I could to help you do it.

"I need to talk to you about Jenna," I tell Ophelia, cutting right to the chase.

"What's there to talk about?" she asks dully, pushing her tray of food away. I've spoiled her appetite.

Archer looks over curiously, but he doesn't say anything. He and Mathers are aware of the strange situation I have with Neil, and although Archer doesn't have all the details, he's been pretty good about not probing into them.

I can't help but wonder if he carries any guilt about what happened to Luke, even though he shouldn't. I never blamed him, and I still don't. We haven't discussed it, but sometimes when we talk, I sense a question simmering beneath the surface. To his credit, he has enough self-control not to pry, unlike me.

"What was her childhood like? You were all friends growing up, right?" I press.

Ophelia looks away. "Yes. Why?"

"So you knew her as a kid."

"Yeah," she answers, a tinge of annoyance laced into her voice. "What are you getting at?"

"I need you to tell me about her family. Please. It's important." I take a breath. "Was she adopted?"

"No," Ophelia says plainly.

"Well, technically she could have been," Archer interjects with a shrug. "No one ever mentioned anything about it, and she looked like her parents, so we assumed she wasn't. But that doesn't mean it's *impossible*."

"I would have known if she was," Ophelia snaps. "She would have told me."

"She didn't tell you she was in a cult."

That shuts Ophelia up.

"Do you know where her parents are now?" I ask. "I need to speak with them. It's *really* important."

"They're on the mainland, not far from here," Archer supplies. "I can take you."

"Seriously?"

He nods. "Her parents have been questioned pretty

extensively, though. I'm not sure how much you're looking to get out of them."

"I just need answers."

Because if Jenna's father is Astaroth, then maybe I can learn how things became like this in the first place.

Dear Maria,

Archer visited you today. I was in the kitchen of Allegra's dormitory house. He spoke with you while I was preparing a meal. Involving the kitchen knives.

And then he dared suggest that he could tutor you instead of me. Him. Maria, my love, he is a fool. Both academically and socially. If I could pursue you now, he would not even be on your radar.

Perhaps I sound overconfident.

Yours,
Rhys

Dear Rhys,

If you had seriously pursued me, it wouldn't have even been a contest. I would have seriously questioned your taste in women, of course, but that's another issue entirely.

Mar

Chapter Fourteen

On Sunday, Archer and I take the ferry to Jenna's childhood home. We need to rent a car with a ramp for my wheelchair, and Archer has to lift me up to get me situated. Then, he wheels me down the walkway to the house.

It's smaller than I imagined, tucked away in a quiet neighborhood. Frankly, it's the type of house I would have killed for as a kid—like some sort of fairytale cottage. Except every single house on the street is like it, in various shades of pastel and overflowing with fresh flowers.

The sun is shining, the birds are chirping, and I'm here to ask a teenage cult leader's parents if she was adopted.

I take a deep breath and try to calm myself down as Archer knocks on the door. A woman in her fifties with curly hair and dark eyes answers.

Immediately, I notice that she doesn't look much like Jenna. They have the same mousy brown hair, but their facial features are different. This woman is slender, almost hollow, though that could be the grief of losing a child. She wears a dress that looks vintage, with polka dots and a wide skirt. Is she going somewhere? Her hair is in pin curls, and she's carrying a small purse, which, from the looks of it, can't fit anything but her house keys.

"Oh, Archer Kinsey." She says his name like it's a curse, her frown deepening the wrinkles near her mouth. "And who is this?"

"This is Mar. She's my friend." Archer sticks out his hand to shake it, but the woman just stares. "Mrs. Cooper, we were wondering if we could ask you a few questions about Jenna."

She doesn't budge from the door. "What do you need to know? She was a screw-up."

I'm taken aback by her frankness, especially when we're talking about her own daughter. A daughter, mind you, she thinks is dead. Maybe she's hiding her true emotions?

"We just wanted to know a few things about Jenna," I say. "Can we talk?"

Mrs. Cooper scoffs and shakes her head. "No. I've already told the police everything."

"Mrs. Cooper, was Jenna adopted?" Archer blurts.

Her eyes widen, and for a second, she hesitates. But her expression quickly returns to a hard, cold stare. "No, she wasn't adopted. Now, if you don't mind, I have things to do. Please leave my property immediately and never come back here again."

Archer steps closer to the woman, his head bowed. "I'm very sorry, Mrs. Cooper. We didn't mean to disturb you."

Her lips tighten. "Just don't come back again."

Archer wheels me away, back toward the car, and helps me inside. Mrs. Cooper watches us, waiting until we're out of sight before she goes back in. As Archer pulls away from the curb, I tap his shoulder.

"Pull down this street," I urge him, pointing toward a side street.

"What?"

"It looked like she was heading out. We'll wait for her car to leave, and then we'll break in," I reply.

"*What*?" he repeats.

"Are you new at this?" I demand.

"We can't just break in."

"Don't worry, I have a kit in my bag." I hold up my backpack. "We'll go around back and see what we can find. That woman is hiding something."

"She's a grieving mother," he argues. "Well, maybe not grieving, but she's Jenna's mother. She's shadowborn. She probably got rid of all Jenna's stuff, already."

"We won't know until we take a look."

Archer sighs and pulls down the street. After a few minutes, her car zips by, a forest green Jeep. As soon as she's gone, we pull in front of her house.

The backyard is small but well maintained, with flowerbeds lining the perimeter and a small fountain in the middle. A wooden fence surrounds it all and acts as a barrier between the Coopers' house and their neighbors' yards. At first glance, there is nothing suspicious about it—until I spot a padlock on the back door. It's hilariously big, larger than my fist, and it almost doesn't look real.

I pull out my lockpicking kit and wheel myself over to the door. I feel along the pins with my pick until they click into place one by one. As soon as I hear the click of the last pin, I know it's done—the lock is open.

I open the door quietly, and Archer and I slip inside. My

wheelchair makes moving difficult; I can barely get around the tight corners, so it's a slow process.

We head upstairs first, which requires a lot of heavy lifting on Archer's part. Once he carries me and my wheelchair up, I immediately spot a door marked with a big stuffed 'J' pillow hanging from the doorknob. I take a deep breath before entering, knowing that this is where Jenna lived her life—where she laughed and cried and dreamed. And plotted to kill me.

But when I open the door, my heart sinks. Jenna's bedroom has been turned into a storage room. There are boxes stacked from floor to ceiling, filled with who-knows-what. A single bed sits in the corner, looking lonely and out of place. The walls are bare—all of Jenna's posters and pictures have been taken down—and there is no sign that this was ever her bedroom, aside from the J on the door.

It hits home, hard. The Coopers essentially erased Jenna's existence once she disappointed them. And God, she's *dead*.

"Let's keep looking," Archer urges, looking out the window obsessively. He's worried we'll get caught, I take it. I'm less concerned, not because I'm prepared to explain myself—I'm not—but because it's more important that I get this information.

We move on, searching through the other rooms in the house: the kitchen, the living room, and even Mrs. Cooper's office. There is nothing in any of those rooms that could help us—just more boxes and furniture pushed to the side to make room for them. I don't even know how they live like this, with some of the rooms just used to store things in boxes.

Worse, the boxes are filled with knickknacks. There are

no secret diaries or blood magic memorabilia. Nothing that could clue me in to Jenna's origins. I can't even find a copy of her birth certificate.

And then, just when I'm about to call it quits, Archer calls me from the living room.

"Come here! I found something!"

I make my way over to him and see what he has in his hands: a photo book. The cover is old and worn but still beautiful, with a picture of Jenna as a child on the front. As I flip through it, I see photos of her growing up—with friends at school, playing in the park, celebrating holidays with her family—all captured in striking moments that tell a story of who she was before.

The last photograph catches my attention. It's flipped over, and on the back, some names are jotted down with a date. I gingerly tug the photo out of its cover to examine it.

Mrs. Cooper stands in front of a sign for Southeastern College. She must have been a teenager in this, flashing a huge smile that looks just like Jenna's. Standing beside her are a few other women I don't recognize, two men, and one very familiar face.

Neil Abbott.

Last week, Dr. Jones got a new diffuser and asked me to choose my favorite scent for it. I picked lavender, which is supposed to have a calming effect. However, as we begin our session, I don't feel calm at all.

"I want to talk about Max today," Dr. Jones says.

Subconsciously, my body tenses. "What's there to talk about?"

"We've discussed him before, I know, but I would like to know your feelings on the matter."

"I don't want to rehash it. I told you everything." I can feel the sweat on my palms as I clench them into fists.

"You told me what happened, but you certainly didn't tell me everything," she says. "I imagine you have a lot of feelings that maybe you don't know how to express."

"What makes you think that?"

"Well, during our sessions I feel like you hold back sometimes. I don't think it's intentional, but I get the impression that certain subjects are very difficult for you to talk about. When I have patients who go through things like you have during their childhood, it's especially hard because as a child your brain isn't fully formed and you don't know how to deal with such trauma. But when you don't deal with the trauma, it lingers and festers like a wound."

"So you think I don't want to talk about Max because I don't know how to deal with what happened?" I ask.

"Am I incorrect?"

Unfortunately, she's spot on. "I don't even know where to begin. I really have told you everything that happened."

Unlike my other therapists, I didn't even bother lying to Dr. Jones. Maybe it's because she's different from the rest, or maybe I'm the one who's changed. Frankly, I can't say for sure if she's actually making a difference. I haven't noticed any major breakthroughs overnight, but talking to her doesn't make me want to pull my hair out either. Plus, her sessions fit perfectly into my busy schedule, so I keep coming back.

"Why do you think he started assaulting you?"

God I hate that word, especially when it's used to describe the situation between Max and me. "I don't know.

Because he could? Because he enjoyed it? I'm pretty sure he was a psychopath or something."

"How did it start?"

"He pushed me down the stairs. I thought it was an accident, and that's what I told everyone. When he realized that he could make things look like accidents, he started hurting me more frequently."

"Why did you think it was an accident?" she asks.

"I don't remember," I say truthfully.

She jots something down in her notepad. A new one, I notice. I guess I give her enough material to go through notebooks like tissues. "How did you feel after it happened?"

"I don't remember."

"When was the first time you realized something was wrong?"

The world around me feels like it's closing in, and I can't escape the suffocating feeling of anxiety that's taken over my body. It's a familiar feeling, one that I've experienced many times before, yet it never seems to get any easier. "Look, I don't remember specifics. All I know is that he hurt me, and no one did anything about it, and it changed my entire worldview. It was the start of the characters."

"I see," she says. "Can you compare how your worldview was changed? How did you look at the world before, and how did you look at the world after?"

"I was a pretty pessimistic kid, but I guess I thought that the world was cruel and uncaring. After what happened with Max, I thought that the world was just being cruel to me. And that's a hard pill to swallow when you're eight." It's a hard pill to swallow at any age.

"Do you think his actions shocked you?"

"I knew people could be capable of cruelty and violence. I'd seen movies and stuff. But I guess I just didn't expect everyone to react the way they did. In the movies, children are always saved from danger. They are protected by adults. But there were no superheroes to protect me. And I guess that's a cold awakening that every kid has to go through. When you realize that people are fallible. They can die."

"The adults in your life let Max abuse you is what you're trying to say, correct?" Dr. Jones asks.

"Yeah. They didn't stand anything to gain from helping me. To them, I was just a criminal's daughter. There were no consequences if something happened to me. No one would even care if I went missing. And that meant that anyone could do anything to me and it wouldn't matter."

It's a suffocating feeling when you're convinced that the world would keep spinning even if you disappeared, and no one would even notice you were gone.

"What you're describing is dehumanizing. Did he feel like they saw you as less than human?"

"I don't know. They might've seen me as human and not cared, or as just some object to use and discard." I honestly can't tell which is worse.

"That must've been frustrating."

"When you're hurt so often in the same spot, you get used to it."

"You told me that when you faced a Nightmare last semester, you saw Max. You also saw your elementary school principal and some adults who were in your life around that time. Ones who you think failed you."

"Yeah. They kind of just let everything happen. But after the fact, when everything came out and they were afraid of looking bad, they blamed me. And that fucked me up," I explain.

"That was wrong of them. As adults, especially educators, they had a responsibility toward you, and they failed to protect you. They only blamed you in a panic because of their own personal failings." Hearing her say that feels oddly validating.

"I know," I reply, "but I don't know how to *unlearn* what they taught me. Even though I know logically it wasn't my fault, that victim-blaming mentality is still so deeply rooted within me. I hate that about myself."

"Do you think you harshly blame others when bad things happen to them? Or is this mentality mostly aimed at yourself?"

"I don't know." I hope it's only aimed at myself.

She continues, "When you felt this shame and frustration, is that when the characters were born?"

"After what happened, Max went away for a while. He took a little vacation and healed up. But I still had to live in his hometown. I still had to go to school with everyone who knew what happened and didn't do a good job of pretending like they didn't," I say, shaking my head with a derisive laugh. "He got away with everything and now I was stuck living with that shame. I just wanted it to stop. I wanted to be someone else. And it made sense, you know? All my life I had been changing my habits and adapting to every new home I went to. You know, not a lot of people think about it, but every household has a different place where they put things. Every household has different rules and etiquette to follow. So this was just like that. I was adapting to achieve a goal. Mari helped me deal with the frustration that I felt, and allowed me to feel as angry as I wanted because she was just a character. I told myself that she wasn't *really* me. It was the only way I could accept that ugly part of myself."

"And do you still feel that anger?" Dr. Jones asks.

"Of course I do. Because everyone who hurt me got away with it. That's why I pushed Max. I hated how he smiled, I hated that he could be happy even though he was making my life hell. He didn't deserve that. He deserved to be as miserable as I was. And if I couldn't make him miserable, then the next best thing was to make him dead."

"If I'm understanding this right, you didn't necessarily want to *kill* him," she says. "You didn't feel any joy from it. You just didn't want him to be happy."

Is there a difference?

"I never wanted him to be happy. I didn't want him to be capable of feeling happy. I still don't. Do you know what he's doing now? He's a *father*, if you can believe it. He's got a good job and he's married. He's happy. All the while I'm here with you and I'm still seeing his face every night in my nightmares."

"What would you want to happen to him now? What do you think would help you overcome this anger you feel toward him?"

I snort. "Realistically? Or in my fantasies?"

"In your fantasies."

I think about it for a moment before responding. "In my fantasies, I never see Max again. I don't know what happens to him, and I never will. But everyone who sided with him is on their knees begging for my forgiveness. They tell me that they were wrong and that I was right. That they're so sorry. That they should've done something. But you can't make someone feel something that they don't. You can't make someone regret something. I know that this is just a fantasy, and that it won't ever happen."

"Yes, but it is natural to want someone who has wronged you to repent in some way. To make them feel the way you think they should. I wouldn't have been alarmed if you had said that you wished they were dead. You are justifying your anger, and while I would never condone violence, from what I understand some things are just unforgivable."

"The thing is, even if this fantasy were to miraculously come true, I don't know if it would make me feel any better," I admit. "It doesn't *undo* anything. I'm still this screwed-up individual who doesn't know how to handle my past trauma, much less my current issues."

"Mar, it's okay to feel that way, and it's very common. But let me remind you that you've taken the first step in seeking help, and that takes a lot of courage. It's not easy to confront your past traumas and current issues, but you're doing it. And with time and the right tools, you can learn to handle them and live a fulfilling life."

Dear Maria,

Today, you asked Allegra if her and I were an item. I was unsure whether or not to be upset or find the situation humorous. I suppose you were asking out of curiosity and not jealousy. Still, I hope you do not misunderstand. Not once has Allegra expressed interest in me romantically, and of course, the feeling is mutual.

Allegra is a lonely girl. She only seeks my companionship. I am nothing more than a servant in her household.

On the other hand, the rumors Archer has spread truly make me regret not dueling him on the night of Allegra's birthday.

Yours,
Rhys

Dear Rhys,

That would have been hilarious. But I thought you guys were fighting over Allegra that night. You two seemed so intimate. I thought you had feelings for her.

Mar

Chapter Fifteen

I place the photograph on Mathers' cluttered desk, amidst a pile of papers and books. The upcoming midterms have undoubtedly consumed most of his time, yet he still manages to make time for me.

"Any idea who these people are?" I inquire as I hand the photograph over to Mathers.

He leans in closer to inspect the image, taking his time before eventually shaking his head. "I barely recognized Neil Abbott. He looks different, not just younger. Where did you manage to get this, anyway?"

"I robbed Jenna Cooper's house," I say bluntly.

"I should be surprised, but I'm findin' that nothin' you do shocks me anymore, Mar."

"Is that a challenge?"

"No," he says quickly. "These folks look vaguely familiar, but I'm afraid I don't recognize 'em."

Damn. I was really hoping he would; wouldn't that be convenient? But since he's a provost and he probably meets a lot of people every year, this is to be expected. He probably can't remember *everyone*.

Unfortunately, the photo is too grainy to do a reverse-image search online. I tried already last night.

I asked Archer to take a photo on his phone, hoping that he could snoop around and find out more. We're being cautious, though. The last thing I want is for Neil to catch wind of me checking up on him. I'm pretty sure he's the suspicious type, but he hasn't given me any trouble since the semester started. I'd like to keep it that way, so I'll tread carefully.

"You might be able to ask the chancellor," Mathers suggests. "He's returned briefly to check on things at the university. But be warned: he's on good terms with Neil Abbott. I'm not sure if you want to ask him. The choice is yours."

"They're on good terms?"

Mathers nods. "The chancellor is friendly with most people. A few years ago, he did an exchange program with several truebloods and placed them as employees in several prominent households. It was to help them assimilate to the mortal realm."

"Do *you* trust the chancellor?"

"I do." Provost Mathers' stare is unwavering.

"Fine," I say. "How soon can I speak with him?"

"I'll arrange for a meetin' soon," he promises. "Until then, please try to stay out of trouble."

"That's like asking a fish to stay out of water."

Mathers actually laughs. "Alright, you leave this to me. In the meantime, take it easy. What class are you goin' to?"

"Combat." My leg is still in a cast, so it's just going to be a day of notetaking. Again. "I go for my checkup later this week, though. Hopefully I can get this thing off soon."

"Remember, don't take any unnecessary risks," Mathers warns. "And don't forget that you have people who are here to help you."

"Thanks, Provost."

I leave his office and wheel myself to the elevator. The gymnasium is already buzzing with activity by the time I arrive. A dozen students are paired up around the room, practicing with wooden weapons while Professor Johnson offers feedback and ensures everyone's safety. I take a seat in the corner of the room and take out my laptop, but it's just for show. Johnson doesn't care whether I take notes or not, and he hasn't checked up on me or given me any assignments. He's just marking my attendance.

I watch as each student pair completes a practice round before switching partners and starting again. Lilly is fighting with a girl whose name I don't know, but she matches Lilly well. They're both around the same size, parrying with wooden swords.

Lilly's strikes are precise and powerful, sending her opponent back with every blow. Even with my limited knowledge of combat, I can tell that she is a formidable fighter. She dodges and blocks each attack easily and responds with swift counterstrikes until eventually her opponent falls to the mat.

Despite the fact that she's a horrible person, there's something to be admired in her fighting skills. She's confident and obviously talented. Meanwhile, I'm here stuck in a cast, unable to do anything. And let's face it: even without this cast, I still suck. The only punch I can throw is a punchline.

When the class ends, Lilly approaches me. She's still clutching her wooden sword and her face is red from exertion. She looks me up and down before finally speaking. "Keep your eyes off me, freak."

"What?" I sputter.

"Stop *staring* at me."

"I wasn't staring, I was observing," I clarify. "There's not much else I can do in this cast. You're actually a good fighter."

Her eyes narrow. "What did you say? Are you mocking me?"

"No!" What the hell? I was trying to *compliment* her. Serves me right, I guess. "Are you brain dead or something?"

"Excuse me?"

"And I thought *I* had a victim complex. Good Lord." I begin to wheel away from her, but she stops me with a hand, unable to let me go without having the last word.

"Don't you dare talk to me like that," she says through gritted teeth. She grabs me, probably with the intention of spinning me around to face her, but she's too strong. The wheelchair spins out of her grasp and sends me to the floor, cracking my cast open.

But the pain I expect doesn't come. My leg feels stiff, sure, but not broken. Not anymore.

Even with my shadowborn healing, the nurse said my leg wouldn't be fixed for another week or so. As I rise, adrenaline floods my body like never before. Stretching, I shake my leg for confirmation—it's good as new.

After a tedious visit to the nurse, who confirmed that my leg had fully healed, I start making my way back to the dorm. Archer should be joining me soon as I had given him a call to discuss our next move. Now that my body has finally recovered, I can't afford to slack on my training anymore. But when I arrive back at the house, Allegra and Nic are just sitting down to eat.

"Good evening, Maria," Nic greets. His friendliness is unsettling; he's up to something, I'm sure of it. "Looks like your leg is all better."

He doesn't sound surprised.

"Yeah. I'm all good now," I answer.

"What a shame," he says. "Care to join us for dinner?"

This is the first time they've invited me to dinner. Or, the first time *Nic* is inviting me. Allegra doesn't look too pleased by the offer. But Rhys is in the kitchen cooking, so I don't think the food is poisoned.

I walk over to the dining room table. The spread boasts an entire roast chicken garnished with rosemary, mashed potatoes, stuffing, vegetables (ew), and fresh biscuits. Rhys outdid himself tonight. Is it a special occasion?

Well, Archer is coming over, so it's probably best to steer clear of…whatever this little game is Nic wants to play.

"Sorry, I've got plans," I answer, swiping a biscuit off the table anyway. "Enjoy your meal."

"Plans?" Allegra repeats. "But you have no friends."

"And you're a slut no one likes," Nic adds.

"Thanks for the reminder."

Archer comes to the back door just in time, knocking on one of the glass panes. I wave him over, but when he tries the knob, it's locked.

Rhys sets down his spatula and gets the door, his expression wooden. "Why are *you* here?"

Archer glares. "I'm here to see Mar."

Rhys is about to close the door in his face, but I manage to jog over and catch it with a hand.

"I invited him," I tell Rhys. It's times like these I wish I could telepathically communicate my thoughts to him.

"*Why*?" he asks.

"None of your business," Archer interjects, making the situation much worse for both of us. His eyes flit over to Allegra, but he doesn't say anything in greeting.

"Come on." I open the door to the basement. "Let's go. We've got a tight schedule."

"What are you doing here, Archer?" Allegra demands, standing up. Is it just me, or does she sound...*hurt*?

"He's helping me study," I explain, mostly for Rhys' benefit. "Come on, Archer."

I lead him downstairs, locking the door behind us. We go directly to the bathroom, hand in hand, and I turn on the shower.

"What are we doing in here?" Archer asks, closing the door. "Are you coming onto me?"

"Are you for real right now?"

He holds up his hands. "Look, Mar. We're good now, but I just don't feel that way about you."

"The feeling is mutual, trust me. This is just the only room that's relatively safe, and it's less suspicious than the laundry room. Anyway, there are hidden cameras and audio recorders in the basement," I explain, lowering my voice. "I think Nic put them in here. Or Neil. Possibly Allegra."

"Or Rhys," Archer says with disgust.

"It wasn't Rhys," I defend immediately. "Anyway, I

called you here to look at the Divinities Sword. I want you to try and lift it."

"Where is it?"

"My closet. I couldn't bring it in here," I explain, washing my hands. "But we need to put on a show for the cameras. I don't want Nic, or whoever's watching, to suspect anything."

"What's your plan?"

I take off my shirt, revealing a tank top underneath. "Give me your T-shirt."

"What?"

"Give me your shirt," I repeat. "I'm going to take my pants off and walk into my closet. And you're going to follow behind me."

Nic or Neil, whoever's watching the cameras, can get a good show.

"You're crazy," he says, pulling his T-shirt over his head and shoving it at me.

"I know. Now turn around. After I leave, wait a few seconds, turn the shower off, wait another minute, and then follow me."

He grumbles, but he does what I ask.

I take off my jeans, throwing them on the towel rack. I open the bathroom door and slip out, wearing a huge smile as I go into my closet. Quickly, I turn on the light and throw a set of sweats on. When Archer comes inside, I throw him his T-shirt.

"You're crazy," he says again. "Where's the sword?"

I point to it on the floor. I managed to drag it into the corner, but haven't moved it since.

Archer rolls his shoulders, getting on his knees and pulling at the hilt with difficulty. "Did you glue it to the ground?"

"Obviously not. I *told* you it was heavy."

Gritting his teeth, he applies more force and I hear the sound of metal clanging against metal. Slowly but surely, Archer manages to pull the blade out of its sheath, though he still can't lift it from the floor.

"This is it?" he asks, running a finger over the engraved Chinese characters. "The Divinities Sword?"

"With this, we can defeat Astaroth. If we can find someone to lift it."

"I can't lift it, and you can't. What about a trueblood?" he wonders aloud.

"Where are we going to find a trueblood?" I can't ask Rhys, and all the other truebloods I know are stuck in the past. I'm *not* going to ask Neil.

"I don't know. Let me try again." Archer's face contorts with effort as he bends his knees and grips the sword's hilt with both hands. He heaves it upward, but it only lifts an inch or two off the ground. I reach out to help, but my fingers are too slow to catch the blade before it falls back to the floor with a resounding clang, making Archer jump. As it drops away, it scrapes my hand, drawing blood.

"Crap!" I yank my hand back.

"Are you okay?"

"I think so. My fingers are intact," I say. "It's just a shallow wound."

"It's bleeding a lot."

"Get the first aid kit from the bathroom. Medicine cabinet," I tell him.

He nods and hurries off.

I inspect the cut, which runs from the base of my thumb to my wrist. It's not deep, but it's longer than I expected. I dab at the wound with a corner of my shirt to stem the flow of blood, wincing when I press too hard against the tender flesh.

Archer returns with a small white box. He sets it down and kneels beside me, taking out a tube of antiseptic ointment and some bandages.

"Let me do it," he says gently, unscrewing the cap on the ointment. I hold my breath as he applies it to my cut, stinging and cold against my skin.

The wound won't stop bleeding though, no matter how hard I press against it or how many times I reapply pressure. It's almost like our efforts to tend to it only make the pain worse.

Is this...because I practice blood magic? The sword is supposed to defeat blood magic practitioners, and I've been studying it with Jenna. I just didn't expect it to work like this, and certainly not on me. Damn it.

I lay on the ground beside the sword, my head swimming.

"You look pale," Archer says, alarmed. "Mar, what's going on? Crap, that's a lot of blood."

"The sword is enchanted," I manage, all the energy draining from my body. My vision tilts and blurs, my breath caught in my throat as my heartbeat grows sluggish. Every second feels like an eternity between breaths, and my limbs are heavier than the sword.

"Mar? *Mar*!" Archer calls, panicking now. He quickly types something on his phone, applying pressure to the wound and lifting it. When the blood soaks through, he grabs one of my T-shirts from the rack and wraps it around my hand. "Shit. Don't die, okay? You don't want to die in a closet with *me*, do you?"

It would be a fitting end. I'm supposed to have this grand destiny and whatever. I've survived zombies, cultists, fae princes, ferals, and a pit of snakes… Getting cut and bleeding out in the basement would definitely be the type of death I could expect.

But while I'm still dizzy and weak, I shockingly don't pass out, nor do I kick the bucket. The blood stops, and after half an hour, Archer ties up my hand and carries me to my bed. A little embarrassing, but since I can't move, I won't complain.

"You're not going to die in your sleep, are you?" he asks warily, grabbing a blanket and a pillow from the chest at the end of my bed. He sits on the floor beside me.

"You're going to sleep here? With me?"

"I won't be able to sleep, anyway. I don't…want you to *die*, Mar."

It's strange, but I think he's being serious. But he can't stay here.

"I need to eat something. And drink something," I say. "Can you get me a granola bar from upstairs?"

"Sure. Of course," he replies.

"And…this is going to sound weird, but can you tell Rhys that you're going to be staying the night? Like, to make sure I don't die? But tell him in private. I don't want Nic and Allegra to know what happened," I whisper.

"Why?"

"Because if you go upstairs tomorrow morning and he catches you coming out of my room, he might kill you. He doesn't like you much." It's just an excuse, but frankly I can see the two arguing, which might result in a fight.

Archer frowns. "Alright, whatever you say. I'm not going to argue with a sick person."

He jogs upstairs. A few minutes later, he comes back down, though Rhys is following close behind him.

"I didn't tell you to bring him," I croak.

"I didn't. He insisted," Archer says defensively, glaring at Rhys.

Rhys' gaze sweeps over me. In a low voice, he says, "Get a protein bar and juice from upstairs. She should eat something." He lifts my injured hand, propping it up on a pillow for elevation. When Archer doesn't move, Rhys barks, "*Now*. Are you deaf?"

"I can take care of her fine on my own," Archer bites back. "I only told you because she told me to."

"Rhys, I'm fine. It's just a little cut. I was just hoping you would be cool about Archer staying here, since, you know. You report to Neil." I give him a meaningful look, hoping he catches on quickly. There are still cameras in here, and an audio recorder.

Rhys' jaw clenches. "No. He cannot stay here."

"I'm not leaving," Archer declares. "She looks like she's got a hand on death's door."

"It is *my* job to tend to her. Neil will not allow you to stay in this house, Archer Kinsey," Rhys says.

"You are Allegra's attendant. Not Mar's. How do I know you won't just ignore her and let her die?"

"I will—" Rhys stops himself. "I am tasked with ensuring the well-being of both Neil's daughters. Neil wants her alive, so I will ensure she stays alive. Now, you should leave, while I am still *asking*."

"Mar..." Archer begins.

"It's fine, Archer," I tell him earnestly. "I'll text you, okay?"

Archer's eyes flit to Rhys, but there's not much he can

do. With a resigned sigh, he says, "I'm coming over first thing tomorrow morning. Text me if you need something, okay? I'm putting the phone on my nightstand."

"Thanks, Archer."

He grumbles something under his breath and trudges up the stairs. Rhys follows him out, and I can hear the click of the lock on the back door. When he returns with food, he helps prop my head up so I can eat properly.

I hope the video cameras down here aren't HD quality, because when he's sitting by my bedside like this, his eyes conceal nothing.

"I'll be fine," I tell him, trying to sound cheerful. "It was just a little mishap. Could happen to anyone."

"But it did not happen to *anyone*. It happened to you." Rhys' voice is low, but it carries a weight that makes my chest ache.

"I've survived worse," I say. "When I was twelve, I had a brief stint as a daredevil and ended up falling off the roof. The aftermath wasn't pretty, and I had to wear a neck brace for a while. The pain was excruciating, but the embarrassment was worse. Just to clarify, no one pushed me. It was all my idea to impress my friends, and well, let's just say it didn't go as planned."

Rhys looks at me solemnly, his mask having returned. "Sleep. You need to rest. I will take care of everything else."

Although the wound inflicted by the Divinities Sword is healing slowly but surely, it's unfortunately put me out of commission for a few more days. This delay has also meant that my training with Archer has been postponed until further notice.

Rhys doesn't have to wheel me to class anymore since my leg is fully recovered. Even though we used to go in silence, it was kind of nice just *being* with him. I barely get to see him anymore, and I can't help but wonder if he's purposely avoiding me or if I'm just overthinking things. Maybe he's been busy, but my mind tends to overanalyze situations.

I've been less busy due to my injuries. I haven't been working at the library, and classes have been less intense after midterms. But now, it's Friday, and Provost Mathers has called me back into his office. Today, we are going to visit the chancellor. I'm not sure what to expect, but my only hope is that he recognizes the people in the photograph I took from Jenna's house. I also hope that he won't tell Neil what's going on. However, from what Provost Mathers said, their relationship was only a business one, and not necessarily personal.

As I walk to the main building, my pace quickens. Since my leg is better, I take the stairs instead of the elevator to the top floor. Mathers is waiting for me in the office where all the other admins work.

"Oh, Mar. You're here, and you have a new injury today. Why is it that every time I see you, you're hurt?" Provost Mathers asks, noting my bandaged hand.

"I'm just clumsy, I guess," I reply.

He shakes his head. "No matter. Come along now. The chancellor is quite a busy man. Luckily, he had time to meet with you. Did you bring the photo?"

"Yes."

We walk down the hall toward a big set of wooden

French doors. The doors are open, and when I step inside, I feel like I've been transported to another world. Not the Veil, mind you. It's more like a storage room in the back of a movie theater with all the marketing materials from the movies. Posters are everywhere, and there are even stands. These aren't current movies, either. Some of them are old, and some are even animated.

"Well, well, well," the chancellor says, turning around. He wears a huge smile, and he has an American accent, but there's something a little off about it. A slight inflection. "If it isn't Maria Rochester."

My jaw drops. "Theodas?"

Chapter Sixteen

Theodas sweeps me up in his arms, twirling me around in a way I can only describe as cinematic. Sadly, this is the kind of reunion I'd imagined having with Rhys.

Theodas sets me on my feet, his face split in a wide grin. "Did you miss me?"

"Of course," I say, still a little shocked to see him. I'd asked Provost Mathers to look for Theodas and the other elves, but I never expected he'd be in the mortal realm. And so close, too.

Theodas has aged. He looks to be in his late thirties, early forties now. But that's pretty great, considering his true age is over three hundred. His chestnut brown hair has been cut short, showing off his elf ears. And he must have adopted the cowboy style from Mathers—or, I guess Mathers could've been inspired by *Theodas*, considering he's older—because he's wearing a bolo tie, button-down, and intricate boots with spurs.

"Chancellor, you should not be huggin' students," Provost Mathers warns finally.

"She's not a student. She's just Maria," Theodas states.

"She *is* a student."

"It's fine. We're, uh, old friends," I explain.

"Indeedaroo."

"Please don't say that." Seeing him here like this is already enough of a surprise, but hearing him speak English is like a double whammy that reminds me of the different timelines we're running on. It's difficult to wrap my head around it all. His accent is similar to Rhys', but less pronounced. I suppose that's because he's been here longer. "It's weird, coming from you."

"It's been centuries, Maria. I've been speaking English longer than you've been alive, along with several other mortal languages. I've had plenty of time to learn English, and all your American expressions. Caprice?"

Good God, I think he meant *capisce.*

"I'm very confused," Provost Mathers announces, looking between the both of us. "Can one of you please explain to me what is goin' on?"

Theodas casually leans against one of the bookshelves that line the room. Half of them are stocked with DVDs and CDs instead of books, and movie posters cover what little wall space is left, overlapping like a chaotic collage. I catch a glimpse of a prominent Sandra Bullock poster out of the corner of my eye.

"Maria here is a time traveler I met in my youth. Oh, don't worry, Maria—Richard is trustworthy. You remember his great-grandma, don't you? Chaela? She married Lyari, by the way. *Twice.*"

What? The kid from the auction house's treasure room? And what does he mean by twice?

"That's a lot to unpack. First," I whirl around to Mathers, "your given name is Richard?"

"Yes."

"Huh. I would have guessed Allen."

"Is that really the point right now, Mar?" Mathers asks, shaking his head. He raises a hand to his temples, like he's got a headache coming on. He must not have known Theodas' and my connection all this time. Which means he's probably a better man than I gave him credit for, helping me out like this. "You are a time traveler?"

"Yes. I *was* keeping it a secret," I say pointedly, "but I guess that's out the window. Instead of training like Neil claimed, I spent last year in the past."

"It's a small world, isn't it?" Theodas chimes in. "Or should I say, small *realm*? Well, regardless, we're all reunited. Oh, I'll have to tell Iacar you're here. He'll get a kick out of this."

"Iacar is okay, too?"

"He's married with seven kids."

I can't imagine him with *one* kid, let alone seven. Maybe he's mellowed out. "And Siraye?"

"Ah, the princess is no longer *technically* a princess," Theodas explains. "The monarchy was dissolved."

I learned that in class, but we didn't dive into specifics. "Where is she now?"

"Richard didn't tell you? Siraye started these schools," Theodas says. "After you and Rhys disappeared, she said she had a 'feeling' she'd meet you again."

A feeling? So, she used her intuition? I know she's a bit psychic, but maybe her powers are stronger than she initially let on. Either way, I'm glad everyone is alive and well. I didn't expect Siraye to be founding magic schools, and I certainly didn't expect Theodas of all people to be running one.

"If you've been here this whole time, does this mean you and Rhys have met?" I ask hopefully.

"I was waiting for him, yes. He wasn't here a day on his own before I found him," he assures.

I let out a breath. Rhys wasn't alone in this unfamiliar realm. My guilt remains, but it's comforting to know that he had some help. It's not every day you get thrown into a world without magic, you know? And let's not forget about the horrors of adjusting to a new time period. At least he had some company, and he wasn't just twiddling his thumbs and waiting for me while working for Neil.

"Rhys?" Mathers cuts in. "You mean Allegra Abbott's attendant?"

"Ah, yes. Richard, he is the Prince Vesryn I once served. Lyari and Iacar, as well." Theodas' stomach rumbles, and he pulls something out of his drawer. Judging from the label, it's some sort of Asian shrimp chip. "He and Maria are something of an item."

"Really?" Mathers looks to me for confirmation. "I don't see it."

"What does that mean?" I demand. Not that I want to talk about my love life (can I even call it that?) in front of my teacher.

"I thought you and Archer were seein' each other. You certainly get along," he says innocently.

"I think you should spend less time worrying about your students dating."

"Alright, kiddos, let's settle down," Theodas says nonchalantly, munching on his chips. "Richard, Rhys is undercover, like Channing Tatum in *21 Jump Street*. He can't act freely because of Neil Abbott. I placed him in that household to keep an eye on Neil; Rhys requested this because he wanted to help you, Maria. But Neil is one slippery snake who doesn't trust anyone. Unfortunately, we haven't been able to gather much intel."

I'm not surprised. "So, what have you found out?"

"He's always been suspicious of outsiders, but he's a demon after all, and they're all pretty shady. I didn't pay much attention to him until Rhys returned, but I knew something was off. It's like in *Scream,* where I correctly guessed the killer—"

"What makes you say that?" Mathers interrupts, genuinely confused. "The Abbotts have always been generous donors to the school. I thought they were payin' us off to keep Allegra enrolled, but Neil has never done anythin' to distinguish himself from other demon families. Sure, most prominent ones on the Ruby Council have their fair share of strange dealings, but there's nothin' particularly remarkable about Neil."

"I'm *very* good at reading people," Theodas says firmly. "That's why I can't watch whodunnits. I always know the killer."

"And Neil Abbott is a killer?"

"He killed my dad," I say.

Both men turn toward me.

"What?" Mathers demands, and at the same time Theodas says, "I'm so sorry."

"Rhys told me," Theodas continues. "We're keeping a protective watch on the rest of your family members now. I have my people on it, twenty-four/seven. As soon as we see an opportunity, we can extract them. But Neil's people are watching as well, and I'm afraid doing anything would tip him off. We don't want to show our hand just yet."

That's a small comfort.

Don't get me wrong—I trust Theodas, and if he says he has people watching my family, I believe they'll do a good job. But I won't be fully relieved until I see them for myself. And even then, the moment will be bittersweet at best, because I'll have to explain what happened to Luke.

"I have the Divinities Sword. That's why I went back to the past," I say, "but I have no clue how to defeat Neil. I don't think shooting him outright will work."

Not that I can even handle a gun.

"Until we figure out his operation, I would advise against murder," Theodas replies.

"Mar, I have a question. How did you go back to the past in the first place?" Mathers asks. "Perhaps that is somethin' we can use against Neil."

It doesn't escape my notice that he said "we." Like we're a team. I shouldn't be as happy about that as I am.

"I have to open a rift and think about where I want to go," I explain. "When I went back for the sword, I was solely focused on retrieving it, not on a particular time period. I've only used time travel in this manner once before, so I don't know all the rules and limitations. But hey, the timeline seems to be holding up pretty well so far. I went back, snagged the sword, and the world didn't end."

"Hmm. You have to open a rift, which takes time and concentration. And you don't always know where—or when—you'll end up," Mathers summarizes. "You haven't tried to go to the future, have you?"

"I haven't tried it again. It just seems too risky." Ironically I don't have the time to be messing around with time travel. It's not practical to use against Astaroth. As Mathers just pointed out, it takes time and concentration, which I won't be able to spare during a battle.

"What if you opened a rift near a volcano and shoved Neil inside," Theodas suggests. "You could place him in Pompeii and close the rift behind him."

"As you said, I think it will be a lot harder to kill Neil. He could always use another rift into the Veil to escape," I reason. "He could also pull *me* into the rift, too. And that's all with the assumption that I could overpower him, even for a split second."

It's not as if I can just teleport behind him and slit his throat. Trust me, I've thought about it. The fact that I need to open a rift makes things much more difficult.

"We're getting sidetracked," I say, pulling out my phone. "The reason I came to you in the first place is because of this photo. Do you recognize any of these people?"

Theodas walks over and peers at the screen with a frown. "Interesting. I didn't realize the Coopers were familiar with Neil. They're werewolf shadowborn."

"And the other couple?"

"I don't recall who they descend from, but those are the Everleighs," he says, pulling away. "Thompson and Sabine. Odd couple. They work at Northeastern College, up...well, northeast."

I'm familiar. Though, my short visit there wasn't very pleasant.

"They worked here twenty-odd years ago," Theodas continues. "Thompson Everleigh and Neil Abbott conducted research together, but something went wrong with the results. The Everleighs lost a substantial amount of money and decided to sever ties with Neil, relocating their family to New York State. I can't say I recall much about them, other than the fact that they left a resignation letter in my mailbox one morning and vanished without any prior warning."

Research? Rhys mentioned something about a secret basement under the plantation. Could it be a lab?

Suddenly, all these puzzle pieces are clicking into place. Allegra said she was born with the body of a human, and she has experimental seals tattooed all over her body to contain her magic. And Faith was way stronger than she should have been, for a human. Could Neil have experimented on them?

Could he have experimented on *me*?

"What kind of experiments were they doing?" I press. "Where can I find out?"

"It was all very hush-hush. They weren't funded by the school for these experiments; they received grant money from the Ruby Council," Theodas says. "Richard, it was before your time, but do you remember hearing anything about it? You're friendly with Everleigh, aren't you?"

"Thompson's a good fellow. Smart, too," Mathers says. "He's currently leading research in a cure for the feral illness. But that's a recent epidemic—not what Neil would have worked on all those years ago. I can ask him, though."

"Do you think he's still in contact with Neil Abbott?"

"No. Not with Neil's reputation."

"He's part of the Ruby Council. That doesn't earn him some respect?" I know it earns him money. Lots of it, too. Otherwise, how could he afford those ugly statues in his house?

"As much respect as a mob boss," Theodas replies. "I've

never liked Neil Abbott. But his involvement with you feels downright sinister. I'm certain he's hiding something."

"Chancellor, if you have these suspicions, why wouldn't you report him to the Ruby Council?" Mathers asks. "He's a danger to us all, not just Maria. No offense."

"He's as slippery as an eel. Let's face it, the justice system, especially one based in the Veil, isn't going to work out for us. We need a vigilante, and since Batman isn't available, we'll have to settle for the next best person."

I scoff. "I hope you're not suggesting me, because I can't go against Neil. I'm not ready, and I certainly can't do it alone."

Theodas leans forward and says, "Who said you were alone?"

"Neil wants me to kill Astaroth. That's been his demand since last summer. But truth be told, I can't even lift the Divinities Sword to use it against anyone. Neither could Archer."

I conveniently leave out the fact that I nearly bled out because of my attempt.

Mathers interjects, "Chancellor, you cannot go into a student's bedroom, regardless of whether or not you are old friends."

"Right. You're right." Theodas taps his foot. "Do you think you could bring it here, Maria?"

"No. It's way too heavy, and there are cameras in my bedroom. I'm keeping it in my closet for now."

"In that case, can you open a rift in your closet and meet me in the Veil?"

That sounds...more doable. But I'll need Archer's help again, which requires him to come into my room, possibly inviting misunderstandings.

And that's way less important than my mission right now, I remind myself.

"Alright. Set the details, and we'll aim for next week," I decide. "Provost Mathers can relay the information to me in person. No matter what, Neil can't find out what we're up to."

"Agreed," Theodas says. "This will be our little secret."

After my conversation with Theodas, the deadline to kill Astaroth and Neil looms over me like a dark cloud. Although I don't have a set date, it's best to prepare myself for anything that could happen. It's been weeks, and I haven't been attacked once, except for in combat class and that one hunting trip to the Veil.

Okay, so maybe I haven't been physically attacked by Neil, Nic, or Allegra since returning, but the verbal attacks keep coming. As they say, sticks and stones may break my bones, but words will never hurt me.

Anyway, in preparation for the big day (or night, who knows), I've decided to take training more seriously. That means I'll be hitting the gym with Archer bright and early in the morning. And when I say "bright and early," I mean the kind of early that makes roosters reconsider their life choices.

"Are you sure you're ready?" Archer asks. He still can't believe my leg is completely healed. Neither can I. "I don't want to push you."

"I'm fine. There's no need to treat me like I'm made of glass."

"Well, you almost bled out the other day from a cut on your hand. I'm allowed to be a little worried."

I shrug. "I'm fine. The worst part about that was falling asleep with contacts in. I hate these things. But anyway, what's on the agenda today?"

He holds up two wooden swords. "We've been doing a lot of strength training, but you need to learn some technique as well. I reserved a private sparring room."

"Fancy." I follow him to the back after our warm-ups, in a separate mirrored room covered in mats. It reminds me of one of those padded solitary confinement rooms in movies.

Archer hands me a sword. It's insane how much easier holding a weapon has become in the last month. I know we've been training for a while, but now it almost feels natural.

We square off in a circle of tape.

"Ready?" Archer says.

"Ready." I tighten my grip on the wooden sword.

We start slow, testing each other's moves and defenses. Archer is patient with me, showing me where to place my feet and how to angle my sword for the best results. As we move around the circle, I become more comfortable with my weapon and more confident in my skills. I begin taking risks, aiming for openings in Archer's defense and attacking with swift movements that surprise even myself. His grin widens every time he blocks or counters my attacks, urging me to keep going.

Our swords clash together in a rhythm that echoes through the room, and I can feel the sweat starting to bead on my forehead. But I don't stop. I can't afford to stop.

As we continue to spar, I can feel myself getting lost in the moment. It's just me and Archer, and I'm determined to win this battle. My heart is racing, and my muscles ache, but I push through the pain, knowing that I need to be stronger and faster.

Just when I think I'm about to gain the upper hand, Archer makes a move that catches me off guard. With one swift motion, he disarms me, and my sword flies across the room. My heart sinks as I realize I've been defeated. But before I can even process what happened, Archer lunges at me, his sword raised and ready to strike.

In a split second, I react and reach out, and with a loud crack, the wooden sword breaks in half in my hands. The room falls silent as Archer stares at me in disbelief. He slowly lowers his weapon and takes a step back.

He looks at me, his eyes wide with disbelief. "What the hell just happened?"

I follow his gaze to the jagged pieces of wood clutched in my hands, evidence of what just occurred. "I think training is paying off after all."

Dear Maria,

Allegra had another fit today. Sometimes, I wonder if she is more ill than she lets on, even to me. She visited the doctor, but those conversations always take place behind closed doors.

You should be wary of her. Sometimes, she looks at you with a dark expression. Almost as if she is envious of you. But it always disappears as quickly as it comes, and I must wonder if she is even aware of her own feelings toward you.

Yours,
Rhys

Chapter Seventeen

As I stumble through the back door, feeling like a sentient Jell-O, I check the time. 10 PM. I definitely overdid it today. I started off with a morning gym session, attended Combat class, and then caught up with Archer again in the afternoon. It's just exciting to *finally* see progress. My hard work is paying off, and damn is it satisfying.

Without wasting a second, I head straight to the bathroom, throwing my clothes carelessly into the laundry basket. Once inside, I turn the shower on full blast, the hot water soothing my aching muscles. Ah, pure bliss.

The steam fills the bathroom as the hot water pours down my body, and I close my eyes, allowing myself to relax. The tension from the day starts to melt away, but there's still something missing, or rather, someone missing. Several someones.

The water runs cold by the time I get out. Stepping out of the shower, I quickly wrap myself in a towel and walk over to the mirror, wiping away the condensation to look at myself.

Progress is good, but it doesn't change the fact that I miss my family.

With my contacts out, my eyes are still as bright yellow as ever. Even though I wear colored lenses during the day, I've gotten used to seeing myself with yellow eyes at night. It's almost *natural* to me, which is strange since yellow eyes aren't natural on anyone. Cats and snakes, maybe, but not people.

Even though I shouldn't worry about it, I wonder what Rhys will think. He hasn't seen me without the contacts. What will my family think? They'll know immediately that I'm not human, as they thought.

I never planned on keeping my supernatural identity a secret from them. But I had hoped to ease them into the idea. Now, as I fabricate speeches and go over scenarios in my head, nothing seems to feel right. How do I explain to them that I'm not entirely human without sounding like a complete lunatic?

I'm not sure what I'm going to say to Rhys, either. I feel like I owe him a massive apology for everything that's happened, and for not trying everything I can to get him out of his servitude to Neil. But it's difficult to balance all my priorities when I have so many people to worry about.

Getting some sleep tonight is crucial if I'm going to be of any use to Rhys or anyone else. I mean, I can't save the world if I'm sleep-deprived, right? So, after brushing my teeth and slipping into my PJs, I fall into bed and turn off the lights, hoping that a good night's rest will rejuvenate me and prepare me for whatever comes my way tomorrow.

Just as I'm drifting off, the room fills with a loud, shrill squawking. I look around in confusion, before realizing that several birds have flown through the window. Seriously? Screaming, I drop to the carpet and roll into a ball as they peck at my skin with razor-sharp beaks.

The commotion wakes everyone else in the house up, and I hear lights turning on and footsteps racing downstairs. Allegra turns on the light, letting out a shrill scream when she sees what's going on. Nic follows, cursing and rushing over to me. Well, there goes my good night's rest.

Without a moment's hesitation, he reaches out and grabs each bird with his bare hands. Even though they're flapping and squawking furiously, he doesn't seem to mind. He snaps their necks one by one until the room falls silent.

Finally, I rise, bloody and battered. Nic and Allegra stand before me, shocked. Considering this is the most genuine I've ever seen Nic look, I don't think he's involved with this. Allegra either.

I survey the room. My carpet is ruined with blood and bird carcasses, which Nic leaves on the ground. I guess I'm grateful none of them are in my bed.

"What was that?" he asks.

"I have no idea." But this feels all too familiar. It reminds me of the night I was attacked at Foley-Hill, the night I was framed for murder. Except that time, Faith was the culprit. She's dead now, so who could have done this? Is it a copycat?

"Are you okay?" Nic presses, which is just unnatural coming from him. Nic Woolridge should *not* be worried about my wellbeing. Unless he's concerned someone is trying to kill me before he gets a chance to.

"I'm not okay, actually," I say. "I'm bleeding, there are dead birds on my floor, there's glass in my bed, and—oh

God. Do you think I can get a disease from this? Some sort of bird flu?"

"You'll be fine. Probably," Allegra says, unsure of herself.

She kneels down and starts picking up the glass, only to gasp when her hand lands on something big. A brick? She picks it up, flipping it over.

An envelope?

"It's addressed to you." She hands it to me, her eyes wide.

With shaking hands, I take it from her and open it, breaking the wax seal.

Dear Maria Abbott,

I am waiting for you in the Veil, Timekeeper's Daughter. The Midnight Hour grows near, and the serpents slither in anticipation of your arrival. You are cordially invited to join me, and meet your fate.

Best Wishes,

Astaroth

"THE FREAKIEST PART? HE SIGNED IT *BEST WISHES*. I'M not sure I *want* 'best wishes' from a blood-magic-practicing demon," I say, pacing the room.

Provost Mathers turns the invitation over, studying it along with the envelope and wax seal. "This is most certainly a trap."

"Oh, I agree. How does he even know where my room is?" I swear, nothing is adding up. Nic and Allegra's reactions were too genuine for it to be a prank. And let's be real —neither of them can act to save their lives.

If this message is indeed from Astaroth, then what the hell has he been up to all this time? He's been out for over a year, and I always assumed he was hiding somewhere. Maybe he was just biding his time, waiting for the perfect moment to strike...but why would he be after me? We never even had a proper introduction. Is he working with someone else, perhaps a member of the Ruby Council?

I feel like I'm in a hellish episode of *Scooby Doo,* except the monster isn't just a real estate scammer in a costume.

"Yes, it's all very odd indeed," Mathers murmurs. "If he knew where you were and sought to send you this message while you slept, why not just kill you? Drop a poisonous snake in your bed or a pipe bomb through your window instead?"

"Um, I'm glad he *didn't* do those things. I'd be dead as a doorknob."

"Door*nail*. But yes, you'd be dead. What if his goal isn't to kill you?"

It's possible that he *does* want to kill me. His cult used moon phases to dictate when they practiced blood magic, so Astaroth could be doing the same. But Jenna and I don't follow the phases of the moon when we practice, and she hasn't mentioned it.

"I actually don't understand why he wants me in the first place. I want to kill *him* because of Neil." And because it's my fault he was released from his time prison. Oops. "But I can't think of a reason he'd want to kill me. We didn't even meet, and the cultists were under the impression I was going to be used as a sacrifice and nothing more. They picked me because I was with Allegra, and they thought I was a virgin."

And the cultists haven't bothered me since I left the cruise ship for good. I thought they attacked me once, but it turned out to just be Faith. So why strike now? Is it possible one of them knows my blood opened the time prison?

I'll have to consult with Jenna about all this. Awkward, considering Astaroth may or may not be her dad. I still haven't gotten confirmation on that, and whenever I bring it up, she doesn't give me a straight answer. A lot of our interactions these days take place when I'm lightheaded due to blood loss.

"Even more of a reason not to go," Mathers says. "This could be from a third party. Or it could be a test from Neil."

"Neil doesn't need to trick me or test me like this. He owns me, and he'll never miss an opportunity to tell me that. If he wanted me somewhere, he knows he doesn't even need to threaten me to get me there." I'm in the palm of his hand, for the time being.

"Then, what do you plan on doing?"

"I don't know. That's why I came to you for guidance."

"I won't tell you not to go," he says slowly, "but if you do, you need backup. And a solid plan. But without any solid details of a time and place, I wouldn't worry about this meetin' just yet."

Fighting off Astaroth will be difficult enough, and frankly I don't think I'm ready quite yet. But managing his cult following as well? Near impossible. I'll need to take some help. If Archer and Ophelia agree to go with me, will they be enough to stop Astaroth's minions?

"We can discuss it with Chancellor Aeynore. He's waitin' for us in the Veil."

"Sure." I grab my bag. "I'll run back to my dorm and open a rift to bring the sword through. But how will I know where to meet you?"

"Rifts open in a general fixed area in the Veil," Mathers explains. "Imagine there's a dart board in front of us right now. Openin' a rift is like throwin' a dart. We probably won't land in the same spot, but we'll still be on the same board."

"Speak for yourself. I'm horrible at darts." But I get the idea. "Okay, so there are limits to how far you can land based on your location in the mortal realm."

"Usually, yes. If you open a rift here, you can only land within a certain radius in the same spot in the Veil. The Veil roughly mirrors mortal continents, so we're fairly confident that you won't find yourself landin' in a volcano. Even if you open a rift underground in the mortal realm, we've found through testin' that you'd still land safely in the Veil."

"That's a relief." At least I won't get buried alive.

Mathers takes a deep breath. "Right then, you better get goin'. I'll see you in the Veil soon enough."

I walk back to my dorm quickly, not wanting to have Mathers and Theodas waiting on me. Going downstairs, I shut the lights off, close the curtains, and play music on my desktop. Heading into my closet, I turn on the light and take the dagger from my safe.

Mathers explained a bit about how rifts work, but since my process is somewhat different, I try to focus on Mathers. I imagine him in the Veil and slash through the air. Unfortunately, nothing happens. I try a second time, and then a third, but still nothing.

Damn. I guess I need my blood for everything.

With a silent prayer that I won't end up in the past

again, I nick my finger and run the blood across the blade. Taking a deep breath, I slice through the air in front of me, and this time, it works. I use all my strength to pull the Divinities Sword with me as I enter the rift.

When I emerge on the other side, I find myself in a forest of dead trees and shrubs, with the air chilled and crisp around me. The sky is grey, oppressive, and heavy with clouds, making it difficult to tell what time it is. The only sound is the gentle rustle of leaves.

"Mar!" Mathers shouts, jogging over. I guess I was right to wear red. Theodas follows, dressed casually in a T-shirt and jeans.

However, my attention quickly shifts to someone else who's present. It's Rhys, walking slowly toward me.

Chapter Eighteen

"He asked to come along," Theodas says with a wry smile.

Rhys dips his head in acknowledgement. "Maria."

I can feel the nerves twisting in my stomach, reminding me of the time I showed up to prom covered in rotten eggs and tried (unsuccessfully) to hide it from Luke and Isabelle. It's been a while since I've felt this anxious, but the familiar feeling has a way of creeping up on you when you least expect it. So many "what if"s bubble up in my head, each one more negative than the last. I try to push them down, but the steady stream of negativity seems to have a life of its own.

"This is the sword," Mathers says, breaking the silence. He kneels down, brushing his fingers along the sheath.

"Are we secure in this area?" I ask, looking around. My heart races inside my chest, pounding like a drum. Despite my body betraying me, I force my lips into a thin smile and will my trembling hands to still.

"Rhys and I have been walking around, but no one's

here. We're safe," Theodas assures, looking between us meaningfully.

Rhys ignores the sword completely and walks toward me. "How are your injuries?"

"I'm fine. I mean, I'm traumatized by birds now," I babble. Alfred Hitchcock was onto something. "Um, are you…okay?"

God, that sounds lame.

He doesn't answer, looking at all the bandages on my arms and legs.

"Let me try and lift that," Theodas says jovially, brushing Mathers aside. He wraps his hand around the handle, but he can only lift it a few inches off the ground, and the tip of the sword doesn't move at all. "I think I'm going to get a hernia. I'm too old for this. Rhys, you're still a youngling. You try."

"If you cannot manage, I know I will be incapable as well," he replies calmly.

"Well, this was a waste of time then," I say, shaking my head. "Sorry for dragging you all out here like this."

"No, this is good. We know now that the sword is magic, and not even a trueblood can lift it," Mathers says. "The question is, who *is* able to lift it?"

"Perhaps we will need to pay the Wisdom Tree another visit," Rhys suggests, turning to me. "Do you think you could transport us directly there?"

"It's worth a try. But I can't be gone too long. It might be better to do it at night, when everyone is sleeping," I say.

"Agreed. We must be careful. I have not been able to keep track of Nic recently. His absence is concerning," Rhys says. He turns to Provost Mathers and Theodas. "Are we finished here?"

"I suppose," Theodas says glumly. "I'll leave the rift open. Give you two some privacy. Come on, Richard."

As the two men walk away, Rhys turns to me. There's so much I want to tell him, so much I want to ask, but now that the moment is finally here, all I want to do is cry.

As Rhys takes a step toward me, his voice is strained as he hesitates for a moment before taking my hand in his. I can feel the warmth radiating from his skin as he says, "Maria, I apologize for being absent last night. Theodas and I were arranging this meeting, and I did not realize what transpired until I returned."

I can't let him apologize to me. It should be the other way around. "I'm okay, really," I rush to say.

Rhys sees right through me, as usual. "I have been concerned about you as of late."

"I don't mean to make you worry. I'm okay," I say again. "I just hate this situation that I've put you in. Being in that house with you, living like strangers. Sometimes, I wish I could just say 'fuck it' and run away with you."

But he shakes his head. "You would never do that to your family. I would not ask that of you."

"I know. You're too good for me." I smile wryly. "I don't deserve you."

"Maria, that is not true. Do you remember the Wisdom Tree's words? We are soulmates," he says. "Even if we were not, I cannot think of a single other person, not even in my imagination, who I would want to be with more than you."

He takes a step closer to me, his hand still clasping mine. The air between us crackles with tension, and I know that he can feel it, too. We've been dancing around each other for so long, but we're finally face-to-face. No pretenses, no pretending. Just him and me, the way it's supposed to be.

Love shouldn't be this hard, and I suppose I should count my blessings that our obstacle is external. Our love isn't unrequited—I know that deep down, even if I sometimes doubt my own worth. Like now, when I question if all of this effort is worth it for Rhys. If *I'm* worth it.

People are so fickle; they change their minds faster than a chameleon changes its colors. One minute, you're the center of their world. The next, your things are by the curb and you're being sent away, left to wonder what you did wrong. Rhys is different, though, I know that. But there's always an undercurrent of fear lurking within me that I still can't shake.

"Rhys, I have a mission to complete. But that doesn't mean you have to stay here," I tell him. He's too much of a gentleman to abandon me, but I want to give him an out. Even if it hurts. "I don't want to put you in danger. You can just disappear for a while and stay in a safe house until this is over. It might be better for you."

"I would go mad with worry. I want to stay here, with you," he says, his voice low and intense.

"It's not fair to you. You've put your life on pause for me. Everything you've given up..."

"I won't give up *you*."

My throat constricts, and I'm momentarily frozen. His words carry a weight that's hard to ignore, and it's overwhelming. Frankly, my initial instinct is to self-sabotage. I want to say something insensitive, build walls around myself, and run as far away as possible. But what good would that do? I take a deep breath and try to steady my thoughts.

"The reality of the situation is, there are no guarantees. I don't care what a talking tree says about my fate. Nothing in the world is certain. Even as a time traveler, I don't know what's going to happen next," I say softly. "There's a real possibility that I won't make it. Like, *truly* die. And this could all be for nothing. You would have wasted your efforts for a dead girl."

"Nothing I do for you is ever a waste. You are worth every effort, every moment, and every struggle we may face together. I wish you believed that about yourself," he says fiercely. "I would rather have a few fleeting moments of happiness with you than a lifetime without you."

"I don't deserve you." I laugh. "But I'm grateful for you. More than I can say."

"You do not have to say anything," he replies, moving closer to me until we're just inches apart.

He leans in, his lips brushing against mine in a gentle, tender kiss. I melt into his embrace, feeling the warmth of his body against mine. His touch is so comforting, so familiar, and for a moment, all my fears and doubts fade away.

This is going to make living together a lot more difficult, but right now, I don't give a damn.

When we finally break apart, Rhys' mask is broken. There's raw passion in his eyes, and part of me doesn't want to stop. I don't think he does, either. He's been holding back for longer than I have, and now that we've broken that barrier, there's no turning back.

"That goes against the rules of courtship," he says finally, a small smile playing on his lips.

"Oh really?" I laugh. "When this is all over, you'll have to tell me all the rules again."

"Is that so?"

"Yep. I'll make a list," I tease, "so I know which ones to break. One at a time."

"Is that a promise?" Rhys' eyes twinkle with mischief.

"Definitely."

After meeting with Rhys, I feel like a weight has been lifted off my chest and I can finally breathe a little bit easier. But now, it's back to business.

"Are you sure you want to do this?" Jenna asks. Dressed in casual jeans and a T-shirt, she looks like she's in her late twenties now. It's a wonder how she manages to keep track of everything despite the time travel thing. I think she keeps a list of events in the notepad she carries, but I haven't gotten a chance to look at it.

"I'm positive," I say, although my tone is far from convincing.

Jenna looks at me, sensing my uncertainty. But I hold her stare until she backs down and we pass through the rift together.

Now that I've gotten stronger, I have a hankering to hunt some ferals again. I need their blood, and I want to make sure I'm on top of my game. The only problem is, I can't use my blood magic in front of anyone else. It's ironic, really. I need the blood to practice my magic, but I can't use my magic to obtain it. I wonder how many times I'll end up saying "blood" in this chapter. Let's keep count and make it a drinking game.

Unfortunately, I couldn't find anyone else to help me out. That's where Jenna comes in. Well, to be more accurate, I had to beg her and she agreed. As a Time Agent, Jenna has her limitations, so I'll mostly be on my own. But having her around for moral support will be a big help.

We're not exactly friends, but I trust her…for the most part. Hey, at least she's not trying to kill me anymore, right?

Concentrating, I cut my finger and rub my blood on the blade of my dagger. The motion has become second nature to me now. Along with blood magic, I've been practicing opening rifts—not through time, just to the Veil. It takes more concentration, and I need to be gentle about it. It's like there are two pieces of paper stacked on top of each other, and I need to cut only the first one—I can't cut all the way through.

I'm not as practiced as I'd like to be, but I manage to open a rift and pass through without landing in a different time period. I think. Jenna follows, though she doesn't stay too far from the rift. I don't think she's able to stray from the Infinity Hallway for long, and I doubt she can do much in a fight against ferals. I'll just have to rely on my own strength.

But there's something liberating about that, too. After being thrust into this magic world, I've hardly been able to take care of myself. Now, I'm stronger. I just hope it's enough.

I end up in the forest again, despite having pictured a lake when I envisioned the rift. Damn. I thought that maybe, by using blood magic, I could bypass the radius restriction with the rift and teleport anywhere. I was able to do it when I time traveled for the sword.

"Okay, now how do I draw a feral to me?" I mutter, looking around.

"Blood offering. You have to spend money to make money," Jenna replies. "I think. I've never actually been crazy enough to draw a feral to me."

I hold my dagger firmly, not letting the blade slip. I draw a line across my palm, and close my eyes, picturing a feral from the borderlands in my mind's eye. A zombie hyena staggering toward me, its skin and fur matted and sagging. It oozes black goo from slashes on its side and from its gaping maw. Its eyes are pitch black, sunk deep into its skull.

As soon as my blood hits the ground, I hear a growl from behind me. I can't tell if the spell worked or if this is just a lucky coincidence, but either way, there's a feral here. And it wants blood.

But so do I.

At first, it might appear to be a canine, but on closer inspection, you can tell that it's something else entirely. This feral is much larger than your typical dog and its spine protrudes from its body. Its flesh is barely hanging on, and its face looks like it's seen better days. With no lower jaw and bloody teeth, it's definitely a zombie. Slime oozes out of its grotesque wounds and when it turns my way, its black eyes seem to cut right through me. It sniffs the air around me and starts sprinting without warning.

I quickly draw a spell bag from my pocket and throw it at the charging dog, rolling away as a bright light blinds us all. Although it recovers from the flash bang quickly, I don't panic because I came prepared. I reach for another spell bag from my belt and blow the contents directly into the dog's face, temporarily stunning it.

Using a plastic water bottle, I pour a mix of herbs and oils on the ground in a circle around the dog. Squeezing out another drop of blood, the oil ignites into a roaring flame.

The feral howls, throwing back its head. I pull thick rubber gloves on over my hands and stab the creature in the head, killing it swiftly before it can fight back.

Jenna claps from a distance. "Very dramatic, Mar! Don't let that goo get in your wounds!"

I grimace. I've never hunted before, but I looked up some methods for blood draining yesterday. Not pleasant, but necessary. Pulling a wooden rack from my closet through the rift, I hang the feral and set a bowl beneath it, slitting its throat.

It's pretty gnarly, and I don't plan on making a habit of this, but I need to keep my goal in mind. If this will help me kill Astaroth...then I guess I have to do it. More importantly, blood magic will help me defeat Neil.

But there's no pleasure in violence, no satisfaction, despite the fact that my training is paying off. I've definitely gotten stronger and faster.

To defeat a monster, I have to become one.

God, that sounds cheesy.

Chapter Nineteen

The feral blood disappears faster than a paycheck after a trip to Sephora. Three jars weren't nearly enough, and after a week, I need to replenish. Now that I know the blood works just as well as my own in spells, I've been able to practice all night long without stopping. Sure, it's unhealthy for me in a different way, but I'd rather be sleep-deprived than lightheaded due to blood loss.

At least now I don't have to continuously cut my hands. That *hurts*. But if I can use another's blood for a spell, Astaroth probably can, too. And that brings me right back to square one. Ugh, why does magic have to be so complicated?

The thing about blood magic is, there aren't many restrictions. Sure, there's no instant "kill" spell (bummer, right?), but I'm not limited to just cleaning up messes or playing with the elements. The downside is, without any guidelines, I have no idea what Astaroth's weaknesses are.

I've been playing around with my own spells to see what works and what doesn't. When Jenna isn't breathing down my neck, I try out some off-the-wall methods. Some spells do the trick, while others fail miserably. But just because a spell doesn't work for me doesn't mean it won't work for Astaroth.

Basically, I have zero clue how to prepare for this face-off. It's like going into a blind date, but instead of a potentially awkward conversation, it's a potential life-or-death battle. No biggie, right? All I can do is become as powerful as I can and hope it's enough.

People go to great lengths to attain power, especially under the guise of protecting those they hold dear. I'm no different.

The whole blood magic thing might be spiraling out of control, but I've come too far to turn back now. Even if I'm walking straight into the fiery depths of hell, I'm not about to stop.

It's Saturday again, and I find myself taking a ferry to the mainland. From there, I catch a ride to the forest, where I walk thirty minutes off the main path until I'm properly stranded in the middle of nowhere.

I think I listened to a true crime podcast that started like this…

I cautiously scan the area, ensuring that there's no one around to witness what I'm about to do. Retrieving my sword from my bag, I hold it in front of me and run my finger across its sharp blade. With a swift movement, I swing the sword down and tear a rift into the Veil. As I step inside, I find myself in the midst of a desolate forest, its trees stripped of life and left to rot. The deafening silence is unsettling, and I strain to hear any sound that could break the eerie stillness. But there's nothing, no rustling of leaves, no chirping of birds. The world around me is utterly devoid of life.

As I survey the forest around me, I realize I have no idea how to track ferals, but I figure I'll stumble across one eventually. With that in mind, I reach out and pull both sides of the gaping rift together, sealing it shut. The rift knits itself back together with a barely audible hum, and I start wandering through the trees.

I haven't told a soul where I am going. But just in case things go south, I've scheduled an "in case of death" email to be sent out tomorrow morning. I don't plan on dying, but you never know what kind of trouble you can get into when you're out hunting mythical zombie creatures, right?

It's not like I could tell anyone where I was going anyway. If I did, they'd probably want to come with me. And how do you explain to your friends that you're off to collect blood and test forbidden spells? "Hey, guys! Want to join me in performing some illegal magic rituals in the middle of the woods?" Yeah, that conversation would go over like a lead balloon at a birthday party.

Weaving through the trees, eventually I come across a carcass. It looks like a giant deer, but only its skin has been stripped. Two of its legs are bent unnaturally, the bones jutting from greying flesh. Shockingly, it doesn't smell.

My heart races as I hear the crunching of branches ahead, the first sound I've heard since arriving. Could it be the creature responsible for this mess? I take a few more steps, and all of a sudden, I hear the crackling of fire coming from somewhere ahead. My curiosity piqued, I duck behind a series of trees and inch closer, trying not to make a sound.

As I approach, black-robed figures come into view, an all too familiar sight. There's a group of people, hoods covering their heads and obscuring their faces. They cluster around a fire, circling it as they whisper. The fire flares every so often, reaching at least ten feet into the air. What the hell are these cultists doing out here?

I mean, I know this is the Veil, but still, most of the cultists Jenna gathered were humans, right? She said she taught them how to use blood magic, but if that's the case, they still shouldn't be able to open a rift. And even if they managed to get to the Veil, why on earth would they come to a place crawling with ferals? At least shadowborn have a fighting chance, but humans? I doubt they'd be able to defeat a rampaging feral, blood magic or not. These cultists are either incredibly foolish or incredibly powerful.

I should get out of here. I came to kill ferals, not humans. Even if they are worshipping a trueblood demon. But just as I'm trying to slip away unnoticed, one of the cultists looks directly at me. How the hell did they sense me? I don't have time to ponder that, as the moment the rest spot me, they make creepy clicking noises with their tongues. If I make it out of this alive, I may just have a horror movie pitch to present to Netflix.

Ten cultists fly at me at once. My palms are slick with sweat, but I swing my sword up, slashing at them just as Archer taught me.

Remember your training, I remind myself, lunging forward.

There's no time for hesitation. If they catch me, they'll kill me.

I dispatch the first two cultists with ease, cutting their throats. The blade is so sharp, their flesh shreds like tissue paper. Blood splatters onto the forest floor and on my face as I move.

The other eight cultists reach me before I can move any further. They swarm me, surrounding me in a tight circle.

One cultist steps forward and points his bloody palm at me. He starts to chant something under his breath and before I have time to react, a bright light shoots from his hand. It pierces my skin, searing into my flesh so intensely that I drop my sword to the ground.

If they want to use blood magic, so will I. Swiping the blood from my face, I coat my fingers and grab a fistful of dirt. This is a spell I modified, ironically based on a cleaning spell that allows you to turn your palms into Brillo pads. When another cultist steps forward with a spell, I claw his neck.

Instead of turning my skin into abrasive metal pads for scrubbing dishes, my fingers become sharp as razor blades. The more blood splattering onto my skin, the more powerful I become. And as much as I hate to admit it, I enjoy it.

I understand now why blood magic is forbidden. I've always understood at the textbook level, but Jenna never warned me how good it feels to use so much blood magic your body buzzes with it. It's like I overdosed on caffeine and my physical body vibrates in perfect sync with my soul.

I can feel the cultists' flesh like raw meat under my fingers, tearing away at their bodies with minimal strength. It almost doesn't feel real, and I completely disconnect from the fact that these are people. And I'm murdering them, using their blood against them.

When it's all over and I come down from the high, it takes a second for everything to sink in. To see the corpses littered on the ground and realize exactly what I've done.

It's a slaughter.

I didn't realize how powerful the blood would make me, and during the act itself, I didn't care. I liked feeling powerful. I didn't like killing them. But when the power I gain comes from killing, it's hard to distinguish between the two.

My clothes are soaked in blood. I'm not sure how I'll be able to board the ferry to Kingsmarch. The cultists lay around me, a mess of torn limbs and guts. I didn't decapitate anyone, but some of their necks are hanging by a hinge of flesh. My hands cut through bone.

Wiping the blood and dirt from my hands and face, I pull back the hoods of every cultist. There's no point in checking for a pulse on any of them.

My stomach knots, but I can't tell if it's from the blood magic coursing through my veins or the shock of the situation. Maybe I should have tried harder to escape, but who knows if that would have made any difference. In hindsight, I could have been smarter and tried to resolve this peacefully, but where would that have left me? These damn cultists would have inevitably interfered with my final showdown with Astaroth.

As I make my way toward their camp, my body buzzes with adrenaline, still on high alert. The flickering flames from the now-dim fire illuminate the area, and I scour the surroundings for any potential clues or evidence. Alas, it seems that luck isn't on my side. There's nothing that could tie them to the cult except for the obvious fact that they were practicing blood magic. It's frustrating to come up emptyhanded after all this effort, but I won't give up that easily.

Going back to the bodies, I begin taking off the robes and rummaging through their pockets. I scan the group of cultists, taking note of their varying ages, but surprisingly, I can't seem to find a single cell phone on any of them. It's as if they've completely disconnected from the outside world.

My curiosity piques when I spot a necklace on a woman in the group. She's blonde, or was, her pale hair spilling from her robe. Her blue eyes stare at the open sky, wide and unseeing, and an unsettling smile stretches over her lips.

I try to open the locket, but it seems to be locked tight, leaving me curious about what could be hidden inside. Nevertheless, my mind races with possibilities, and I know I'm not out of ideas yet.

I wrap the locket around my hand, smearing blood on my sword. With a deep breath, I open another rift, hoping to find the answers I need. I've been racking my brain trying to look for answers in the present, but maybe I should have been looking in the past this whole time. I might not be able to change anything, but no one said anything about me poking around for clues.

As I step through the rift, I find myself on the beach, surrounded by the sound of waves crashing against the shore. I take a moment to wash my hands in the cool water, tuck the locket securely in my pocket, and close the rift behind me. Now, it's time to start searching.

As I look around, my eyes land on a small wooden boathouse nestled up the beach. It appears as though it hasn't been used in years, but my curious mind wonders if someone or something could still be living inside. The hut is an old red wooden structure with peeling paint, giving it a slightly eerie feel. I approach cautiously, my heart racing with every step I take toward the building.

The door swings open easily, creaking loudly. It's dark inside, with light filtering in from a single boarded-up window. An oil lamp hangs on the wall, along with a life preserver riddled with holes. Because, you know, someone might need to be saved from the horrifying sight of this place.

The rest of the room is filled with wooden crates and boats coated in a thick layer of dust. In the center of the room is a table, upon which rests a map. Studying it for a moment, I realize it's a map of Kingsmarch Island.

Is *this* Kingsmarch? I've been to the beach a bunch of times, but I don't remember seeing this hut.

As I start to dig deeper, my thoughts are abruptly interrupted by the sound of voices outside. Without hesitation, I quickly jump behind some discarded crates, my heart pounding in my chest. I strain my ears to listen, but can't make out much yet. However, it's clear that two people are approaching the boathouse, and they're getting closer by the second.

I recognize the girl immediately as the one I pulled the pendant off. Although, she appears younger now than she was when I last saw her. So, I suppose my time-traveling scheme worked out in my favor. However, the guy standing next to her is a stranger to me. He's clearly a grown man, probably in his mid-thirties, while she looks like a mere freshman in college. Her blonde hair is piled up on her head elegantly, and she's dressed in a pristine white blouse and pencil skirt, looking like she just stepped out of a fashion magazine.

The man hisses through gritted teeth, "You cannot do this." I'm caught off guard by his deep, melodious voice. He looks mousy, short with light brown hair and thick glasses. "Sabine will find out, and—"

The girl interrupts him, her voice filled with contempt. "Sabine hasn't been the same since her maternity leave. I can sense her weakness. And Neil does not give a damn.

He's the only one worthy of our concern, Damon. Don't tell me you've gone soft, too."

The man, Damon, responds with caution, "I am cautious. *You* are bloodthirsty."

"I thought this was a cause you believed in, too." The girl puts her hands on her hips, her tone defiant. Given the fact that this man is probably her professor, if this is truly Kingsmarch and she's a Southeastern student, she's got some serious guts. Or maybe she's just an arrogant idiot. I'm not sure which one it is yet.

Damon snaps back, "I never said I changed my mind about our cause."

The girl's voice rises, her tone heated. "Then what? You *knew* your role in the grand design before starting this project. You've only met that girl once. She's barely even considered a daughter. If anything, the experiment is your child. Not some lowborn bastard you sired with a dental assistant."

He snarls, his tone almost animalistic now. "She isn't lowborn."

The girl scoffs. "She is fodder. You know as well as I do that she was never supposed to be born. You would sacrifice our mission for that? Once this girl plays her role, you can have a new daughter. A pure born. How can you not see that?"

"I—"

"What are you two doing here?" A voice cuts through the tense conversation. Suddenly, a stunning woman appears in the boathouse. She's not as young as the female student, but just as gorgeous with icy hair and piercing dark eyes. I don't think her hair is naturally that pale, but it suits her.

"Sabine." Damon jumps away from the blonde student, lowering his gaze.

Well, well, well, the plot thickens. Sabine is here, and she doesn't look happy.

"Hello, Damon," she says, narrowing her eyes. "My husband wishes to speak with you, Elisabeth. Hurry up. He's an impatient man."

The student exits the boathouse and ducks her head, her fire seemingly extinguished. Sabine turns to Damon, her expression cold.

"So, what were you two discussing?" she asks pointedly.

Damon shakes his head and replies, "Jenna."

Jenna? Could he be talking about Jenna Cooper?

Jenna's mom was a dental assistant or something, right? That can't be a coincidence. But what does this mean? Is Damon her biological father? Or does he just *think* he is?

"You're having second thoughts," Sabine says, though it's not an accusation. She almost sounds *relieved*.

"I saw her yesterday in the park. Her mother took her for a stroll," he says, his voice breaking. "She's so small, Sabine. I don't care that she's just shadowborn. Even if I'm not part of her life, I want her to live."

Sabine raises an eyebrow. "Even if it means going against the grand design?"

The grand design? The Wisdom Tree mentioned that phrase before. From what I can gather, it's just another fancy term for fate—the timekeepers' plan for the entire universe or something like that. Regardless, the Wisdom Tree made it clear that I wasn't part of their original plan. That's supposed to make me feel special in some way. However, the conversation I'm overhearing now between Sabine and Damon leads me to believe that being "special" in this case might not be a good thing at all. What is this cause they keep talking about?

"Yes," Damon says. "The timekeepers claim the grand design cannot accommodate for all the extras, but I don't believe that anymore. They can fix the timeline, they just don't want to—because they need soldiers."

"You are having regrets now," Sabine says slowly, "and yet, you've sacrificed countless children for the cause. But your child is different, isn't she? You love her."

"Don't be a hypocrite when you're in the same situation," Damon counters. "There are whispers about you, Sabine. Elisabeth and the other interns think *you* regret it. Elisabeth wonders if you even believe in the cause at all."

Sabine's body stiffens. "She looks just like Rory, you know. Thompson doesn't see it."

"She's a baby."

"She's *my* baby. And Neil is going to do God knows what to her." Sabine takes a moment to regain her composure. "It's not too late, Damon. We can turn things around."

"How? The last person who dissented got locked in a time prison," Damon whispers. "I cannot end up with the same fate."

"You have a choice to make. But choose wisely—because the fate of the two realms hangs in the balance."

"And you?"

"I've made my choice," she says simply. "I will not allow *my* daughter to become Neil's weapon, or the timekeepers' breeder. This entire plan is horrible. I see that now."

"I—"

My body chooses this exact moment to react to the dust floating around the room. I try to hold it in the best I can, but the sneeze comes out anyway.

Damon and Sabine jump, now on high alert.

"Who's there?" Damon demands, rounding the corner.

He peers over the crates, seeing me crouched near the floor.

"Uh, hi," I say. "Didn't mean to interrupt. You can continue now."

He responds by pulling out a dagger. *Great*.

Chapter Twenty

"Wait!" Sabine grabs Damon's shoulder before he can do anything.

"She overheard everything," he argues. "She might be a spy for Neil. If he learns of our doubts—"

He doesn't finish his sentence. Sabine smacks him in the face, her hand coated in green powder. I have no idea where she got said powder, but I'm guessing it's the same memory dust Jenna tried to use on *me*, way back when.

Damon goes down hard. Sabine sidesteps him, letting him fall straight to the ground. I'm afraid she's going to advance on me next, but she wipes her hands on her dress.

"You must be Maria," she says.

My jaw drops. "How do you know my name?"

"We don't have much time. Once Damon wakes, he'll report me to Neil. I have to spin my own story first," Sabine says quickly. She reaches out to me, but quickly draws back, second-guessing herself. "If you're here, then the experiment must have worked. My suspicions were right. How old are you right now?"

"Nineteen," I answer. "How do you know me? Who *are* you?"

"My name is Sabine Everleigh. Listen, I'm not sure why you've come, but you must return. You being here will create a paradox," she explains. "You can't be in the same place as your younger self or meet any biological relatives. And I have no idea how many spies Neil has around campus. He's a suspicious man; if I'm gone for too long, he'll begin to suspect something. You must never trust him."

"I don't."

"Good. Good. I don't know how much he's told you about the mission, or the timekeepers—"

"No one will tell me anything! All I get are cryptic half-answers!"

"Look up Damon Harper. Angeline Willis. Faith Scott. Mary Williams," she lists. "Elisabeth Randall. Mikayla Larson. Katherine Himes."

As she speaks, a rift tears open behind me. It's like a vacuum. The wind blows everywhere, whipping our hair around us and rattling the old boathouse.

"The Shadowborn Genome Project!" she yells. "Don't trust anyone, Maria. Not—"

I don't catch the end of her sentence.

My body is ripped backward, through the rift. I'm launched onto the pavement, right next to a pad of nice, soft grass. Typical.

Looking around, I'm back at Southeastern. Coincidentally, Ophelia passes by, stopping to stare at me. The rift closes in front of us on its own.

"What's all over your clothes?" Ophelia asks, wrinkling her nose. "You smell awful."

I get up, dusting the gravel from my scraped elbows. "What day is it? When did we last see each other?"

"It's Saturday, freak. And we saw each other last night for dinner." Ophelia rolls her eyes. "You're so weird."

"You're so nice. Has anyone ever told you that?"

"Plenty of people." Ophelia struts away, flipping her blonde curls over her shoulder.

Okay, so not a lot of time has passed. That's promising, right?

I need to talk to Theodas and see if he knows anything. I also have to do some research on what Sabine said. But first, I've gotta shower.

"The Shadowborn Genome Project?" Theodas asks. "I don't recall the specifics. I didn't have much to do with it, to be honest. I wanted to fund shadowborn comic creators, but Princess Siraye thought this genome thing took precedence."

After a nice, hot shower and a change of clothes, I managed to catch Theodas and Mathers in the main building. We sit around Theodas' desk, on which sits a large robot modeling kit. I'm sorry—*mecha* modeling kit. Theodas kindly corrected me when I asked about it.

But that's not the point.

I recounted everything that happened between Sabine and Damon, leaving out the involvement of blood magic. I hoped Theodas would have been more involved, being a chancellor and all. Apparently not.

"Did you help with the project, Provost Mathers?" I ask.

Mathers hesitates. "How old do you think I am, Mar?"

"Richard wasn't a provost yet," Theodas supplies. "I'm sure the library has files from the project. You could take a look."

"Damon Harper's dissertation should be there, as well," Mathers says. "I had him as a professor, back in the day. Brilliant man. A shame what happened."

"What happened?"

"He went missin'. He was on the Ruby Council, actually. I heard he was caught embezzlin'. Never heard from him again. But that's how the Ruby Council does business."

He went missing? Could it be because of Sabine and Neil?

"Damon said that the timekeepers needed soldiers. There was a cause, some sort of plan that he was working on," I explain, still trying to wrap my head around it all. "I think Jenna Cooper was his biological daughter."

It aligns with what I know about her. She's a dental assistant's daughter. She's a Time Agent because she was never supposed to be born. That *must* be what Damon was talking about when he said that the timekeepers could accommodate the "extras" like Jenna—they're being used as soldiers by the timekeepers. But why? And where do I fit in?

I'm not like Jenna, who needs the Infinity Hallway to time travel. I can do that on my own, clearly. But I'm also not part of the original grand design. Why am I special?

And if I'm reading things correctly, is it possible I'm related to Sabine, too?

I don't look like her. But whatever she and Damon were working on, she was willing to give it all up for her daughter. The one Neil wanted to use as a weapon. The one the timekeepers wanted to use as a breeder. I don't even want to know what *that* would entail.

I don't look like Sabine. But I don't look like Neil, either.

"Do you know an Elisabeth? She would have been a student of Damon's. Blonde. Blue eyes. She worked on a project with him and Neil, and the Everleighs," I say. "I think her name was Elisabeth Randall."

"*Her* I remember!" Theodas grins, snapping his fingers. "She was a nut."

"Chancellor, you cannot say that about a student," Mathers chides, like a father reprimanding his son.

"I think it's time we visit the princess, Mar. Why don't we go Monday afternoon?"

"How about tonight?" I want to get these answers as soon as possible.

"No can do. The princess needs more notice. She has to travel across continents." Theodas leans over his desk, inspecting his purple robot toy. "Do you think I should put a Polly Pocket in its hand?"

"No. And isn't she in the Veil?"

"Currently, she's in Kuala Lumpur on business. And I can see from your blank expression you don't know where that is, which makes me question the quality of our gen ed classes. Malaysia, Mar. It's the capital of Malaysia."

"Right. Totally knew that."

Theodas grins at me, looking up. "Liar."

Ah, crap. I forgot about the whole elf thing. "Okay. Monday, then."

As I walk out of the office, I can't help but feel a heaviness in my chest.

I need answers. Answers about my past, about my

family, and about the timekeepers' plans for me. I'm going insane with all these fractured pieces, none of which seem to fit together. Is Damon Astaroth? Sabine mentioned she needed to "spin a story" so he wouldn't report her (and me) to Neil, but is that the reason he was locked in the time prison? Because I meddled?

The more I think about it, the more I'm beginning to suspect that Sabine is my mother. She said that I couldn't travel to a biological relative or near a past version of myself. She might know more about time travel than I do.

I step into the elevator, trying to shake off my anticipation of meeting Siraye tomorrow. Unfortunately, as soon as I get to the first floor, the elevator opens to Nic and Allegra.

"Maria. What a lovely surprise. What brings you here on a Saturday?" Nic asks, putting an arm around me.

"Can you not touch me, please?" I try to shrug him off, but he grips my arm tightly. I'm stronger now, though. Using more force, I shove him away. A momentary look of shock passes over his face, but he quickly hides it with a smarmy grin.

"Let's not fight. We're family, after all."

"I don't have time to deal with you right now," I mutter.

"Did you have a nice trip to the past?"

That stops me in my tracks. How could he possibly know about that? I turn to face him, but my reaction is too hasty. Nic laughs, poking my nose.

"Ah, so you *did* take a trip today. My, my. Busy little bee, aren't we?"

Shit, he was just tricking me to see my expression. And it worked. "I'm doing what Neil asked me to do. But I don't recall him saying you should micromanage me, Nic."

"Father is getting impatient. If it were me, I could have defeated Astaroth already," Allegra cuts in unnecessarily.

God, if that isn't the biggest lie I've ever heard.

She's even weaker than me! No offense. She might have grown up in the shadowborn community, but physically she can't do anything about Astaroth.

"But Neil didn't assign the task to you. He assigned it to *me,*" I tell her. "I wonder what that says about you."

Her fists clench at her sides. "You think you're the only one who can handle this task? You're just a pawn in Father's game. He doesn't care about you. If he cared, he wouldn't have killed someone you loved."

"Don't mention that," I warn, simmering.

But Allegra just keeps pushing. "You know what I hate most about you, Maria? You're a hypocrite. You get angry over that, but when it comes to my mother…you don't even apologize."

"What do I have to apologize for? The fact that she tried to kill me?" I grit out. "I don't owe you *anything*."

"You owe me *everything*!" Allegra screams, drawing the attention of other passing students. "You took everything from me. From *us*. You took my place, and you think that you can just go around and pretend like nothing happened?"

"You're a psycho! Neil made his own choices," I yell back. "I didn't steal anything from you! And I'm not pretending like nothing happened. I know what happened, and I'm trying to do what I need to so my family can survive. Do you even know the meaning of family, Allegra?"

"Yes, I know what family means. I know that family is about blood, and that blood ties are supposed to be unbreakable. But you? You're not my sister. So I don't understand why Father is pretending that you are when you're not even related to us!"

"What are you talking about?"

"The DNA test! I had us tested and you and I are *not* biological sisters," Allegra shouts, her face getting red. "You're just some charity case that Father—"

"You only had my DNA tested with yours?" I cross my arms. "That just means we're not sisters. That doesn't mean I'm not Neil's biological daughter."

"You don't look anything like us," Allegra sputters.

"In a world where magic exists, and eye colors can change," I say, pointing to my eyes, "I don't think that's much of a concern."

I spin on my heel, powerwalking away from her.

No, I don't buy that I'm actually Neil's daughter. Now that I know Allegra did a DNA test, if the results can be trusted and she wasn't lying...

Well, then what Sabine was saying all falls into place. Neil conducted experiments, which were obviously not kosher, since Damon *and* Sabine mentioned Neil keeping an eye on them. And sacrificing babies for the cause, whatever the cause is.

Technically, Neil could still consider himself my father. If I was an experiment, and he was a scientist running the experiment, then he had a hand in my birth. And I suspect Sabine did, too.

But if I'm an experiment, then what did he do to me? Did he give me the ability to time travel artificially, somehow? What's the end goal there? A time-traveling assassin? A...breeder?

As soon as I go home, I refer to the list of names Sabine mentioned and begin looking them up. I wasn't sure how much information I'd find by a Google search, but interestingly enough, I manage to get news articles from the early 2000s.

Every single woman on the list was marked as missing. Cold cases—they were never found. And even more curious? They were all pregnant when they disappeared.

Dear Maria,

Neil has been spending more and more time away from home. I wonder what he is planning. He went to the Veil earlier this morning to visit the Ruby Council. He returned in a poor mood. Perhaps not everything is going to plan.

Yours,
Rhys

Chapter Twenty-One

We decide to meet Siraye in the Veil instead of having her come to campus. I guess I'm not the only one paranoid about Neil's spyware, which makes me feel a little less crazy. But that's what happens when you spend all your spare time thinking about horrible what-if scenarios.

You know, before all this shit, I *never* thought of myself as a worrywart. Now, it's a completely different story.

Mathers and I need to make an excuse to leave campus together, so we pretend we're going on a hunt. At least this plan allows us to take backup, in the form of a blonde werewolf and an ex-turned-ally.

Neither Archer nor Ophelia has been clued in. It's not that they aren't trustworthy, but we're not entirely sure who's listening on campus. We pile into Mathers' Jeep and drive through the rift, since according to him we'll need a car to get to the meeting spot.

"Nice Wrangler," Ophelia comments, rolling down the window. She puts her sunglasses on, despite the sky in the

Veil being overcast as per usual. Her hair blows directly in my face, not that she cares, and I catch a taste of her hairspray. Gross. "It almost distracts from the fact that this bitch is a big fat liar. Again."

"I didn't technically lie," I defend. "That was Provost Mathers! And move your big feet. You're hogging all the legroom."

"Big feet? Excuse me? How is it my fault you're a shrimp?"

"You're not that much taller than me. Your feet are just disproportionately large."

"*You* look like you're a size eight, too!"

"I think I'm going to be sick," Archer announces, looking a bit green in the face. He clings onto the grab handle above him, leaning out the car window.

"Please do not vomit in my car, Mr. Kinsey," Mathers says dryly. He's stiffer than I've ever seen him as he weaves through the winding dirt road. There aren't any other cars, and there are no street signs or GPS navigation to guide him. He has to rely on Theodas, who has a paper map in his hands. How archaic! "And while I lied to get you on this trip, we *are* goin' huntin'. Just not for ferals."

"We're gathering intel, not hunting. I didn't even need to bring my sword," Ophelia grumbles.

"Research *is* an integral part of the hunt, Phoebe," Theodas chimes in cheerfully. At least one of us is smiling.

"It's Ophelia, Chancellor."

"Yes, sure it is. Anyway, you wouldn't walk into a dragon's nest blind, would you? Besides, the Veil is the perfect place to talk. Wi-Fi and cell towers are very limited. If Neil Abbott wanted to record our movements, he'd have a tough time."

To her credit, even when speaking to authority figures, Ophelia doesn't seem to have trouble standing up for herself. "Why not just use a spell to block out recordings?"

"We have spells placed in some rooms of the main office, but we can't put them everywhere. They cost too much to maintain for the entirety of campus, and we have to prioritize student safety," Theodas explains. "We don't want Neil to know that *we* know he's spying. As long as he uses human methods of eavesdropping, we can counteract it. But if he uses some sort of spell, we'll have a much more difficult time. And you missed that turn, Richard."

Mathers curses, coming to an abrupt stop and making a K-turn. The dense woods can't be fun to drive in, and since ferals are still lurking around the realm, I can see why he would be on edge.

After a few more missed turns, we finally arrive at the cottage. The building is a secluded stone structure that looks like it's waiting to be blown over by a big bad wolf. The roof is hay, and there hardly seems to be enough room inside for one person, let alone six.

"This belongs to my grandfather. Unfortunately, he's on vacation at the moment," Mathers says, opening the door for us.

He leads us through the side door, into a dimly lit hall. The ceiling is just high enough so Mathers and Theodas don't bump their heads, but I bet I could reach it if I stood on my toes.

It's warm inside, providing shelter from the chill of the Veil. Compared to Georgia, it's much colder here, though it's not quite snowing.

In the dining room, a few wooden tables have been pushed together to make one large table, filled with food.

Siraye stands when she sees me, her face splitting into a wide grin. She looks to be in her mid-thirties, with hair flowing to her waist in orange-red waves. I know she's not technically a princess anymore, but she still has a regal aura, a way about her that screams elegance and grace.

"It's been so long, Maria. I have missed you," she says, pulling me into a big hug. We might not have known each other well in the past, but I can feel the authenticity of her words.

I'm a little bit relieved she isn't angry with me. I would be, if I were in her shoes. I'm the reason she lost her brother.

Speaking of Rhys, he's here, too. I don't notice him at first until he clears his throat, looking straight at me.

I haven't seen him around the house for a while, but now that he's here, my stupid heart does a little flip.

"It's good to see you," I say finally, looking at both elven siblings.

"I would love to have a touching reunion, but we have business to conduct," Theodas interrupts. "Princess, did you make all this?"

"Of course. Anything for my favorite henchmen," she teases.

"Hey, I'm not a henchman. I'm a *minion,* there's a difference."

"Semantics." She settles at the head of the table, beckoning me to sit. I do, pulling out the chair beside Rhys.

Archer, Allegra, and Mathers settle around the table while Theodas takes a seat at the other end, filling his plate with bread, cheese, and salami. It's quite an elaborate spread, and the bread looks handmade. It reminds me of my time in the past.

"I'll introduce myself," Siraye says. "I am Siraye Torren. I founded the five magic colleges in the United States, as well as several in Europe and Canada."

Ophelia and Archer look surprised, but Mathers doesn't. Given his relationship with Lyari and Chaela, he's probably met Siraye before.

"I have come because Theodas tells me you have discovered some interesting things about Neil Abbott, Maria. I will need a full recap of events. Theodas explained, but he speaks so quickly, I had difficulty understanding."

"Sure." I take a deep breath and start my story. I don't leave anything out, except maybe the bits about Rhys. I don't want to spill my guts about my love life to the whole table, though it's clear Theodas and Siraye would find that entertaining. "In short, I think Damon Harper is Jenna Cooper's biological father. And Sabine might be my biological mother. Oh, and Neil was conducting experiments involving children. It's all very textbook bad guy, isn't it?"

"It's a subversion of the 'Luke, I am your father' thing," Theodas unhelpfully adds. "Have you all seen *Star Wars*? If you haven't, you really must—"

"Maria, do you have a list of the people Sabine Everleigh mentioned to you?" Siraye asks.

I pull out a packet from my bag and hand it to her.

"Wow. There must be a hundred pages in here," Mathers comments. "You didn't use the library printer for this, did you?"

"Jenna is a Time Agent?" Ophelia questions, her blue eyes narrowing. "Why didn't you say anything before?"

"I'm still confused," Archer says. "Why is *Rhys* here? He works for Neil!"

"Why is Archer in attendance when he has the emotional intelligence of a fruit fly?" Rhys counters, glowering.

"To be fair, I'm also curious as to how you're here," I say carefully. "I didn't think Neil would give you time off."

"I am contracted through Theodas. Neil has no say in my time off," Rhys explains, his voice gentler when speaking to me than Archer. Admittedly, it's a little bit funny to me how biased Rhys is against Archer. Just a little. "I have not managed to find out much by working with Neil, but as you suggest, I believe Damon Harper is an earlier version of Astaroth. It makes the most sense, given Jenna's claims that Astaroth is her father."

"Astaroth is supposed to be centuries old," Ophelia points out.

"The name is derived from a Christian demon; Damon Harper simply stole it. Either that or Jenna rebranded him as Astaroth to appeal to more cultists. Astaroth likely already had a following amongst humans, and she needed recruits to use in her blood magic schemes."

"There's no way Jenna was a cult leader," Ophelia insists. "I've known her for practically her entire life."

"Jenna admitted to this herself. Moreover, I do not believe she is *helping* you, Maria, however it may seem," Rhys says. "The timekeepers are working with Neil, and by extension, so are the Time Agents. To what end, I am unsure. But for some reason, they want you to kill Astaroth."

"It sounds like Neil imprisoned Damon because he believed him to be a dissenter. Sabine reported him after your trip to the past," Mathers says. "But in that case, why not outright kill him? He was involved in the experiments and knew many of Neil's secrets."

"It's not very Machiavellian of him," Theodas chimes in, crumbs on his lips. I'm not sure what part of his conversation makes him hungry, but all this talk about cults and demons and Neil makes me sick to my stomach. "Maybe there's a reason why Maria, specifically, has to kill him."

Siraye taps her foot, deep in thought. Finally, she says, "Damon and Neil were mapping the shadowborn genome. They did a lot of work with DNA, with the justification that this could be used to cure diseases. I believed it was never completed, as Neil and Dr. Everleigh had a falling out, but perhaps that was not the case. Admittedly, I am not well-versed in the sciences, so I allowed them to do as they pleased for the greater good of the community. But it sounds to me like Damon and Neil were further along than I would have guessed. The pregnant women you believe they abducted—according to your findings, each of these women was no more than three months into their pregnancies. And, had they given birth, the children would probably be around Allegra Abbott's age."

"Allegra?" Archer asks worriedly.

"When humans were mapping the genome, there was concern about gene editing," Theodas says. "Maybe Neil played God. It would explain Maria's ability to time travel. In all my years, I've never heard of anyone having that power—and it fits in with the timekeepers and Time Agents."

He's right. That makes the most sense right now—Neil claiming to be my father, my connection with the timekeepers, being someone who shouldn't exist…

My throat constricts, and suddenly this information is a little too much to handle. I push up from my seat, standing.

"I need a minute to process all this. I'm going for a quick walk."

"Mar—" Archer begins.

"I'm fine." The three elves in the room look at me pointedly, so I amend my lie. "I will probably be fine."

I walk out the back, but the cold air does little to calm my nerves. Then again, I'm not sure if you can call the air in the Veil "fresh." The sky above me is a depressing canvas of clouds and smog, and the backyard looks like it's been through a ten-year drought. I don't venture too far—I don't want to worry anyone. Going out to the garden area, underneath a metal archway with dead vines hanging from it, I settle on a wooden swing.

Isn't the hero's journey supposed to be more clear-cut? I'm not sure what the right decision is here. Do I kill Astaroth or not? Because if Neil wants me to, then nothing good can come out of it. He's working for the timekeepers, who ordered Jenna and Todd to help me. But why? What's their end goal? I'm back to the same questions I had months ago, despite all this new information having come to light. If I make the wrong choice, are people going to get hurt because of it? If I *don't* kill Astaroth, what if he goes on a rampage?

Engrossed in my thoughts, I swing back and forth, savoring the cool air that washes over me as I close my eyes. There's something so peaceful about being away from the others. However, my tranquility is short-lived as I hear an unfamiliar sound…the distinct crunching of gravel beneath footsteps. With a jolt, I open my eyes to find Rhys strolling toward me.

"May I sit?" He gestures to the space beside me.

Feeling like a total idiot, I bob my head up and down. "As you can probably tell, I didn't walk very far."

"Good. There could be ferals lurking beyond the property."

Well, he has a point. "Don't take this the wrong way, but what are you doing here?"

"Unhappy to see me?"

"No. It's more like…I keep showing you the most pathetic parts of myself, and I'm hoping someday soon I can prove that I really *am* a good time. Minus these continuous threats to the safety of myself and everyone around me," I ramble.

"You are not pathetic," he says. "I am. I worked with Neil for three years, and yet you have discovered more than I have in all the time I spent actively attempting to uncover information. I wanted to be useful to you, so that when we finally reunited, you would not be bound by these burdens."

"Neil is a squirrely asshole. I'm not surprised he'd be secretive, especially now that I know he's doing all this shady shit with gene editing. He's a goddamn mad scientist!" I exclaim. "But that's not your fault at all, Rhys. I just don't know what to do from here. I feel like whatever I choose is going to have some horrible consequence."

"You can only work with the information you have. Whatever happens cannot be pinned on you," he says gently, reaching for my hand. "That being said, from what I have gathered, the timekeepers do have one weakness. The Divinities Sword."

"The sword? Why?" I thought it would only work against blood-magic users.

But Rhys explains, "The timekeepers are essentially fates,

almost like gods. They should be omniscient. They determine the lives of everyone. And yet, they did not know where the Divinities Sword was. The Wisdom Tree claimed it was in their blind spot. Perhaps we use this 'blind spot' to our advantage."

"So you don't think the timekeepers are the good guys, right? To put it simply."

Rhys hesitates, choosing his words carefully. "If they are working with Neil, I am under the impression they are aware of everything he has done in order to ensure your compliance."

Taking my family hostage. Wiping their memories. Killing Luke.

If Rhys is right and they *are* omniscient, then of course they would know about all that.

"What if they're right?" I ask. "What if all this is for the greater good, and if I go against them, I'll be damning us all?"

"I do not see how hurting those you care about is justified. They could have found another way to convince you. If they designed your life and determined we were soulmates, they must know a great deal about you. I find it difficult to believe that this was the only way to ensure your compliance."

"God, that is so..." I can't even find the word for it. I just want to scream!

"Even if this is all for the greater good, I would never comply with those who would harm the people I care about," Rhys says. "Regardless of what you decide, I will do whatever I can to aid you."

"Even if it means walking straight into hell?"

"Perhaps it is more fun down there."

"Well, before we go party with Satan, it might be worth

it to visit the Wisdom Tree again. Despite its weird way of relaying information, it *did* give us a lot to chew on." And now that I know what's in store for us, I'll bring a notepad this time.

"I will accompany you."

"I wouldn't have it any other way." Even though we've been apart, I trust Rhys completely. I've had doubts about myself and my place in his heart, but now, being like this, everything feels obvious. No matter how crazy things get, Rhys has my back. I want to tell him all this, but when I open my mouth, a stupid jumble of words comes to mind instead of anything remotely eloquent. I blurt, "There are a lot of things I'm not good at, and I think grand declarations of love are one of them."

"What a coincidence. *I* am not good at receiving grand declarations of love," he replies easily, a smile spreading across his face.

"What about mid-sized declarations of love?"

"Hmm, it might be best to stick with comfortably-sized declarations of love."

"What would that look like? A greeting card?" I tease.

"No, it would be more than a greeting card, but less than a skywriter," Rhys concludes.

"Somewhere between a skywriter and a greeting card. I think I can manage that." I lean forward, wrapping my arms around his neck. When our lips meet, it's like a spark igniting a fire that has been smoldering for too long.

When we pull apart, I say, "I think that was a comfortably-sized declaration of love, don't you?"

"Inconclusive," he replies, unable to keep a straight face. "We might need to test it out more, just to make sure."

"I think you're relying too heavily on those rusty

chains," Siraye cuts in, folding her arms over her chest. How long has she been standing there? And why is this the *second* time she's caught us kissing? "That swing looks like it's going to fall."

"I'm happy for you two," Theodas chimes in. He's on his second (possibly third) sandwich.

"Chancellor, you cannot comment on a student's relationship. It's inappropriate."

"Oh, lighten up, Richard."

"Wait! *What*?" Archer yells, more surprised than angry. He looks between Rhys and me, pointing. Hasn't anyone told him that's rude? "When did this happen?"

Can I just disappear now? Please? I want to move away, but Rhys has an iron grip on my hand. Ironically, as an elf, he can't touch iron. "Before *you*, chronologically."

"Time travel gets messy," I add, my face on fire.

Archer's mouth hangs open. "I thought you liked Allegra. Even if Mar isn't her biological sister, it's still messed up."

"That is the pot calling the kettle black," Rhys sneers. "I have explained to you numerous times that I am not involved, nor do I have an interest in being involved, with Allegra Abbott."

"If you aren't secretly in love with Allegra, why did you give me so much grief when we were dating?"

"I knew you would kiss Maria one day. And I simply do not like you," Rhys replies flatly. "I never interfered with your relationship, however."

"You turned the sprinklers on me when I was outside Allegra's window!"

"I was not trying to prevent you from climbing up. I simply thought it would be amusing."

"Mar, do you see what kind of person he is?" Archer demands, waving his arms wildly as he speaks. "If you need a boyfriend, there are *plenty* of guys I could set you up with."

"That's not true," Ophelia says dryly. "You don't have many friends, Archer. And no offense, but Mar isn't my type at all."

"As entertaining as this all is," Siraye says, "we aren't meeting to discuss my brother's love life. We are here to discuss Neil Abbott's plan."

"Yes, if we could all get off this *exciting* topic and get back to business, that would be great," I add, looking at Rhys pointedly.

"He started it," he replies, which is very mature of him.

"Me? You're the one who started it!" Archer accuses.

"You kissed my girlfriend."

"I didn't know she was your girlfriend! Hell, *she* didn't know she was your girlfriend! And *she* kissed *me*!"

"God, I just need some popcorn and a slushie," Theodas says, thoroughly entertained. I'm glad someone finds this amusing. He nudges Siraye with his elbow. "I told you she would be fun. You should have come sooner, Princess."

"It's been a long time since I've seen my brother so worked up," she confesses. "Maria, I looked over the packet you printed. There is someone who stands out to me—Elisabeth Randall."

"I saw her in the past, talking with Damon." I pause. "I...kind of killed her. In the Veil. She was a cultist, and she attacked me with blood magic."

Not that it justifies what I did to her—tearing her throat up. But I decide to leave that part out. This isn't the time or place.

Siraye doesn't seem surprised at all. "Elisabeth Randall was a student. I remember her because I was called in to make a final decision about her attendance at Southeastern. Unfortunately, we had to expel her. She was barred from attending any of the schools in the United States."

"What did she do?"

"She wrote her final paper on eugenics. She wanted to use gene editing to create a master race," Siraye says. "In other words, she was a neo-Nazi."

"*What*?" Was that the cause Damon was talking about? A "master race"?

Oh my God, if that's true, then it makes Neil evil incarnate!

Before Siraye can reply, a rift forms in front of us. The ground shakes, and the wind blows cold as a deep, unnatural mist covers our surroundings. I stare at the churning purple and black vortex, unable to look away.

The rift starts to pull in the rocks and sticks on the ground close to it. It's like a black hole, inexorably drawing us closer to it with its gravity. The air ripples from the pressure and I feel the force of it against my face and body. Then, all at once, it pulls me through.

Chapter Twenty-Two

I land unceremoniously on my ass.

The stone floor is cold, and I roll to my feet as soon as my head stops spinning. I'm in an underground chamber, and thankfully my eyes adjust quickly to the darkness. The only light emanates from a single flickering wall sconce.

Huh, it's almost as if I'm in Medieval hell.

I'm not alone, either. Soon enough, someone else is flung through the rift, smacking the ground hard. Thankfully, Rhys gets up, wincing as he touches a wound on his forehead.

"Shit!" I rush over, pulling Rhys to the side. "Are you okay? Why did you follow me? I could have landed in…a volcano or a landfill or something!"

"I was not thinking clearly. Are you alright?"

"I'm not the one bleeding."

Archer and Mathers follow close behind, with Ophelia landing on top of the two men. She gets up, unscathed as the rift closes, while Archer and Mathers are left groaning in pain.

"I think I chipped a tooth," Archer says, holding a hand over his mouth.

"Did any of you bring a sword?" I ask.

They all shake their heads, which is great. We're in a dungeon and we have no weapons, which means we have no way of opening a rift and escaping.

"This feels like a trap," Archer complains.

"Gee, you don't say." Ophelia grimaces. "What do we do now?"

"We have to move ahead," I say. "There's one way out. Even if it is a trap, our only other option is to sit here and rot."

"How can you even see anything?"

"You can't see?" The lighting is pretty bad, but it's not pitch black. I can make out the corners of the room, along with a doorway shrouded in darkness. It's foreboding and not a single part of me wants to go in, but I'd rather face the darkness than die here like this.

"No, I can't," Ophelia replies, annoyed.

"Huh. Maybe my yellow eyes give me night vision."

"What? That's the stupidest thing I've ever heard."

"I don't make the rules." I take Rhys' arm and guide him to the wall, doing the same for the others. We need to make a human chain, with me leading the way. The hall is a short maze, and we backtrack twice to reach a red wooden door. When I open it, light floods in and finally I can see clearly.

This is a throne room, and a lavish one at that. The walls are adorned with paintings that tell ancient tales of long-forgotten legends, while the floor beneath our feet is made of gleaming marble, adding to the grandeur of the room. As we approach the center, my eyes are drawn to a figure sitting on the ornate throne, decorated with intricate carvings and mysterious symbols. Above the throne is a large, gilded chandelier hung with shining chains. The figure waits for us, tracking our movement with dark eyes.

It's a man, his chest fully exposed by the robes he wears. His skin is covered in a myriad of scars, and he doesn't have a single strand of hair on his head. Not even eyebrows or lashes. As he stares at us with a piercing gaze, it's as if his eyes are boring into my soul, and I involuntarily shiver under his intense scrutiny. The room is heavy with his presence, and I struggle to keep my breathing steady.

"Welcome," the man says in a deep, rumbling voice. "I have been waiting for you."

"Why did you bring us here?" Rhys asks, his voice steady and controlled. I can always count on him to be the rational one. He doesn't show any fear, which I admire. Myself, on the other hand? I'm shaking in my boots. Well, sneakers.

The man smiles, but the movement is that of a puppet. His mouth curves, but the rest of his face holds no emotion, no amusement. "I don't recall bringing *you*. As far as I know, I only brought Maria here. But I won't kick you out just yet, since she seems to want your company. I'll do anything for the timekeeper's daughter, after all."

His tone drips with sarcasm as he emphasizes the last part, making it clear that he's not impressed by me.

"You're Astaroth. Just…in a more human-like form," I guess, though I could hardly call his current form humanoid. His skin is a bit too smooth, too ashen, and his scars are too clean, even, and straight. When I last saw him, he was literally a giant. Now, he's still fairly tall, probably at least seven feet, but it's hard to tell when he's sitting down.

His movements are startlingly quick, almost unnaturally

so, and his head jerks from side to side with mechanical precision. It's as if he's completely unfamiliar with human behavior and is simply mimicking what he's seen or remembered. "You are Maria Rochester. The girl who should not exist. Did you receive my message?"

"Yes. It looks like someone needs to go back to etiquette school, because that's *no* way to deliver a message," I say, attempting to mask how freaked out I am. I hate how he looks at me. Call me crazy, but I feel like he's fixin' to eat me.

"They said you'd be amusing." Astaroth clearly doesn't agree, judging by his tone. "Thank you for releasing me, Maria Rochester. You have my utmost gratitude."

"Enough games. Why did you summon me here?" I demand. "How did you suck me into that rift?"

"That's simply a parlor trick."

And *that* isn't an explanation. But I guess I shouldn't expect one from him.

A hissing noise fills the air, and from behind his throne, dozens of snakes pour onto the floor. They're silver, so metallic they don't even look like living creatures, but rather statues molded from metal. Their bodies are thicker than the circumference of my head.

"Shit!" Archer curses, leaping back. They curl around his legs, rooting him in place, along with Mathers and Ophelia.

"They are my greatest allies," Astaroth says softly, petting one in his lap. "It all started with them, you know. I was studying the breeding habits of beastbloods, originally. But after the first few shadowborn came into existence, I became curious. You are so much weaker than truebloods. It is a step back, when really, evolution should always move forward. Suffice to say, nature doesn't always listen to us. Sometimes, we have to force its hand."

Ophelia, despite the situation, glares at the demon. Obviously she's taken the statement personally. "Shadowborn can open rifts from both realms. Truebloods can't. We may be weaker in some ways, but we have a power you need."

Astaroth concedes, "That's true, but why can't we bioengineer a trueblood to do that? In fact, why can't we create a new generation of stronger truebloods? With science and magic combined, anything is possible."

"You failed," I tell him firmly, taking a step forward despite my natural instinct not to get closer. "Allegra isn't a trueblood, and neither am I."

"That *was* our goal." Neil steps out from behind the throne as well, emerging from the darkness. The shadows seem to cling to his skin like black smoke, and I wonder if it's some kind of blood magic that allows him to hide from even *my* eyes. "And yes, Allegra was a failure. Nic, too. But you, Maria? Certainly not a failure. You are perfect."

I never thought I'd hear those words coming from him, and frankly, it's not something I want. Because Neil's version of "perfect" is vastly different from my own.

"Neil." I stagger back, dragging Rhys with me as snakes hiss at us. "What are you doing here?"

"Waiting for you. I must say, Maria, it took you quite a long time. But I believe you're ready now," Neil muses, his green eyes glowing. "Did you really think I would fall for Sabine's lies? You certainly didn't inherit your lying habit from her."

"You've known everything this whole time." From the ship, to Astaroth, to the Divinities Sword. I knew he was involved, but I didn't know to what extent. Everything has gone according to his plan, maybe even the stint with his own wife. Everything led me to this moment, and Neil has me right where he wants me. I was just too foolish to see it.

"Damon went willingly into the time prison," Neil confirms, patting his accomplice on the back. "As soon as Sabine accused him of questioning our *noble* cause, he became even more committed. But his role had to change. I received word from the timekeepers, and Damon agreed to go into the time prison. Do you know why, Maria? The time prison moves throughout history. That is why it is so difficult to find; it is constantly traveling. To me, it seemed like eight years. To Damon, the time he spent imprisoned spanned centuries. And he spent those years practicing blood magic."

"Your pitiful attempts never measured up to my abilities," Astaroth adds smugly. "But do not fret, Maria. Those nights you spent practicing the forbidden arts haven't gone to waste."

"Maria, you have been practicing blood magic?" Mathers questions, horrified.

Okay, so maybe I left that little detail out of my explanation earlier. "Look, I needed to defeat *him*. Though it feels lame saying that now."

"You will never defeat Astaroth," Neil says sympathetically. "It was an impossible task from the start. But I needed a goal to drive you forward, to make you come face to face with Astaroth again. To make you so desperate you would turn to blood magic as a solution."

"I have been waiting for this moment for eight hundred years," Astaroth says, rising to his bare feet. His toes are notably ugly and gnarled, and he could use a pedicure. I swear he grows in size as he stalks toward me. I take a step back, but the snakes around me root me in place. "My blood is refined, *perfect*, just for you, Maria. Everything was done for your sake."

"This really isn't sanitary!" I protest.

"Neil, stop this at once," Rhys demands.

"You are a prince no longer, elf." Neil grabs Rhys by the throat, lifting him off the ground with ease. "You are just my servant."

"Hey!" I bend down, grabbing the snake by the neck. It hisses at me, and for some inane reason, I hiss right back, tearing it away from me and chucking it against the wall. That distracts Neil enough for me to jump on his back, clawing at his face.

"Enough!" he roars, releasing Rhys and sending me to my back, flat on the ground. More snakes pin me in place, crawling over my arms and legs. Rhys is beside me, in a similar predicament. "Do not be disobedient, Maria. I am your father."

"Like hell you are!"

"I might not have raised you directly, but your entire childhood was my design. Every hardship you faced was a lesson *I* wanted you to learn. Every major event that happened, every time you cursed the world for its cruelty, every single person in your miserable life…that was because of me. All is according to plan. I'm a meticulous man, as you probably know."

"Is that a nice way of saying you're a control freak?"

"Your childhood was modeled after my own," Neil continues, ignoring my remark. "I, too, was the son of a criminal. And that is what defined my entire being. My father wasn't even guilty—the Ruby Council decided he was, based on no evidence and a joke of a trial. They needed to blame someone, and their small brains could not figure out the true culprit."

"You don't—"

"I don't understand?" Neil smiles, caressing my cheek. "My dear, I am the one person who understands you most. All your pain, all your anger...I know it well. But every experience has made me the man I am today."

"A cold bastard?"

"A brilliant scientist. A wave-maker. An agent of change. The world cares too much about outside factors—who your parents are, how much money you're born with, and what you look like. I envision something different. A world where everyone is created equal. Doesn't that sound nice?"

"You don't want a world where everyone is created equal," I say, though I know it won't make much of a difference. "You want a world where everyone is just like you—and you'll do anything to achieve that."

Kidnap pregnant women. Bioengineer babies. Trap people in time prisons. Kill innocents.

"All I truly wanted was one person to understand," he says quietly. "But why limit it to just one person? Why not...everyone?"

He's gone too far. I don't think Neil can be reasoned with anymore—he's too convinced that what he believes is right. And frankly, I don't *want* to reason with him. I want to kill him.

Because how *dare* he?

He made my life hell so I would understand him? I get it, the world sucks! That doesn't mean you can use people like puppets. Like their lives don't even matter.

"So what? Your way of thinking is right, and everyone

else in the world is wrong? Isn't that a little bit too textbook supervillain?" I scathe, struggling to free myself.

"Maria, you can resist *me* all you like. But you will succumb to your destiny, whether you like it or not. When the timekeepers learned of my plans, they thought it aligned with their own," Neil continues, circling around me. "They, too, wanted to eliminate the weakness of the realms. But unfortunately, there is a finite number of timekeepers, and they are all male. They couldn't reproduce. And that is where you come in."

"We tried to create female timekeepers." Astaroth kneels down, grabbing my wrist and cutting open my palm. I squirm, crying out as he smells the blood flowing from my hand. "It didn't work. Most of the babies died during the first trimester. We also tried to turn humans into time-keepers—also a failure. Finally, we made *you*. In a way, I am also your father."

"But *I* created the correct combination," Neil says proudly, unable to allow Damon to take any credit for this. "You are perfect. Even if Sabine selfishly tried to keep you from me, in the end, she played her role."

"Where are the timekeepers?" I demand. "They're basically making you into their lackey, Neil. I'm surprised. I never thought of you as a follower."

"The timekeepers?" Neil takes another step forward as the snakes continue to crawl up my body, constricting against me and holding me in place. One of the snakes is right beside my head, leaning forward and allowing Neil to pet it. "The timekeepers are right here."

Chapter Twenty-Three

I think I liked it better when I was just half demon. Being part snake doesn't sit well with me. Excuse me, part *magic* snake. Because that makes it *much* better.

At least Neil is humanoid. I know that I was made in a lab, but the thought of a human-snake hybrid is still pretty icky. And I have no idea what this means for me now.

Astaroth suckles away at the wound he created on my hand, his face finally showing some genuine emotion. Too bad that emotion is ecstasy. Ew. He's getting his saliva all over me, like a dog, except he's not cute and furry. He's a bald demon.

When he's had his fill, he cuts his own hand open and shoves the gaping wound toward my mouth. I suppress a gag.

"Drink," he commands. "It is your destiny. Drink my blood and become the true savior of our realm."

I'm gonna need to see a blood test first! I think.

I try to turn away but I can't move—the timekeepers are too strong. He pries my mouth open with his dirty fingers and presses his palm against my lips. I feel like I'm about to drown in his blood as it pours into my mouth, the taste almost sweet…almost like honey.

The timekeepers release me as I cough, trying to hack up the blood to no avail. My body burns and wounds begin to open as if my skin is bursting with magic. Blood drips from my eyes and mouth, and I can hardly see. Can hardly *breathe*.

My head is going to explode and my vision shakes. I might be dying. I think Rhys is shouting for me, but I can't make out what he's saying.

"I did learn something from Allegra," Neil whispers in my ear, grasping my shoulders. I can feel his breath on my cheek. "If a child is born with too much power, they will die. Their body rejects the magic. But Everleigh discovered that, through blood magic, we could achieve the desired results without killing you. As an adult, your body should be able to handle this much. And in a few more doses, Maria, you will be perfect."

I think we have two *very* different definitions of "perfect."

The air crackles with tension as a sudden shift in the atmosphere is accompanied by a grinding noise that fills the room. Before I can even react, a partition grows in the center of the room, moving so fast that it nearly slams shut on the snakes writhing around me. The partition cuts the room in half, leaving Neil and Astaroth on the other side. Neil shouts a curse, his fists slamming against the stone, but he doesn't manage a spell fast enough.

My vision begins to clear as Rhys rushes to my side, helping me to my feet. He tosses something to Archer, barking out an order. "Open a rift!"

"I can't!" he exclaims, frustration etched on his face. "The blade isn't sharp enough!"

The stone wall trembles and cracks, as if a giant is trying to smash through it. It's only a matter of time until the wall gives way.

As tired as I am, I need to do something. Looking at the blood from my palm, I take whatever small stones I can find from the ground and rub them in my palms. It hurts, but coated in my blood, I manage to perform the same hand-sharpening spell I performed the other day in the Veil.

Once complete, I only have seconds before it wears off. The few stones weren't a strong enough anchor. With my mind muddled, I envision a safe place and tear a rift through the floor.

"Let's go," I croak. My body lags behind my brain, and I fall into the rift instead of jumping through. Luckily, it's not that far of a fall. As soon as I land, I roll away so I don't get squished by the others. My legs are jelly, however, and I can't find the strength to stand.

Rhys follows after me, pulling me into his arms and tilting my chin up to meet his eyes. "Your pupils are dilated. You need a doctor. How do you feel?"

"Like I just drank demon blood," I mutter, leaning against his chest. He's so warm, I don't want to move. I could probably fall asleep. Yes, that sounds like a very good idea.

"I'm traumatized," Archer announces. I never noticed before now, but he's so loud! Not just his voice, but every time he moves I can hear the whooshing of his jacket and his feet stomping in the dirt. "I have a phobia of snakes now. The one that crawled on me stared into my eyes, *daring* me to move."

"Where the hell did you bring us, Mar?" Ophelia asks.

"Away from the huge, time-traveling snakes. You're welcome."

"If they can time-travel and open rifts like you, can't they follow us?"

She brings up a good point. I just can't find it in me to give a shit. What did Astaroth's blood *do* to me? I can barely even form a real thought.

Rhys shifts me, lifting me from the ground and onto his back. "Hold on, Maria."

"Better than a princess carry. More comfortable," I mumble. "I hate being princess carried."

"Let us walk," Rhys tells the others. "Look for metal on the ground, or any medium-sized stones."

"There's nothing here but dead trees," Ophelia complains.

"A wooden sword will be unable to tear a rift," Mathers says. "I believe we're in the Veil, but where and when…I don't know."

I wish I could be more useful, but I'm just so tired. My eyelids are like lead, and each time between blinks feels longer. It doesn't take much time before I'm dead asleep. I'm not sure how much time passes, but when I wake up again, I'm still on Rhys' back. I lift my head, glancing around.

Oh, thank *God* I didn't drool on him! That would be embarrassing. More embarrassing than falling asleep directly after escaping certain death.

We're in a grove of trees now, with Rhys still carrying me without complaint. He's not even winded.

"This forest is completely dead," Archer says beside me. "We're screwed. We're going to die here. We're going to go insane and eat each other."

"I'd prefer starving to death," Rhys tells him.

"I'm already going insane," Ophelia announces, rubbing her arms.

"Set me down. I can do the same thing I did earlier to get us here," I rasp.

"Did you have a nice nap?" Ophelia asks sarcastically.

"I could still sleep for a week straight." But I need to get us out of here first. I'll worry about the rest later.

Still, this grove looks familiar. Dead, yes—all the trees around us are withered and shriveled, but still packed quite close together. Almost impossibly so. I can't imagine how they grew like that.

Rhys sets me down on my feet. My legs are numb, so I shake out my limbs and head toward the edge of the grove.

"What were you thinkin' when you made that rift?" Mathers asks. It's not an accusation—he genuinely wants to know what I had envisioned.

"I didn't get a chance to think anything over," I admit, running my fingers along the peeling bark of the tree trunks in front of me. "I just wanted a safe place, away from the timekeepers."

And that's when it hits me. A safe place? We're probably near the Wisdom Tree. The grove looks different, and there are no guardians, but being near the Wisdom Tree *would* be safe from the timekeepers. I think.

I couldn't understand the timekeepers when they, uh, *hissed*. And aside from their size and color, they didn't look much different from other snakes, nor did they act differently. But I won't be fooled. Just because they seemed like animals doesn't mean they are. They're beastbloods, the same as truebloods, except without a humanoid form. And they can time travel.

Not sure how they created the Infinity Hallway without opposable thumbs, but I guess magic can explain everything away. And somehow, they communicate with Neil. Oh, and they can time travel and control fate.

So yeah, I'm really second-guessing how safe we are.

But for now, I guess Neil got what he wanted. I drank Astaroth's blood, and the effects were immediate. I'm not sure what other consequences will come of that, but I'm praying to God, Buddha, or whoever that I don't turn into a snake myself.

At least I couldn't have prevented this situation. That makes me feel better, in a way. Astaroth sucked me into a rift (unavoidable), Neil appeared and made his not-so-grand villain speech (unfortunately unavoidable), and now we're somewhere in the Veil.

Now I know what Neil's goals are, so that's a positive, right? Or am I just grasping at straws here? Because his goals are pretty fucked up, and if I understand correctly, he's going to find a way to "dose" me with more of Astaroth's blood.

One thing's for sure: I can't rely on Jenna anymore. I wonder if she knew about all this, or if she's been just as in the dark as I have.

Either way, we need to get out of here.

I try not to make a sound as I squeeze blood out of my hand injury, swiping it on the trees. I'm not sure if this will work, but I will them to open, throwing dirt and fallen branches at the bloody marks.

The trees shift with a groan, almost like a death rattle. They part, making a narrow path for us to enter.

"Come on," I tell the group. "We need to move."

"Mar, I don't think you should be using blood magic in

this state." Or at all, Mathers *wants* to say. He's just looking out for me, I'm sure, but what else am I supposed to do? We can discuss my (mis)use of blood magic later.

In the next grove, the Wisdom Tree is just as I remember. Sort of. Like the other trees in the grove, it looks aged, though not quite *dead* yet. Its face, etched in the bark, seems to sag as it smiles at me. Well, I *think* it's smiling. You can never be too sure when it comes to sentient trees.

"Maria Rochester," the tree croaks, its branches rustling. "It has been a long time."

Ophelia and Archer are too tired to be surprised anymore, but Mathers' jaw is slack. "Mar, where did you bring us?"

"The Wisdom Tree is an all-seeing tree." I pause. "Do you count as a beastblood?"

"Perhaps, to some," the tree replies, its branches rustling. "You've arrived at the perfect time, Maria. I was just thinking about dying. I am withering, you see, and my guardians have fallen. The timekeepers will come for me soon, as well."

Maybe now isn't the time to be joking, but I have to ask, "How are snakes going to kill a tree?"

"Poison," the tree answers casually. "I can do nothing to defend myself, and I accept this fate. But have you accepted yours?"

"I don't think I'll ever be able to accept being used for eugenics. Or snake breeding."

"You have come to seek counsel about how to defeat your foes, but I have already told you, Serpent Queen. The White Swan is the blind spot."

"Who is the White Swan?" Rhys asks. "How do we find them?"

"The White Swan has her wings clipped at Northeastern."

Northeastern? As in, the magic college?

"The timekeepers cannot see the Butcher. They cannot control her, for she has the gift of free will," the tree explains. "And that gift will extend to you, should you accompany her. Your whole life has been spent following the timekeepers' rules, playing into Neil Abbott's trap."

"The timekeepers don't just control Mar's fate. They control all of us, if I understand correctly," Mathers says, walking around the tree. "What's to stop them from usin' us against her?"

"Fate cannot change as easily as they would like. Once the Butcher is in play, it's anyone's game."

"I need more than just these code names," I urge. "What is her name?"

The tree begins to wilt, leaves falling rapidly from its branches. Its bark pales, and the last word the tree can utter is a name.

"Karina."

And then, it withers completely.

Chapter Twenty-Four

I tear open a rift with my hands again to get us back to the mortal realm, ignoring the disapproving looks from Mathers as I do so. We're all exhausted, and without proper blades, this was the only way to get home.

How long will I justify using blood magic like this? "It was the only way." "I have to do this to protect those I care about." "I have no other choice." I'm sure you're getting tired of those lines, too, aren't you? But it's hard to untangle myself from these situations and look at things from a neutral point of view. Maybe Neil feels the same way.

I try to tell myself that his reasoning is selfish, but a small part of me wonders if that makes it any less important. Don't get me wrong, he's morally reprehensible. But I'm not sure if I'm that far off from him.

I've killed people. Those cultists in the Veil...I didn't even check beforehand to see if they were followers of Astaroth before I tore into them. Yes, I wanted the power to defend myself, but is that really what I'm doing? If I'm not certain these choices I'm making are really for the greater good, maybe I shouldn't be making them. The uncertainty weighs heavily on my chest, but I try not to let it show.

We land on Kingsmarch Island, right next to the ferry and the welcome sign on the island. The wooden board is faded, the paint chipping, but I've never been so happy to see it.

"How did we get here?" Mathers asks, closing the rift. "The Wisdom Tree is outside of the location limit when travelin' around the school."

"Mar's powers probably grew when she drank the demon blood," Ophelia suggests, rolling her shoulders. She looks just as exhausted as I feel, her usually perfect blonde hair sticking every which way and her eyes drooping.

We all want to get some rest before processing what happened, but Rhys insists we see the nurse first.

Aside from my torn-up hand, which is nothing new, I'm fine. She slaps a Band-Aid on and sends me on my way while the others wait to get checked out.

The first thing I do is shower and get ready for bed. It's still light out, but I need at least twelve hours of sleep.

Forcing myself to stay awake for just a little longer, I finally take all the cameras out of my room, along with the voice recorders. I don't see the point of pretending anymore, now that everything is out in the open. With the timekeepers being so powerful, if they choose to come for me, there's nothing I can do about it tonight. Until I find this White Swan, I'm still vulnerable no matter how much blood magic I practice. In a way, it's a small comfort—Neil needs me alive. Granted, he needs me alive to harvest my eggs. After which, he's going to fertilize them with snake semen. And I'll have biological snake babies running about. Oh, the more I think about this, the grosser it becomes!

Just as I'm about to turn the lights off, I hear the front door opening. Rhys must be back.

Dragging myself up, I walk up the stairs. He comes through the door, turning the lights on.

"Are Nic and Allegra out?"

"I guess so." I haven't heard them since coming back, not that I've been very attentive.

Rhys checks upstairs and I follow. Allegra and Nic's rooms are both empty.

"Maybe they're having a meeting with Neil to go over everything," I say. "Either way, I suggest we barricade the doors."

"We might have to find other living arrangements," he agrees. I like how he says "we."

"Well, after your shower, you should come downstairs. My bed is big enough for both of us. And I removed the cameras," I add. "Unless that would be against the rules of courtship."

"It would, and while exceptions can be made, we both need sleep. Which will not happen, should I come downstairs tonight," he says. "Good night, Maria."

"Good night." I walk back downstairs to my room, crawling into bed. And as soon as I close my eyes, I fall into a deep sleep.

Waking up to scratching on my bedroom window feels like something out of a horror movie. It's probably a branch—though there are no bushes near the window—and I roll over and try to ignore it. It's still dark outside, which means it's far too early for me to be conscious.

However, the scratching turns into knocking, which is now a series of frantic, wet slaps. Finally, I pry my eyes open.

Allegra's bloody face presses against the glass. A scream tears from my throat as I fall out of bed, dragging my sheets with me. Oh God, it's 3 AM, I'm in a basement, and a vengeful ghost has come to kill me!

She moans. "Maria."

I creep toward her, grabbing a letter opener from my desk and holding it out before me. "What are you doing?"

"Help me..."

I can't determine whether this is a trap or not, but on the off chance that it's *not,* I exchange the letter opener for a dagger and head upstairs, turning on the lights. Rhys pads down, probably having heard my scream.

"Allegra, or something that looks like her, is outside," I tell him. "Did she come to bed?"

"No," he replies, cautiously heading toward the back door. He gets a heavy-duty flashlight from under the sink and turns on the backyard lights, only to find that they aren't working. So we *are* in a horror movie, and he's playing the stupid spouse who goes outside unarmed! Not that I think of him as my spouse.

I follow close behind, sticking to his side like glue. Allegra lies a little ways away, her body drenched in blood. It can't all be her own, otherwise she wouldn't be breathing. One of her legs twists at an unnatural angle, and judging by the path she left in the grass, she must have dragged herself here.

"Shit, what happened?" I exclaim.

Rhys sets the flashlight on the ground, bending down to

examine her injuries. "You need medical attention. I must call the campus nurse immediately."

"No! No doctor, no hospital," she insists, grabbing his arm.

"You look like you're going to keel over," I argue, watching her. "Were you *stabbed*?"

"I never wanted this," she babbles, her words slurring. I get the feeling she isn't talking about her injuries. She must be delirious from blood loss and the beating. Underneath the blood crusted to her skin, her face is swollen. "I swear. I never knew what he wanted to do."

"Enough talk. Let's get you help."

"No, no. I need you to believe me," she cries, grabbing my arm so tight I'm afraid she might snap it in half. I don't know how she even has the strength to do that. "I didn't want any of this. I was angry with you, and with my father, but I didn't want to *hurt* you. I told Nic that. I told him that I wouldn't work with him if he was going to harm you, and he agreed."

"I can't tell where the blood is coming from," Rhys mutters.

I peel up her shirt. While she's drenched, there don't appear to be any massive wounds on her stomach. That's a good thing, right?

And yet, I distinctly remember she had tattoos all over her body. She doesn't anymore. I fold her sleeves back, too, but there's nothing—just fair skin.

Archer said they slept together while I was gone. I didn't think too much about it at the time, other than the initial ick factor, but he didn't mention tattoos. Maybe because she didn't have any, then or now. But when she showed them to *me*, they weren't fake. She must have gotten rid of them.

How is that possible? The tattoos bound her powers. They were keeping her alive.

"What happened?" I urge.

"Nic promised me that I would be strong," she whispers. "I was going to be strong. I was going to graduate, and I was going to get away from everything."

"*Nic* promised?"

"I tried to stop him. He told me he wouldn't hurt you. I tried—and when I did, this is what happened. He drank more of the formula than he was supposed to. Just like Mom. He hates you, Maria—genuinely. I thought he just liked to tease you, but he really hates you."

"Tease me? He got my dad killed and mocked me about it," I say, but now isn't the time to argue about this. "Rhys, call someone for her."

"No hospitals! They'll see what I've done," she wails, struggling to sit up. But Rhys is already in the kitchen, going for the landline.

"Too bad," I say coldly. "Would you rather die like this? Because when you die, everything is over. You don't get another chance."

"Listen to me. I know I'm not making much sense. It does things to your brain. The blood," she continues. "But I *was* resentful. Part of me still is. Not enough to hurt you, though."

"Look, we can work out our problems after you're not bleeding out," I say with a sigh. "I'm not mad at you. I've barely even been thinking about you lately. We've both said things that weren't so great, but it's not like I hate you. Neil has put us both through a lot of shit, and it's not your fault. I would have lashed out, too, if I were in your shoes."

"Memory potions don't last long, Maria. I overheard my

father talking about it," she explains quickly. "Your family has been looking for you for months. Dad never renewed the potion, and it wore off. It was easier to block the news about your disappearance, and convince the investigators that you were a drug-addicted runaway. No one was taking it seriously."

"*What?*" So Isabelle has been looking for me this whole time? She's been torturing herself over this... And probably Luke, too, before he died. He must have been so stressed out. And here I thought I couldn't hate Neil any more than I already do.

"Nic has been running surveillance on them. I thought it was on my father's order, but it's not. While you were gone, Nic went to your house."

My heart drops. "What has Nic done?"

"I'm sorry. I'm sorry," she repeats. "He's playing a game with you, Maria. He wants you to chase him, but it's just a trap. Nic wants to drink your blood, but you can't let him."

"But Nic has had plenty of opportunities to attack me while I'm sleeping. I lock the door, but he could break the window if he wanted to."

"That would rob him of the thrill of the hunt," Allegra says. "He needs more than one dose. He needs to capture you where my father can't see. The stage is already set...and now he's waiting for the curtains to be drawn."

He needs to kidnap me and continuously drink my blood. Dandy.

I always knew Nic was a freak, so this isn't surprising. But is she implying that he's acting without Neil's direction? How? Is Neil allowing this, or is he going to swoop in and intervene?

"Nic can wait until hell freezes over. He's not getting my blood, and I'm not playing his game."

"You will."

"What do you mean?" I ask, just as Rhys comes back outside.

"The on-call doctor is coming," he reports. "He will be here soon with a team."

Allegra pulls me close, whispering in my ear. "The last time I saw him, he was heading to your house. You have to go, Mar."

My house?

He wouldn't. Nic knows not to cross that line—

Except he would. He already has.

"Thanks," I tell her, getting up. "Rhys, I'll be right back."

"Maria—"

I brush past him, running downstairs to my room. I grab my shoes and fling open my closet door. But when I look inside, the Divinities Sword is gone.

Chapter Twenty-Five

The mainland looks much closer to Kingsmarch Beach than it actually is. The water is freezing, and the sword on my back certainly weighs me down. I debated on whether or not the switchblade in my pocket would be enough, given I'm better at blood magic than swordsmanship, but ultimately I decided on both.

Somehow I manage to make it across without collapsing from exhaustion, running purely on anger and adrenaline. That's always a fantastic combo for decision-making, right?

But it's already the middle of the night, pretty much the morning, actually, and I don't give a damn. I left Rhys a note and took off on my own; I can't waste time arguing with him about how stupid my plan is. I already know that. Time is of the essence, and I'm not going to wait around for a ferry and take a chance on my family's lives. Nic sent Allegra back as a message, and it's clear he has no qualms about hurting others. Especially my family.

If I don't make it in time, how will I be able to live with myself?

When I wash up on shore, I wring out my hair and clothes. I'm chilled to the bone and sopping wet, but my waterproof fanny pack kept all my stuff dry, even my phone. I'm able to get a ride share within thirty minutes.

The night roads in Georgia are pretty empty around this time, and we arrive quickly at my house. When the driver pulls up, my heart jolts. This isn't the homecoming I imagined.

Taking a deep breath, I approach the front door and rap my knuckles against it. To my surprise, the door swings open with a loud creak, revealing a pitch-black interior. I can see perfectly fine in the dark, and I scan the living room. It's a mess of overturned furniture, books strewn across the floor, and broken glass. I take a tentative step inside, my heart racing with each passing second. No bodies, and no blood—that's a good sign, right?

But I guess I speak too soon, because as I pass through the kitchen, my blood runs cold. It's a mess, with every drawer pulled open and a broken stool in the corner. The sliding door is shattered, and blood pools on the floor. Again, no bodies, but this isn't a good sign.

On the corner desk, I notice a stack of papers and catch a glimpse of my senior photo. In the picture, I'm wearing a black shirt, and my face is beaming with a big smile. However, the word "Missing" is printed in bold text over my head. My family truly *has* been searching for me all this time, suffering from my disappearance. Meanwhile, I've been stuck at Southeastern, following Neil's instructions and thinking that I was keeping them safe. How stupid was I to believe that?

Walking through the rest of the house, there's no more blood, but I can't find a single sign of them. Still, Nic was here...so where could he have taken them? And even with his powers, would he have been able to capture all three of them alive? If he killed someone, he would have left the body and taken the other two.

Did he go back to Foley-Hill? Would he have? I don't think this was quite in line with Neil's plan. But if Nic has the Divinities Sword, a blind spot, then maybe Neil doesn't know what Nic is doing at all.

I grab the keys from the counter. I'll drive over the whole goddamn state if I have to.

I retrieve my car from the garage and quickly update Mathers, ignoring the fifty missed calls from him. I suspect Rhys had a hand in that, since he doesn't own a cell phone. Sending a text about my destination, I toss my sword in the back seat and speed toward the cemetery.

Grayhill, a few towns over, is where Luke's parents are buried. I'm almost certain he's buried there, too. Allegra said Nic is a fan of theatrics, and what's more theatrical than a fight in a cemetery?

I'm lucky that there are no cops on the road because I'm going twenty miles an hour over the speed limit. As I skid into the parking lot, the rain starts pouring down. I'm already soaked from my earlier swim, so it doesn't matter. But something feels off about the sudden change in weather. Thunder booms and lightning illuminates the sky. Atop the tallest hill in the cemetery, a figure stands, watching and waiting.

Taking my sword out, I make my way up the hill, my grip tightening with each step. As I approach the top of the hill, I can make out Nic's figure more clearly. He's holding a small, leatherbound book, and his eyes are fixed on me.

"Where are they?" I snarl.

"They're safe, for now," Nic says, his voice dripping with amusement. "But they won't be for long if you don't cooperate with me."

I raise my sword, ready to strike, but Nic just laughs.

"Ah, Mar, always so predictable," he says, twirling the book in his hand. "You know, I expected more from you. I thought you would have figured out by now that I'm not your enemy."

"What are you talking about?" I demand, stepping closer.

"You know, don't you? What Neil has done to you. To *us*," he emphasizes. "I was the second batch, you know. The first was an utter failure. None of those babies survived. Allegra and I were the only survivors of our batch, and you were one of five survivors of yours. We were all born to be tools."

"I agree, you *are* a tool."

"Cute. But you're missing the bigger picture, Mar. Why do you think Neil wants the Divinities Sword if he doesn't want you to kill Astaroth? He wants to destroy it, and he asked me to take it. Because he trusts me. But the thing about the Divinities Sword is, with it, I can do whatever I want."

"And what do you want?"

"Neil is playing us for fools. You, me, and Allegra. But I refuse to be a pawn in his game. At first, I thought you might be clever enough to figure things out on your own and defy your fate…but I was wrong. I realized this from our first conversation on that plane," he says, the wind getting stronger around us. "My entire life, I was trained to help Neil carry out his plan. Told I was a *failure,* that I wasn't made correctly. On top of that, I'm a guy, and Neil needed a girl. I looked forward to meeting you, his so-called success… But I don't know what's so successful about you. You can be bred, sure, but is that really worthy of all these plans? All these sacrifices? I don't think so. I wasted *years*, gave up everything, and for what? *You*?"

"You're jealous? Didn't get enough of Neil's attention?" I mock.

Nic's face twists into a sneer. "Jealousy has nothing to do with it," he spits out. "I'm done being Neil's pawn, and I'm done with you, too. You're just as much a tool as I am. But unlike you, I'm going to use my power for something worthwhile."

"Oh? Is this the part where you tell me *your* plans for world domination?"

"No. I'm afraid this is the part where I tell you that I need your blood, and if you don't give it to me, your brother dies."

Fear grips me, but I try not to let it show on my face. I don't think I'm doing a very good job. "You don't have him."

"Try me, Mar. I have nothing to lose," he says, his voice cold and hard. "He's in the trunk of my car, spelled to hell. Only I can open it, and if anyone else tries, he gets crushed."

He's not bluffing, and I don't have much leverage. "Why do you want my blood?"

"Easy. I need to drink it, just like Neil wants you to drink Astaroth's," he explains, his shoulders relaxing. He has me right where he wants me, and he knows it. "Neil discovered during his experiments that a shadowborn can be turned into a trueblood through the use of blood magic and alternative medicine. Hasn't your vision gotten better? Don't you feel stronger? Astaroth's blood is making you more powerful. And your blood will make me more powerful, too. You're squandering your potential...but I promise I won't follow the same path."

Allegra is considered a failure because she isn't strong, but Nic might only be considered a failure because he's a guy. Maybe he can't time travel, but if he drinks my blood, will he gain my powers? He seems to think so, at least.

The wind around us continues to pick up speed, and for a moment, I think there's a storm coming. But then I notice Nic's eyes, and I realize that he's the one behind it. He's using his powers to control the wind and make me feel even more helpless.

"Drop your sword, Mar," Nic orders. "I won't ask twice."

I follow his instructions, tossing it away from us both. His night vision isn't as good as mine, apparently, because he doesn't ask me to toss my fanny pack.

Nic kicks the sword away from us both, unsheathing his own weapon—the Divinities Sword. He can barely hold it up, but I don't dare underestimate his determination or strength. One scrape of the sword was enough to put me out of commission, and if I'm too injured, I won't be able to protect David.

"Let's go," he says in a low voice.

I follow him to an old black sedan. Once we're close enough, he shoves me against it and binds my hands behind my back with zip ties.

"Let me see my brother," I demand. "I need to make sure he's alive."

"Even if he were dead, do you think you're powerful enough to stop me?" Nic challenges.

"You said it yourself—I drank Astaroth's blood, and it made me stronger. You have no idea how strong I am now."

I have no idea how strong I am now. Apparently the lame argument works, though.

Nic opens the trunk. "There. You see?"

David trembles, his wide eyes filled with terror. His brown hair sticks out in every direction and his arms are bound so tightly they are probably numb. His mouth is gagged with a thick cloth that must make it hard to breathe, each breath coming out in desperate gasps.

"Satisfied?" Nic sneers.

"Oh yeah." With a fierce tug, I rip my wrists apart, the zip tie breaking and slicing through the flesh of my arms. Blood pours from the wound as I shove Nic with all my might, sending him stumbling back. His entire body quivers with rage until finally he charges forward with the Divinities Sword held high above his head. With split-second reflexes I dodge out of the way and grab a handful of grass, blowing it directly into Nic's eyes. The spell momentarily blinds him, giving me time to grab David and pull him out of the trunk.

I quickly remove the gag from his mouth and cut the bindings on his arms with my switchblade. I *knew* it was smart to bring it!

"Mar, we have to go now!" David cries, his voice choked with fear.

"You have to run. Go, as far and fast as you can," I say, handing him my cell phone.

"Mar, what about *you*—"

"Go!" I order. He bolts away.

Nic stands tall, eyes burning with rage, clutching the Divinities Sword in a white-knuckled grip. Before I can move, he grabs my hair and wrenches my head back, causing me to gasp with pain. With a guttural roar of defiance, I swing my small blade into his side, desperately hoping for some form of retaliation. But even the force of my strike does nothing to stop Nic's wrath.

Instead, he laughs. "Your little brother might be gone, but I still have you. And that's all I need. New powers or not, do you honestly think you could defeat me? Do you think you're the only one who knows how to use blood magic?"

He slams me against the pavement face first, his strength unmatched. By me, anyway. He's way stronger than last summer, when he beat the shit out of me at Foley-Hill Plantation. I might have come into my own powers, but I'm still not a match for him. In my absence, he must have been training like crazy. Or doing something else to enhance his strength...

Even without the difference in our physical prowess, he's trained in combat for most of his life. I won't be able to beat him through sheer talent, and if you've been following along this far, you know luck isn't on my side. Hence the fanny pack.

I unzip my pouch and take out a hastily-made spell bag, rubbing the fabric against my bloody wrist and slapping it against Nic's side. The impact activates it, causing the bag to detonate on contact, sending an explosion of shrapnel into his side. Nic screams in pain, sputtering curses. I buck him off me, rolling to my feet. I need to buy time for David, and for myself.

"I've been practicing blood magic for months, Nic. Do you think you can win against me?" I goad.

"I don't need you anymore, Maria. I don't care about dosing myself multiple times. I just need one good drink!" he howls, getting rash now.

"Come and get it, then." I throw my second spell bag at him, a flash bang, and race toward the cemetery. I have seven more, and I'll have to use them sparingly. I can create more spells with the dirt and grass around me, but the bags are far more powerful. I prepared them in my closet for situations just like this. And with the bags, at least I can keep track of how much magic I'm using.

Nic searches for me between the headstones, the rain coming down in torrents. It might be hard for him to track me in the darkness, but it's difficult for me as well. I can't hear his footsteps, and my heart is pounding so loud I'm afraid it might give me away. I continue to move forward as best I can, running and hiding between headstones as I make my way deeper into the cemetery.

Hot air presses against my skin as a bolt of blue flames strikes a nearby tree. I know he's getting closer, but he hasn't quite discovered my hiding spot yet. The tree burns to ash within seconds, zapping away any last hope I have that Nic isn't as good at spellcasting as he is at combat. If I get hit by one of his spells, it's game over. Nic is no longer interested in my blood—if he gets the chance to kill me, he's going to take it.

I mean, I assumed he was going to kill me after getting my blood. But his ego is getting in the way of the bigger picture. Maybe I can use that personality flaw to my advantage.

The headstone closest to me explodes in a shower of rocks and dust, signaling that it's time for me to move.

"You can't outrun me, Maria!" Nic shouts over the storm. "You can't hide from me!"

But I *am* hiding from him. Dumbass.

I activate a spell bag with my blood and bury it in the

mud, slipping away quietly as Nic draws near. His foot sinks into the ground and the mud hardens around him, trapping one leg in place.

"Enough playing around!" The ground begins to tremble and light up, the sky opening as blue lines of fire ignite around the cemetery, forming some sort of magic circle beneath us. Nic frees his foot and takes a step toward me. The injury in his side isn't slowing him down in the least.

The wind spirals around us with such force that I can feel the power in the air; the energy is so intense it seems to press on my skin, like a physical manifestation of his dark magic. I have no idea what kind of spell he's casting, let alone how to stop it. It's unlike anything I've ever encountered before, even with Astaroth.

Hands push up from the ground, clawing at the mud and dirt as the dead begin to rise. I know necromancy is possible, but I've never seen someone raise more than one body. When Jenna did it on the ship, it was like a puppet without strings, and it took all her concentration to control. Its movements were jerky, inhuman. And yet, Nic is here raising the whole goddamn cemetery! The storm has yet to stop, either. Just how powerful is he?

Digging into my wrist injury, it looks like I'm going to have to cut open my palm soon as well. The rain is washing away my blood, cleaning the wound and making it a lot harder for me to keep up with these blood spells. My head pounds and my arm radiates pain, but I try not to let it slow me. I throw the bag at Nic, but it hits some sort of force field, bouncing back at me and shooting fire at my back. I cry out as Nic whirls around.

"Found you." He inches toward me slowly, dragging the Divinities Sword on the ground.

The zombies shamble down the rows of headstones, their eyes glowing a faint blue that eerily matches the flames on the ground. They form a tight circle around me, trapping me. But Nic doesn't give the order to attack yet.

"I can kill you with a single swing," he says, sneering. "There will be no more hiding for you."

"You can barely hold that sword up," I challenge, maintaining the distance between us as I clutch another spell bag. I need to stall, to drag out this battle for as long as I can. But it doesn't look like that's going to be as successful as I'd hoped.

Nic is using a ton of power to maintain all these zombies, but he doesn't even seem tired. He lifts the Divinities Sword high above his head with a grunt, but it's so heavy, he has no control over the swing or speed, and he can't change direction midway through. I dive to the side at the last second, narrowly avoiding getting hit by the blade. I feel a sudden rush of adrenaline as I realize that this could be my chance.

I activate another spell bag and throw it at Nic's feet, using what little energy I have left to cast a powerful shield around me and blast him back as he swings at me again. He stumbles backward, surprised by my counterattack but still determined to fight. The zombies continue to shuffle closer and closer, their eyes growing brighter with each passing second.

I plant my sneakers in the mud and with savage determination, draw an intricate circle around myself. I rip open a blue spell bag, letting the herbs spill out, along with the blood from my arm. I'm beginning to get sluggish, lightheaded. Maybe I should have packed a protein bar in here, too. A dome is immediately erected around me.

Nic stops in his tracks, his face twisting in fury as he realizes he can't move further. "You think this will stop me?"

He presses the palm of his hand to the barrier, smearing blood over the surface of the invisible force field. His skin is pale, though I can't tell if it's the freezing rain or the blood loss. Hopefully it's the latter. The sky lights up as a bolt of lightning crashes from the sky, breaking my barrier and shattering it like glass.

Nic drops the Divinities Sword, lunging for me and knocking me to the ground. "I wonder how your blood will taste," he muses.

I struggle against him, but his hands move to my neck, choking me as the zombies' cold, withered hands hold me immobile. But before Nic can bite down, he pauses, looking deep into my eyes. The rain dripping from his hair lands on my face, along with the blood tears beginning to form in his eyes.

"You know what sucks about using too much blood magic at once?" I manage as his grip loosens. "The rebounding."

Nic's eyes widen in shock as he realizes what I mean. He scrambles away from me, clutching at his throat and eyes, blood flowing freely from his nose and mouth. The zombies sag to the ground as his power wanes.

As much as I'd like to gloat, I can't move. I'm on the cusp of rebounding, myself, but I didn't use nearly as much power as he did. I'm surprised Nic is still standing.

The rain starts to slow, and silence overtakes the cemetery once more. Nic stumbles forward, attempting to reach the Divinities Sword one last time.

"Maria!" Rhys' frantic voice cuts through the silence as he runs toward me. But he's too far away.

Nic's hand closes on the hilt of the sword as he drags it across the ground, creating a rift.

I curse, rolling to my knees as I scramble toward him. But I'm too late, too tired. As I throw my final spell bag at him, Nic falls through the rift, taking the sword with him into the Veil.

Chapter Twenty-Six

Even though he's angry at me, and rightfully so, Rhys still brings me flowers while I'm waiting for the discharge papers at the hospital. This is the second time I've been checked out by a doctor in twenty-four hours, so either my life is really exciting, or I'm a reckless idiot with a penchant for trouble.

"Thanks, tulips are my favorite," I say sweetly, but that doesn't do much to dampen his bad mood. I guess running away in the middle of the night headfirst into danger and then dodging his calls really pissed him off.

"We will drive back to the house so you can rest," he says tersely.

"Look, I'm sorry I didn't tell you where I was going. But I thought you'd try to talk me out of it. You'd never have let me leave the house if you knew where I was headed."

"Good guess."

"I needed to face him alone. If you were there, I would have just worried over you."

"Do you trust me?"

"Of course," I answer without hesitation.

"It does not seem like it."

I don't have anything to say to that, but luckily I don't have to respond—the nurse comes in with my paperwork and lets me leave.

The car ride back to the ferry is eerily silent, and I'm at a loss for words. What's there to say? Nic is gone, and Rhys stayed with me instead of following him through the rift, despite my insistence that I was fine. Which proves my point, though I would never tell Rhys that. But if he can't choose between helping me and catching Nic, then he would have only gotten in the way during the fight.

And let's be real, it was barely a fight. If Nic had wanted to, he could have taken me down without breaking a sweat. But he was too busy showing off his zombies and his storm, which gave me an opening. He won't make the same mistake twice. In fact, I'm sure he learned something important from that fight—his magic stamina is far superior to mine.

Not only that, he has the Divinities Sword. I'm not sure how much it will shield him from Neil, but out of everyone who's tried to use it, Nic has been the most successful in picking it up and swinging it.

Rhys pulls into a campus parking lot and the heavy silence continues to hang between us. I know he's not trying to punish me; he's just as lost for words as I am. What is there to say? The walk back to the dorm is stifling, and I want so badly to make it better between us, but I have no idea how. Not without lying.

What does that say about me?

I try to brush my thoughts aside as we approach the dorm. As soon as I open the door to the house, I'm practically tackled by Tasha, who throws herself into my tight embrace. She releases me just as quickly, hitting my arm hard before pulling me into another hug.

But as she holds me close, a lump forms in my throat. I know there are so many things I need to say to her, so many apologies and explanations that need to be made. I can't seem to find the words. All I can do is hug her back, holding onto her tightly as if she might disappear. I'm sure she feels the same.

"Idiot," she grounds out.

"That's the first thing you have to say to me?" I ask lightly, pulling back.

"*Huge* idiot."

"Ah, how poetic." We walk into the living room, where Mathers, Isabelle, and David are waiting for us.

"We'll give you some time," Mathers says politely, both him and Rhys leaving. It's not that I don't want them there, or that I'm ungrateful, but I'm glad they're gone. Because when I finally start to cry, they're already out the door.

Isabelle hugs me next, and it's obvious from her red, puffy eyes that she's been crying, too. She smells like cinnamon and sugar cookies. She smells like *home*. She kisses my head, not letting go of me even when we make it to the couch.

Of all the things Isabelle could say, she chooses the perfect thing every time. "I made a quiche."

"I wouldn't eat that quiche," Tasha immediately chimes in with a sniff. "She's been crying all over it."

"So were you," David reminds her helpfully.

I didn't get a great chance to look at him earlier when he was tied up in the car, but I can see now that my little brother has grown. His light brown hair is a mess of curls, just like Isabelle's, and the smattering of freckles over his face seems to have increased. He's taller, too, though still not as tall as me. He adjusts his wire-frame glasses, being the only one in this family, it seems, to keep himself together.

He sits at my side, taking my hand to examine the bandages on my wrist. "I called 911."

"Thanks, David," I choke out.

"That guy…who was he?"

"It's a long story," I say, which is an understatement. "Let's start with y'all. How did you get here?"

"The rescue squad the school sent," Tasha replies, handing me a water bottle. "Drink up. You get dehydrated easily when you cry."

"I'm not crying!"

"You so are," she shoots back. "Anyway, some guys rang our doorbell in the middle of the night claiming they'd found you. They looked like police, so we went with them—which I realize isn't the smartest move now. David was on his way home from a friend's. We were going to pick him up on our way, but when we arrived, he had already started walking home."

My little brother's expression darkens. "That's when that weird guy got me," he says bitterly. His once happy demeanor has been replaced by a sense of jaded weariness that pains me to see. He looks as though the life has been drained from his eyes. All because of me.

"We were brought back here," Tasha explains further. "That red-haired cowboy told us that magic exists, which at first sounded pretty nutty. He showed us some cool tricks and we've been waiting for you to return all day. David was brought in, too, saying he'd been kidnapped and that you fought off his attacker. Honestly, I thought he was just making it up since you're not exactly the best fighter. You've lost to girls way smaller than you."

"Thanks for the reminder. Really, super helpful."

"In any case, we're together now," Isabelle declares, her voice faltering. "Mar, about Luke—"

"I know. It's a long story," I say quietly. I can barely look at her now. "I don't even know where to begin."

"Start with the ship," Tasha advises, and so I do.

We ditch the quiche and opt for a frozen pizza. As I recount the events of what has happened, the sky outside turns a deep shade of blue. Tasha's incessant questioning, combined with the complications surrounding Luke, makes the conversation challenging. I fumble through my words, trying to articulate what I'm feeling.

David sits in silence throughout the entire exchange, which only exacerbates my anxiety. He must be struggling to hear what I have to say, and I can't help but feel responsible for everything that's happened.

Talking only intensifies the guilt that weighs heavily on me. Each word I speak feels like another weight on my chest. By the time I reach the end of the story, I'm severely dehydrated and my head is pounding.

"You did well," Isabelle tells me, stroking my hair. "You did your best, right?"

"It wasn't good enough," I reply flatly. "I'm not even the one who saved you. That was probably Theodas' team. By the way, did y'all bring anything with you?"

"No. We were allowed to change into regular clothes and came without many supplies. Provost Mathers informed us that the extraction team wanted to get us out as soon as possible, in case Neil Abbott made a move," Isabelle explains.

It's getting late, and I'm exhausted. They probably are, too. "Okay, Isabelle and Tash can take my bed, and there's a spare room upstairs for David. I'll just take the couch."

"Absolutely not. I'll take the couch, and you and Tasha will share the bed," Isabelle argues. "You need to rest."

"We're here!" Theodas announces, barging in. His announcement breaks the somber atmosphere, as he carries in armfuls of shopping bags and places them on the table. Mathers follows close behind.

"We were just talking about sleeping arrangements," I inform him, feeling a bit self-conscious in my disheveled state. My eyes must be puffy from crying. Ugh.

"Nic's room will be cleared out tomorrow. Until then, the rooms here should be sufficient," Mathers says. "Rhys washed the sheets this mornin'. He says someone can stay in his room."

"Where is Rhys?" I ask.

"He'll be staying with me," Theodas says. "It's been a while since we've shared a room. I have a bunch of movies lined up to show him. You know he's never seen *Romeo and Juliet*? The one with Leonardo DiCaprio?"

When would he have had time to watch that?

I wish Rhys were here, even if he's angry with me. I feel bad kicking him out of his room. "Tell him to come back. We can figure out the sleeping situation."

"For now, let's just leave it like this. We'll all reconvene in the mornin' when everyone is well rested," advises Mathers, ushering Theodas toward the door.

"I'll see you out," I offer, walking them both to the porch. It's spring, and I feel the warmth in the air, even at night. The flowers are already beginning to sprout on the lawn. "Thank you both. For everything. I don't know what I would have done without you."

Theodas chuckles. "It goes without saying, Maria. I like you. And Rhys wants you to be happy. He's my friend; I just want you both to ride off into the sunset, like in an old Western."

I shoot a pointed look at Mathers. "I'm not the one who belongs in an old Western, but thank you both. I'll give you a full report on Nic in the morning. Until then, do you think we're safe?"

"As we can be, from omniscient time-travelin' snakes," Mathers mutters. "Rest well, Maria."

As soon as they disappear from view, I slip back inside and do a quick check to make sure everyone has everything they need. Theodas brought pajamas and toiletries for them. I toss their clothes into the washing machine and lead them to their respective rooms. After locking up the doors, Tasha and I head to the basement to take turns showering and getting ready for sleep.

Finally, when we settle into bed, it's like we're kids again, snuggled up and sharing secrets.

"It wasn't the same without you," Tasha tells me, her voice a whisper in the darkness. "It was like…everything soured."

"I'm sorry," I say automatically.

Tasha shakes her head. "I don't want an apology. Do you remember when we were in seventh grade, and you asked me if I would miss you if you died?"

I frown, trying to recall the conversation. "I did?"

"Yeah. And I said yes, and you said that you were glad because at least one person would remember you."

I cringe. "God, that's pretty dark. Why would I say that?"

"You were depressed, maybe?" Tasha guesses. "We were looking everywhere for you. We never stopped."

"I'm sorry," I say again. It's all I can muster, it seems, but the words aren't enough to encapsulate just how awful I feel. "Whenever I try to explain what happened, I can't help but dwell on all the mistakes I made. At the time, they didn't seem like such a big deal, but now I'm cursed with hindsight."

"You did your best. I know that."

"And it wasn't good enough." I turn onto my back, staring at the ceiling, feeling the weight of my regret pressing down on me. "Your life has been ruined because of me. Isabelle's and David's, too. I want to make up for it, but how can I?"

"Are you kidding? After all this time, you're still like this?" she jokes. "How has my life been ruined?"

"I got you into trouble in school all the time."

"You also stood up for me all the time, even when no one else would. You punched Shannon Muroney for me, and subsequently got the ass-kicking of your life."

"She's six foot two and was on the basketball team!" She pummeled me into the gymnasium at recess, and somehow I'm the one who ended up walking away with detention and a broken nose. Okay, so I started it, but *she* shouldn't have started those rumors about Tasha. "I started a lot of trouble, Tash. But with Luke...I don't know how to make that right. I see the changes in David and know that it's my fault. I'm not sure how to cope with it."

"Well, you've never been very good at coping with anything," she says kindly. "Of course David's changed.

And Luke's death was hard as hell, in part because there was no closure. No reason for it. But he loved you, Mar. No doubt about it. He loved us all. And if he were here, he would never blame you. He would just want you to be happy."

"I don't know if I deserve that."

Tasha's hand finds mine. "I know it's hard for you to deal with, and it will take time. Especially since you're so...bad with emotions. And expressing how you feel. And ice skating. Oh, you're not very good at baking, either."

"What's your point?"

"If someone spoke to me the way you speak about yourself, you'd probably try to beat them up. You'd fail, but you'd try," she says with a small laugh. "Don't be so harsh. You're only hurting yourself, and the people who care about you. Like me."

I turn to face Tasha and give her a halfhearted smile. She's right, as she always is. But it's hard to shake off the guilt and self-loathing that has been a constant companion for so long. I'm grateful for Tasha's unwavering support, but it feels undeserved.

"I love you. Even though I hate you a little right now for making me say such sappy crap," I add.

"Right back at you," she says. "Everything's going to be alright now."

As Tasha speaks, I can't help but feel a sudden urge to cry. Everything is far from being alright, and I know it deep down. But the sincerity in her eyes makes it hard to keep up the façade that I've been putting on for so long.

Tasha doesn't flinch, doesn't try to console me with empty words. She wraps her arms around me and holds me tight.

Chapter Twenty-Seven

I'm the first one to wake up, which is a big surprise. Back home, I always slept in. Now, I guess everyone is still tired from the past few days' events.

I thought I'd head upstairs to make breakfast, but Rhys already beat me to the punch. I'm surprised to see him, especially after our disagreement yesterday. I can't call it an argument, because we didn't really fight about it. Maybe it would have been better that way. It's easier to deal with anger than this awkwardness hanging over us.

"Hi," I greet cautiously, all too aware I'm in sloppy PJs and haven't brushed my hair.

"Good morning," Rhys says cordially, which means he's still mad. Right?

It's hard to tell with him, but I'm not brave enough to ask outright. "I didn't think you would be around, after yesterday."

Rhys looks up from the stove, where he's flipping pancakes with practiced ease. "We were unable to have a proper conversation before. About anything that's happened between us. As the situation becomes more complicated, I wonder if you want me around at all."

"Of course I want you here," I tell him, and it's the truth. I'm not sure how to navigate our complicated relationship, but I do know that I want him in my life, in whatever way he's willing to be. "I screwed up the other night. I panicked, and maybe I made some assumptions on how you'd react. That doesn't mean I don't trust you. I guess I'm just bad at this."

"At what?"

"Relationships. Relying on other people. Asking for help. Does that sound cheesy? Actually, don't answer that," I say with a sigh. "I told myself that as soon as this all blew over, everything would fall into place. But now I'm not so sure if that day will ever come. Life always throws obstacles and challenges our way, some of which may be a result of my own self-sabotage. On top of that, I feel like I've misled you and steered you toward a relationship with me without fully disclosing just how complicated it could be. Despite your reassurances, I can't shake the doubts in my head—not about you, but about myself. There's a reason why I haven't been in many relationships before, and as much as I'd like to blame others, it's always been me and my stupidity ruining things."

"You are not stupid," he says firmly, plating the pancakes. They look perfect, evenly cooked and golden brown. "And you did not mislead me. I am here because I want to be. Relationships are indeed difficult, romantic or otherwise. Likewise, life is often complicated without magic intervention. But I will be here as long as you want me to be."

"I want you. Here, I mean. Not in a perverse way," I

babble. *Smooth, Mar.* "Are we okay?"

"Are you going to run off in the middle of the night again, headfirst into danger?"

"Probably," I admit, "but next time, I'll ask you to join me."

"Fair enough."

"Now, I have a very important question for you," I say seriously. "Are these pancakes chocolate chip?"

He gestures to a pot on the stove. "I made a dark chocolate syrup to drizzle on top. But I will heat everything again once your family wakes up."

"Until then, how can I help?"

"Sit down and do not touch anything."

Yeah, that's probably for the best. I sit down at the kitchen counter, watching him as he moves around the kitchen with ease. I can't help but admire him for adapting so well to this modern mortal realm.

"How's Allegra doing?" She didn't come home last night, so I assume she's still in the hospital.

"Better," he replies, getting a carton of eggs from the fridge. "Her injuries were severe, but not life-threatening. I imagine she is still in a state of emotional shock, however. She repeatedly apologized after you left."

"I don't think she was part of Neil's plan," I confirm.

"No. Regardless of what your impression may be, I do not think she would go as far as to put a child in danger."

I don't think so, either. For all that's transpired between us, I believe Allegra's apologies.

"When she comes back, and Nic's room is cleared, where are you going to stay?" I ask. "I don't want you to leave. You can stay in my room; there's more than enough space."

"That would be inappropriate," he informs me, washing

the egg off his hands in the sink. "I doubt your mother would be comfortable with such an arrangement."

"She knows I'm a big girl. And we *have* shared a bed before. Sort of."

"That was different." Rhys whisks the eggs together and sets the bowl to the side. "My sister will be moving into the mortal realm for the time being, on campus. I will stay with her and Theodas."

"That's probably for the best," I say with a smile, and I genuinely mean it. They've been apart for so long, it will be good for both of us to spend time with our respective families. And now that we're not hiding our relationship, we can see each other whenever we want. "So, what are you doing tonight?"

"I have no plans," he says, raising his brows.

"I have a proposition for you. Why don't we take a break from saving the world—or destroying it—and have a beach picnic?"

"Are you asking me on a date?"

"Yep. You, me, some cafeteria food, a blanket...it could be nice. Besides, we haven't shared a meal in this time period." As a servant of Neil's, Rhys always prepared the food, but he never sat down to eat. And besides, isn't this the same crap you'd see in a romance movie? I don't like the ocean, but the beach is okay, I guess. It will give us a chance to talk in private.

Rhys breaks into a genuine smile, and I'm struck by it. "I look forward to it, then."

I would have liked to kiss him, but I can hear my family stirring upstairs. I'd rather not have my siblings walk in on us. It's bad enough *his* sister has. Twice.

The thought of introducing him to my family is nerve-wracking, but I don't have much time to mentally prepare as Tasha enters from the basement and Isabelle and David come downstairs.

"I smell pancakes!" Tasha sings, stopping when she sees Rhys. Her eyes go wide. "Oh. Uh, I didn't think we had company. Sorry, I'll go back and change—"

"I apologize for intruding," Rhys says. "Please make yourself comfortable. I was just about to make eggs. What toast would you prefer?"

"She likes whole grain. I'll make that. Oh, don't give me that look—I can make toast."

"No, you can't," Tasha says. "*I'll* make the toast, and you can make the introductions."

"Good morning," Isabelle greets, shuffling in with David. "Did you girls sleep well?"

"Yeah. Mar's bed is great, and the tea is hot this morning," Tasha supplies.

"Tea?"

"Gossip," she clarifies. "Mar was just about to introduce us to her handsome friend."

My face burns. "Thank you for the great introduction, Tash."

"Oh, you're very welcome."

"Okay. So, this is Rhys. My, uh..." I struggle, looking at him. He's all too amused, just like Tash. They have the same smug look in their eyes. "We're...together. Kind of. It's complicated."

"Not particularly," Rhys says. "Maria and I met when she traveled to the past. I followed her into the future, but landed in the wrong time period, three years prior to her boarding Southeastern's cruise ship for the summer. To help her, I began working for Neil Abbott as a spy. We reunited, but she had yet to meet me due to the time traveling. But now that she does remember, I can continue courting her."

"Um, I thought we agreed that *I'm* the one courting *you,*" I say awkwardly.

"Jeez, Mar, you're so awkward with relationships." Tash rolls her eyes. "Is he your boyfriend like Kyle Merrick was your boyfriend?"

"No, I don't think this will end in setting his porch on fire. At least, I hope not."

"Wow. Well, I have a *ton* of embarrassing stories to tell you about my sister," Tasha says, taking his arm. "Sit down. Should I start with the time she tried to buy lotto tickets when she was eight, or when she got caught in the middle of the football field in—"

"We don't need to talk about my childhood," I cut her off.

"I should finish cooking," Rhys agrees, but Isabelle stops him.

"I will continue. Sit down," she urges. "You're a guest."

"Technically Rhys lives here. He gave up his room last night," I say.

"Even more of a reason he should sit down. Did you offer him a drink, Mar?"

"No," I mutter.

"Well? He's your boyfriend, isn't he?" She can barely hold in her laughter. I'm glad they're all enjoying this. Yesterday I was trying not to get killed by a blood-magic user and his army of zombies. Today, I'm trying not to die of embarrassment.

After breakfast, Mathers and Theodas arrive to discuss the plan going forward. We gather around the dining room table, but Isabelle sends David to watch TV in the living room. She sets up her Netflix account for him and joins us adults at the table, sitting at the head.

"Are you sure you want to be part of this?" I ask her.

She gives me an incredulous look. "Of course. I might not be a shadowborn or trueblood, but I'm still your mother. Besides, Tasha and I might be able to provide some insight into the situation."

"We watched a lot of telenovelas in your absence," Tasha adds.

"Oh, I *love* telenovelas," Theodas says, because of *course* he does. "But we can discuss that later. Most importantly, we have two problems. One is Neil, Astaroth, and the snakes. The other is Nic, who seems to have gone rogue."

"Nic has the Divinities Sword, which gives him an advantage over Neil. I'm not sure how much," I say. "But he's powerful. He's been practicing blood magic, too. That's the only way I was able to fight against him, but if he hadn't rebounded and gotten sick from too much magic, I would've been a goner."

"Yes, we had to…take care of the aftermath," Mathers says carefully. "If Nic has the Divinities Sword, it's likely he will try to attack you again. And unlike Neil, Nic wants to drink your blood and kill you."

"Fitting, I guess. He looks like a vampire in a teen movie," I say, painting a picture for my sister.

Tasha snorts. "Sorry to interrupt, but can you back up and explain where Nic fits into this again? If he's gone rogue, does that mean Neil is going to get rid of him? Maybe they can fight each other and leave you alone, Mar."

"A nice thought, but Neil's top priority is Maria. Nic having the Divinities Sword is concerning, but there's little Neil can do about it," Theodas explains. "He'll want to give you the doses of Astaroth's blood as soon as he can. If he's not making a move now, it's because he can't. And he didn't recapture you, so he must be confident he will be able to find you at any time. During these stretches of time, we should be moving to find the girl the Wisdom Tree spoke of."

"The White Swan. Karina," Mathers says. "We will have to take a trip to Northeastern and go through the records ourselves, though. The school is a mess since last semester. Chancellor Kinsey disappeared, and they haven't found anyone to replace him yet."

"Chancellor Kinsey disappeared?" Archer's uncle?

"Yes. Unfortunately, they have had more trouble with ferals."

"I have a question," Tasha says, raising her hand as if she's in school. "Can you explain why the Divinities Sword is so important again? None of you can use it, right? Why did Neil want it if Mar isn't going to kill Astaroth with it?"

"The Wisdom Tree explained that the sword, along with the White Swan, is a blind spot," Rhys explains patiently. "These blind spots, as the name implies, are objects or beings which the timekeepers cannot see. I imagine they cannot control them for some reason; perhaps their magic is stronger than even the fates."

"A blind spot? And you don't know why?" Tasha presses. "These snakes are like gods, right? All-seeing and pretty damn powerful, with the time-travel abilities."

"But not all-powerful. They needed Neil to help them create Mar," Isabelle reasons.

"They probably can't leave the Veil," David says casually, coming through to the kitchen to grab a drink.

"What?" Theodas pauses, looking at my brother. "What

do you mean?"

"Well, they're beastbloods, right? And Mar and y'all are shadowborn. Children of two worlds. They probably need her because they want to create hybrids and control both worlds. It's classic video game villain stuff. Though I've found it's mostly in sci-fi, not fantasy stuff."

"Oh! That makes sense! They want to make timekeepers with the ability to travel between both worlds and control the fates of humans, too," Tasha adds.

"But they can already control the fates of humans," Theodas says, confused.

David shrugs, taking a sip of soda. "Humans aren't magic. We're probably easier to predict with fewer variables. But you said they had a grand design, right? And it changed? And the first rift was opened in, what, the 1800s? That's probably why the fate of everyone in the Veil changed. An unpredictable variable was introduced."

"How do you even remember all this information?" I ask, staring at my little brother in awe.

"I play a lot of video games. Anyway, you should find out why this one girl is special. She's probably your only shot at beating an omniscient enemy," David says. "Once, when I was playing Gods of Blood—"

"Which I told you that you *couldn't* play," Isabelle cuts in disapprovingly.

"Well, in that game, one of the enemies is programmed to predict all your movements. The only way to defeat it is with a hat you have to pick up at the beginning of the game. It's pretty bogus, but it makes your unpredictability stat max out."

"It looks like we're headed to Northeastern, then," I say. "Road trip!"

Chapter Twenty-Eight

Rhys is nervous about the flight, having never been in an airplane before, but in the end, it's Archer who blows chunks. He's practically green by the time we get off the plane, and we have to wait an hour before he can get in the car. He can take the ferry with no problems, but planes and sometimes cars make him motion sick. Knowing that, I was surprised he volunteered to come.

I didn't ask him. He kind of invited himself, not that I mind. I expected him to run away, after what happened with Astaroth. But he told me he wants to help, which I still can't wrap my head around. It's not like we're sleeping together, or he's getting extra credit. Helping me train is one thing, but risking his life to help me catch and kill a demon is a whole 'nother story.

Part of me is glad he's here—if it were just me, Rhys, and Mathers, that would be a bit awkward. But my relief is quickly dampened once Archer tells me that he wants to see his cousin Ethan. I just nod and smile, but inside, I'm panicking. Nothing good can come from being in the same room as two guys you've kissed, and one you're currently dating. Trust me on that.

Ophelia's presence saves this from being a sausage party, but she doesn't add much to the conversation. She ignores me for most of the journey, and in the car, she sits up front to navigate. I have to sit in the middle, squished between Archer and Rhys, because I have the shortest legs.

Mathers drives across the narrow bridge to Northeastern College. The college sits on a tall hill with rocky cliffs leading to a steep fall into the forest below. The main building is a renovated castle, which is what *all* magic schools should be like. I'm not sure what the architects who designed Southeastern were thinking.

When I get out of the car, I realize immediately that what I've packed won't be nearly warm enough. It's still chilly in New York, despite it being early spring.

Ophelia doesn't seem to mind, wearing shorts and a cropped T-shirt to show off her flat stomach. She must've just hit the tanning salon before we left. Maybe I should get their contact info.

"I'm going to find Ethan," Archer announces, shrugging a backpack over his shoulders. "We can meet up later."

"Sounds good. Ask him about Karina," Mathers instructs, putting a Southeastern ID badge over his head. "The rest of us should head to the main office. Any student records will be there."

"I'm going to find my brother," Ophelia says casually, taking her purse and walking off in the same direction as Archer.

I didn't know she had a sibling, but then again, I don't know much about her at all. She's never mentioned him, so maybe they aren't close. And why would he attend Northeastern instead of Southeastern, like her?

Well, I guess trueblood families are complicated.

Mathers brings Rhys and me to the main building, tapping his phone against a scanner on the door. Being a stone castle, I kind of figured the doors would have to be opened with spells. No such luck. Mathers needs to generate a personal QR code to access the elevator, too, proving Northeastern to be much more high-tech. While the school is secluded in the middle of nowhere, anyone could break in. It's much more difficult on an island like Kingsmarch—though Faith Abbott managed to, when she tried to kill me.

The interior is modern, with monochrome minimalist furniture from Ikea that doesn't quite match the stained-glass light fixtures or the tapestry-covered halls. No students hang around, which is strange since it's the middle of a weekday. Is everyone in class?

We ride the elevator up to the top floor. A receptionist sits at a large mahogany desk and greets us, her eyes ringed with dark circles and her hair clipped up in a messy French twist.

"Welcome to Northeastern College. What can I do for you?" she asks in a tired voice.

"We were lookin' for school records," Mathers explains, showing her his Southeastern ID badge. "Specifically, a list of all active students and faculty on campus. Perhaps recent alumni, as well."

"The records aren't accessible digitally. We're undergoing massive construction repairs from the last feral attack, and our computers have been destroyed with many files getting lost. Any records we have would be in the library archives, and they haven't been updated in a while, I don't think."

"You didn't save to the cloud?" Everything else is pretty advanced here.

But the receptionist narrows her eyes. "The files saved were corrupted. You'd think we'd have enough to deal with, given the monsters and all."

That's suspicious. "Is the school newspaper digital?"

"You can use a library computer if you'd like. Are you looking for something in particular?"

"Yes. A student named Karina. She might go by the moniker 'White Swan.' Do you know anyone like that?" Mathers asks.

"Karina?" She looks up in thought. "Doesn't ring a bell."

A lot of students must pass through here. Of course she wouldn't remember them all.

The library is in the main building as well, so we don't have to travel far. It's twice the size of Southeastern's library, and twice as cold thanks to the big hole in the wall. A feral attack, I assume. The tarp covering it does little to ease the chill in the air, and it's no surprise that the room is empty. There aren't even librarians around.

I log into one of the computers with my Southeastern credentials while Mathers and Rhys sit at the tables, going through the physical archives. The school paper's website is saved to the home screen, but it's pretty outdated. The articles are updated, but there's no search bar.

The first thirty articles detail numerous feral attacks and remembrance posts of dead students, painting a bleak picture of student life at Northeastern. No wonder there's hardly anyone on campus! The school is an epicenter for feral attacks.

I go through hundreds of articles, but none of them mention Karina. There are a few that mention *Katherine* Swan, but not Karina. Which is a good thing, since the Katherine mentioned is being accused of causing the feral increase in the first place.

The Wisdom Tree definitely said we'd find Karina here, but did he mean in the present? Or the past? I assumed the present, but since I can time travel, maybe I need to do that to find her.

After going through about 500 articles, I finish looking at the school website and log out with nothing to report. Rhys and Mathers look equally frustrated, overcome with boxes of books and records to pore over.

"There are too many records," Mathers mutters, looking up. "How did your search go?"

"I didn't find anything useful. Whoever this girl is, she doesn't seem to be very newsworthy." She's supposed to be special, but maybe she's not aware of it yet. She could just be a normal student, keeping her head down.

But if that's the case, can I really drag another innocent person into my mess? I need her, but she's a person with her own life. And, if the Wisdom Tree is right, she might be the only person in the realms with free will. If she chooses not to help, what can I do about it? Kidnap her and force her to come with me? I'd be no better than Neil, then.

I flip through one of the books on the table, going through a list of names and dorm assignments. The writing is small and in cursive, so I look up now and then to prevent eye strain. It takes hours to go through the books on the table, and by nightfall, my stomach grumbles and I'm ready to give up.

"I found it!" Mathers cries triumphantly, shoving a book

in my face. "Her dorm buildin' and room number are listed, too. It's from last year."

K. Swan.

"I saw this name before, too," I tell him. "Her name is Katherine, though—not Karina."

Mathers deflates. "It's the only lead we have. Do you think the school paper could be wrong?"

"Would they get something like her name wrong?" It seems like too simple of a mistake. Besides, they listed the name multiple times. "I think we all need a break. And I'm starving."

"Maybe you're right," Mathers says, disappointed.

We clean up the books and go to the cafeteria, messaging Archer and Ophelia to meet us. I haven't heard from either of them all day.

Archer waits for us at the door, sporting a fresh black eye and a split lip.

"What happened?" I sputter. "I thought you were going to see Ethan!"

"I saw Ethan," he replies darkly.

Ophelia doesn't look any more pleased than he does, crossing her arms. "He's touchy. He used to be easygoing."

I remember. "What did you get into a fight about?"

"It's not worth talking about," he mutters. "I'm hungry. Let's eat."

We walk into the cafeteria, which has a few more students, but not many. Maybe twenty students at most. There are multiple food stations, like at Southeastern, but only one is open. Worse, it's a salad bar.

"Did you find your brother?" I ask Ophelia as we sit down.

"No. He seems to have gone missing," she replies nonchalantly.

"Excuse me, did you just say *missing*?"

"Blake's always been a bit of a womanizing asshole. I figured he would get his ass kicked eventually," Archer says, "but no one's heard from him in weeks."

"His dorm is empty, too. Last time anyone saw him was during a hunt, I think," Ophelia adds, not particularly worried. "If he's dead, maybe my father will create a new heir."

That's cold. "I take it you don't have a good relationship with him, then?"

"My brother used to be alright. A little bratty, maybe, but not a bad person. In college, he changed completely. Now, he's just like my father," she sneers. "I don't care whether it was the ferals or the women he's wronged. Whatever happened to him was probably his own fault."

I turn to Archer. "I know you didn't have a great relationship with Ethan, but I didn't think he'd hit you."

"Well, he did," Archer says, looking pointedly at Rhys. "You have bad taste in men."

Rhys doesn't take the bait, thankfully. "Did you ask about Karina?"

"I didn't get a chance to. He hit me before that, and after getting a black eye, I didn't feel like continuing the conversation."

"I'll text him, then. Give me your phone," I say, stretching out my hand. "What? He's not going to give *me* a black eye."

Archer reluctantly hands over his phone, and I give Ethan a call. He doesn't pick up, so I call him until he does.

"What?" he spits into the phone. I can feel his anger through the line.

"Come to the cafeteria," I order. "I have questions for you. It's important. Life-or-death stuff."

"Who is this?"

"Mar. Come here right now." I hang up and hand the phone back to Archer.

"That wasn't very convincing," he says.

"He'll come." I hope. I didn't want to use my Marilyn voice—that would be a bit embarrassing, since I'm not in character. And I didn't want to remind Ethan that we kissed, not right in front of Rhys.

Sure enough, halfway through our "dinner" (if you can really call a pile of leaves dinner), Ethan enters. Tall and blonde, he and Archer certainly look related, but Ethan is a bit more rugged. Dangerous, even.

He spots our table and makes his way toward us, sitting down. "I don't want to continue our conversation."

"Neither do I," Archer snaps.

"We're just looking for information," I say cheerfully.

He squints at me. "You look familiar. Have we met before?"

"Nope. Not once," I lie. "Anyway, we're here on official school business. We're looking for someone named Karina. She goes to this school."

"I don't know most of the girls I hook up with, much less a random student," Ethan says flatly. I remember him being a lot friendlier last time.

"She might go by the moniker 'the White Swan,'" Mathers supplies. "Or 'the Butcher.'"

Ethan's eyes blaze with anger. "The White Swan? The Butcher?"

"You recognize those titles?"

"I've never heard of anyone calling her the White Swan, but I've heard of the Butcher. Everyone has," he snarls. "You're looking for that bitch Kitty Swan."

"Yes," I urge. "I mean, probably. Do you know where she is? Can you call her?"

"No," he refuses.

"This is important," Archer reiterates. "What happened before, I—"

"This isn't about that," Ethan says coldly. He looks me dead in the eyes, staring me down. "If you'd asked me last semester, I'd tell you to run in the opposite direction. Kitty Swan is bad news."

"I don't care." Even though I do. What does he mean by "bad news"? Is she uncooperative? Shit, if she doesn't want to help—

"Since you're asking me now," Ethan says, "then I'll tell you that it's pointless to look for her. Back in December, ferals attacked the school. There was a huge fight, and Kitty died."

Chapter Twenty-Nine

"You're better off without Kitty," Ethan continues, his frown deepening the more he thinks about her. "I know you're not supposed to speak ill of the dead, but she was a bitch. Good riddance to her. The reason why the ferals attacked is because of her. She reduced the school to its current state."

"She was shadowborn?" Mathers asks, leaning forward.

"A freak is what she was. Her powers were *unnatural*. She didn't belong here," he says, disgust clear on his face. Though his words are already harsh, I get the feeling that he's holding something back. He genuinely hates her. What could she have done to warrant that? "There was something wrong with her. Whenever she was around, it was like…a chill went up my spine and my stomach knotted. I felt sick just looking at her."

"What sort of abilities did she have?" I press. "What trueblood species did she descend from?"

"She wouldn't say. She wasn't ever upfront about how her powers worked," Ethan explains. "I always thought she was lying. She didn't seem like a trustworthy person. Or a reliable one. Her powers were greatly exaggerated. I guess her title suited her, in the end."

"What title?"

"They called her a monster," Ethan finishes dully. "The mortal monster."

"Breaking into the dorm of a dead girl is not what I signed up for," Archer whispers.

"Technically, you aren't breaking in. I am. You're just the lookout," I reply.

"You brought a lockpicking kit?" Rhys asks. "What did you think we would be doing?"

"I correctly guessed we'd need to do a little breaking and entering." The lock clicks and the door of the dark dormitory opens. There's hardly anyone in the building, making sneaking in easy. Mathers turned a blind eye to my plan, going back to the hotel to "lay down" while the rest of us storm the dorm.

The room is small, how I'd expect a dorm to be, with bunk beds on one side and two desks on the other. The beds are still unmade, like whoever was living here just left to get a coffee and never returned.

Archer waits outside. I never thought he'd be superstitious. Okay, so admittedly it is creepy going through a dead girl's things. But I need more unbiased information. Ethan wasn't much help, calling her a bitch and insulting her. Sure, it might be true, but he didn't seem to know any of the nitty gritty details I was looking for. For example, what the heck a mortal monster is.

I start with the desk, turning on the light. There are textbooks and a laptop here, which I plug in. A phone, too, is left precariously in one of the drawers. Rhys goes through the other desk, fiddling through the various books.

On the wall, no intact photos remain. Half of them have been torn down and ripped up, but by piecing one together, I can see why—the eyes are scratched out. On all of them. Ethan did say there was something wrong with her. Maybe she had issues and she scratched her own photos? Or maybe it was her roommate. I'm not entirely sure.

She doesn't keep any physical notebooks, and there are several letters of reprimand in the desk drawers addressed to "Katherine Swan." I'm still not entirely sure if this is the Karina we're looking for, but it's the only lead we have.

"Find anything?" I ask Rhys.

"Vandalized chemistry textbooks," he replies dryly, showing me a few of the pages. "What does this mean?"

I look closer at the words written in bold red ink. "Uh, those are racial slurs."

"It is written on quite a few of these books."

Weird.

Finally, Karina's phone turns on, and it begins buzzing with what must be thousands of messages and voicemails. I turn the sound off as all the texts come in, most from unknown numbers.

It looks like Ethan isn't the only person who disliked her. Karina had quite a few passionate haters. The phone is locked, but I can read the messages on the notification screen. They range from death threats to graphic images, sent repeatedly within minutes of each other. Now I understand why the phone was turned off. Regardless of what she allegedly did—I'm still having a difficult time believing this feral issue is completely her fault—no one deserves this level of harassment.

With this new context, I don't think she scratched herself out of the pictures. Someone else might have done it. It's clear the roommate was getting similar harassment, since the texts contain the same slurs written in the book.

Pushing away from the desk, I open the closet and find a backpack hanging on a hook. Opening it up, I stow the laptop, phone, and chargers inside. I can always come back, but for now, I think it's time to return to the hotel.

"I'M THINKING OF DOING SOMETHING STUPID AND reckless," I tell Rhys. "But I'm telling you now, so you can't get mad."

He steps into the hall of the hotel, closing the door behind him. He has to share a room with Archer, which would be amusing if I weren't seriously afraid they'll get into a fistfight. Not over me—I'm not so arrogant as to assume that. But they rub each other the wrong way, and after getting hit by his cousin, Archer isn't in the best mood.

"What stupid, reckless thing are you thinking of doing?" he inquires.

"Going back in time to save a dead girl, and hoping she'll be grateful enough to help us against the timekeepers."

"I thought you were incapable of saving someone from death." Rhys was an exception allowed by the timekeepers. I doubt there will be more of those.

"I should be. But she's the blind spot, right? The rules are different for her." If the timekeepers can't control her, then I should, in theory, be able to save her and bring her back to the present with me. If I'm wrong, I'm going to create a paradox and possibly destroy the timeline. But I'm hoping I'm *not* wrong.

Rhys nods. "And do you need help with this?"

"Moral support."

"You have it."

"Do you think it'll work?"

"That, I cannot say. Logically it should work, but you cannot change anything else. You must be careful," he warns. "The timekeepers were controlling the paradoxes created when I traveled to the future, but it will not be the same this time. You should avoid interacting with others if unnecessary, and take a weapon."

I show him the dagger in my boot. "I'm going to have to jump as close as I can to her death and save her right before. But she died in a feral attack. What if the feral follows me back?"

"You should leave the portal open. I will guard it, and should a feral come through, I can take care of it."

We head to the parking lot, where there's more space to open a rift. I clutch Karina's cell phone in my hand, hoping this will be enough to lead me to her. I don't know what she looks like, so I can't picture her image in my mind. All I can do is hope I land near her, and that she's still alive.

Finding a few spaces in the corner of the lot, Rhys watches as I cut my finger and swing the dagger down through the open air. I chant Karina's name in my head, picture a vague silhouette of her and hold the cell phone in my other hand. The rift tears open before me, but until I pass through the other side, I have no idea whether or not I've succeeded.

"Be careful," Rhys warns. "If you aren't out within fifteen minutes, I'm coming after you."

"Don't." I have no idea if it's safe for a non-time-keeper to time travel. I'm taking a major risk with Karina already—passing through the rift could have unforeseen consequences on her body. But since she's already dead in the present, it's not as much of a risk for her as it would be for Rhys. "I'll be back soon, I promise."

I step through the rift and find myself in a dark forest. The air is heavy with the smell of earth and decay. The trees loom overhead, casting long shadows on the ground. Dead ferals litter the ground, along with mangled shadowborn corpses. That's not promising.

But I think I'm in the right place. She died during a feral attack, and this certainly looks like a battlefield. Cries and growls sound off in the distance, so I try to quicken my pace as I search for her. The battle was fierce, judging by the dismembered body parts thrown around.

I walk aimlessly around the rift. She has to be here somewhere—if I did indeed make the rift correctly. I don't think she's one of the bodies on the ground, but I don't know for sure. I begin rolling over the intact ones, checking to see if they're dead or not. Most are.

When I near the mouth of a cave, one of the bodies is curled up on the ground. It's a girl, her skin pale as a ghost. Actually, she *does* resemble a ghost, with long black hair covering her face. It's almost not worth it to check if she's alive, but I do anyway, since she appears to be all in one piece.

The body is cold, though that could be the temperature in the Veil and not because she's dead. It doesn't look like she's breathing, and I'm about to leave her alone when I hear a faint sound coming from her mouth.

It feels weird to stare at her chest, but I do, and after a long moment, it moves slightly. She's not dead, but her hand is on the gates of heaven.

Could this be Karina? The dorm room photos showed a girl with dark hair, but didn't reveal much else. Cautiously, I take the girl's hand and press it over the phone's fingerprint scanner. The phone unlocks with a click.

It must be her. This is definitely *her* phone, and her finger unlocked it. Shoving it into my jeans pocket, I try to assess the damage. Her shirt clings to her clammy skin, damp with cold sweat and blood oozing from her stomach. That can't be a good sign. I should've brought a first-aid kit.

When I raise the fabric, the injury is worse than I feared —a gaping hole below her belly button releases an ungodly crimson flow of blood. How can someone survive this? Aside from the deep puncture in her abdomen, there don't seem to be any other injuries.

Pushing the hair off her face, her eyes stare blankly ahead, dark pits of nothingness. Her eerie expression looks like it belongs on a corpse, and in a few minutes, she might just turn into one.

Hurrying, I lift her in my arms and carry her toward the rift. She's silent the whole way, without so much as a whimper. Passing through, I stumble as I reach the parking lot.

Rhys' eyes widen as I return, laying Karina on the pavement. I pull the rift shut and fumble with the phone, dialing 911. The hospital isn't far away, and the operator reports that she'll send an ambulance immediately.

But when I bend down to check on her, Rhys shakes his head. "She is gone."

Her eyes are blank, almost glazed over, and her mouth hangs open slightly. Her entire body is still and her chest no longer rises and falls.

"She can't die," I mutter, taking out the dagger in my boot.

"Maria, what are you doing?"

"Saving her." And, by extension, myself.

Cutting into my hand, I pull up her shirt again and drip my blood into her wound. Smearing it around her stomach, I let our blood flow and mingle.

Nothing happens.

"She is dead," Rhys insists.

"Damn it, I know that!" I take a strand of long hair and tie it with my own, knotting the two pieces together and pressing it into her wound. This isn't a spell Jenna taught me—I'm just making it up as I go. But blood magic doesn't only need *blood* to work. Other body parts can magnify a spell.

Bringing someone back from the dead, not just reanimating a corpse, shouldn't be possible. But with enough blood to make me dizzy and dozens of tied hairs, Karina Swan finally begins to breathe again.

Chapter Thirty

Karina is still unconscious. She was stitched up at the hospital and transported back to Southeastern days ago, staying in the guest room of my dorm where we can keep an eye on her. Not that she's going anywhere anytime soon. Her body is healing, and the doctors say she could wake up any day now. When she does, I have a lot of questions for her.

But I'm trying not to stress about it too much, especially with finals around the corner. Time moves in the blink of an eye, and summer is almost here. With Isabelle, Tasha, and David settling into the house, it looks like we'll be staying on Kingsmarch Island until further notice.

Archer and Ophelia are staying, too, for the summer. No, I didn't ask them. Archer is avoiding Celeste, and Ophelia, as per usual, doesn't let me in on her thoughts. She's formed a friendship with Tasha, ever the diplomat, so it's not that Ophelia is incapable of friendship. Just…friendship with *me*. But I'm not taking it personally. Dr. Jones says that it's normal for some people to have no chemistry, and the best part about being in college is that you aren't forced to be friends with everyone.

I close the door to Karina's bedroom, trying not to make too much noise as I walk down the hall. Rhys officially moved out yesterday, taking all his things to a house across the island with Siraye and Theodas. I hear Lyari and Iacar will be joining us soon, as well.

David lives in Rhys' room, now. Isabelle is in the guest room, and Tasha is with me. Allegra is still in the hospital, but as soon as she recovers, she'll be living with us. I'm not going to kick her out of her own dorm, and with Neil MIA at the moment, she's got nowhere else to go.

Foley Hill is empty. Theodas sent men over there to confront Neil, only to find the plantation being demolished. I guess he's getting rid of the evidence. No one knows where he is at the moment.

There isn't much I can do about that until Karina wakes up and agrees to help me. I'm still figuring the last part out, but I saved her *life*. That's gotta mean something, right?

Isabelle is cooking something delicious and cheesy when I walk into the kitchen. She holds a wooden spoon dripping with Alfredo sauce in front of me. "Are you sure you don't want to stay for dinner?"

"I'll be back at midnight for leftovers," I promise. "I've got a date."

"Oooh," Tasha teases, skipping into the room. "A clandestine rendezvous?"

"I don't know what that means, but I don't like your tone."

She pinches my cheek. "You're so cute, Mar. Have fun."

"Not too much fun," Isabelle warns. "Text me if you're going to be out overnight, please."

My face reddens. That is the *last* conversation I want to have with her. "See you later."

I grab my bag and head outside. The sun nearly blinds me. Thanks to my yellow eyes, I can see in the dark, but I need sunglasses when I go out on bright days like this.

Most of the students are heading toward the library, on their way to cram for finals. I got fired on account of not showing up for work multiple times in a row. The head librarian didn't buy my excuse—that I was a little busy saving the world.

Isabelle can work from Kingsmarch, and Tasha finished the rest of her semester online. David's teachers were gracious enough to let him finish school online, too, though he's told me he already did all the work assigned and spends most days in his room. We haven't talked much since the whole kidnapping incident, and I get the distinct feeling he's avoiding me. Isabelle says to give him space.

The ferry is empty when I board. It's a short ride to the mainland—luckily I don't have to swim this time around.

From there, I order a car. When I arrive at the cemetery, the zombies Nic raised are back in the ground, and everything is back in order. Theodas worked his magic (and money) to put things where they belonged, it seems.

I walk past the rows of headstones until I see Luke's, stopping in front of it.

He was cremated, and his ashes were spread in the ocean. I know he's not really *here,* but I needed to see it anyway.

"I'm not good at goodbyes," I begin. "You know that."

I sit across from the stone, taking a Hostess cupcake out of its wrapper and setting it in the grass. He would prefer the cupcake to flowers.

"I didn't come to say goodbye. I don't know what's next. If there's an afterlife or not. If there are gods, or one God, or a big sentient meatball in the sky controlling us like puppets. Maybe you can't even hear me, wherever you are. And that's okay. I think most of the time, people do this—talk to inanimate objects—for themselves. For closure, or something.

"I don't want closure, though. I don't want this to be over, even if it's painful and I blame myself for the rest of my life. I feel like if I forgive myself for killing you, I can close the door on this whole incident and move on. How can I move on from *you*? How can I start a new chapter of my life without you in it?"

My voice breaks, and it takes me a moment to compose myself. I told myself I wouldn't cry.

"There's so much I want to say to you. *You*, not just a… headstone. But the most important thing is this: I love you. Always. And I'm sorry. The words aren't quite enough, I realize. I'm…so sorry. If there's a way to change it, I'll do it. I'll do anything." I take a deep, shaky breath. "I need to go now. But I'll be back. I promise."

I stand, dusting the grass off my legs and walking to the parking lot.

Rhys waits for me by his car, leaning against the sleek black coupe and staring at his new phone with a furrowed brow. He's still trying to figure out how to use it. Once he notices me, he puts the phone away. "Are you alright?"

"Not really," I answer honestly, climbing into the car. "How'd you know where I was?"

"I stopped by earlier. Tasha was under the impression we had a date. Once we figured out you lied, Isabelle said she thought you might be here," he explains, slipping into the driver's seat.

"I didn't technically lie," I say with a sniff. "I just needed some time alone."

Rhys starts the car and pulls out of the parking lot. We drive in silence for a few minutes before he speaks up again. "Do you want to talk about it?"

"Someday, when I get a better handle on figuring out my feelings. Right now, I want to think about happier things. For example, where you're planning on taking me."

"Back to the island. You have finals this week, and you should study."

I groan. That's *just* like him to be thinking about my grades. "I made you wait three years, Rhys. And now that we finally have a chance to be together, *alone*, you want to study?"

"I want *you* to study. After finals, I will reward you," he offers. "Reward you, or console you, depending on how you do."

"What kind of reward?"

"The kind no one can resist."

He declares it with such confidence, I'm admittedly intrigued. "Can you give me a hint?"

"I can give you more than that." He turns his signal on and pulls over to a small ice cream stand off the main road. "Should I give you a preview?"

"You were talking about ice cream?" I ask dumbly. Am I stupid, or is he making fun of me right now?

"Of course. It is one of the best modern inventions," he says confidently. "What did you think I was talking about?"

"Nothing," I squeak, too embarrassed to admit that I was thinking of something sexier than a frozen dessert.

But Rhys catches on quickly, his expression softening. "There is no need to rush into things. We can go at our own pace, and for now, simply enjoy one another's company."

I try not to feel too disappointed. He's probably right; I've always rushed into things when it came to romantic relationships. Maybe this time, taking things slow will give me a chance to get to know him better.

"Alright," I say finally, smiling at him. "Let's get cones and eat here. I don't want it to melt before we get back to campus."

Rhys nods, and we get out of the car, walking over to the ice cream stand. The sun is setting, casting a warm, golden light over everything. It's a peaceful moment, and for the first time in a while, I'm hopeful things are going to work out after all.

About the Author

Samantha Gao is a New Adult author with a passion for all things fantasy and paranormal romance. Her writing is fueled by her love for paranormal romance, and she enjoys creating compelling characters that readers can relate to and root for. After graduating from college with a degree in a completely different field, Sam decided to pursue her life-long dream of becoming a writer.

When she's not busy crafting stories that will transport readers to another world, Sam enjoys watching Asian dramas (with subtitles, of course!), listening to music, and indulging in her weakness for chocolate.

Sign up for her newsletter here: subscribepage.io/SamGao

facebook.com/imberhousepublishing
instagram.com/imberhouse
amazon.com/author/samgao
bookbub.com/profile/sam-gao
goodreads.com/samgao

Glossary

Astaroth: A powerful demon known for practicing blood magic. Astaroth was once imprisoned in a time prison, but due to certain events, was released. He has a cult following in the mortal realm.

Beastblood: Non-humanoid creatures originating in the Veil. They are often associated with animalistic traits and remain within the Veil, usually unable to get to the mortal realm on their own. Some examples of Beastbloods include lycans, chimera, and dragons.

Blood Magic: A forbidden type of magic that uses blood or other body parts to perform spells. Anyone, even humans, can use blood magic without many limitations. However, it is illegal to practice, and can be dangerous if used too often.

Elves: Truebloods with a distinctive appearance characterized by elongated ears. They possess the innate ability to distinguish truth from lies. In addition, Elves can wield elemental magic, enabling them to control and manipulate natural elements such as air, water, fire, or earth.

Fae: Winged truebloods who inhabit a continent alongside the elves, with whom they are in constant conflict. Fae are known for their trickery and manipulation, and they have elemental magic. They are physically incapable of lying and must always speak the truth, which often leads them to use clever wordplay and misdirection instead.

Infinity Hallway: A corridor used by time agents to travel through time. It contains multiple doorways, each leading to a different point in history or the future. However, the hallway can be dangerous to humans and may cause madness or disorientation to those who stay for extended periods.

Linguist's Orb: A fae device capable of instantly translating any language. It was created because Fae speak many different mutually unintelligible dialects.

Magician: The offspring of two shadowborn. Generally, magic weakens as the generations are mixed with human genes. Magicians can perform spells, although their abilities are not as potent as those of shadowborn. They cannot open rifts like their shadowborn counterparts.

Mortal Realm: The realm where humans and non-magical creatures live. It is separate from the Veil and lacks the magical properties and creatures that exist in other realms.

Psychic: The child of two magicians. While they cannot perform spells, psychics possess limited abilities and are born with a connection to the Veil. They are unable to open rifts, however.

Rift: A magical portal between realms that can be opened by swinging a blade through open air and concentrating on the desired destination. This ability comes easily to most shadowborn, and allows them to travel between the Veil and the mortal realm.

Ruby Council: The governing body of trueblood demons in the Veil. They hold significant political power and are responsible for maintaining order and enforcing laws among demonkind. One of the most powerful and wealthy members of the Ruby Council is Neil Abbott. As a member of the council, he wields a great deal of influence and is respected by many in the demon community.

Shadowborn: A hybrid born from the union of a human and a trueblood, possessing traits from both species. They are considered half-bloods and are often seen as shadows of their trueblood parents. Shadowborn have the ability to open rifts between the mortal realm and the Veil, and are stronger, faster, and more durable than humans. They can also perform magic, with some being born with rare and powerful abilities. Generally, the child of two shadowborn will either be a shadowborn or a magician.

Time Agent: A highly trained agent responsible for maintaining the timeline and ensuring that all events occur as they are supposed to. Time Agents use the Infinity Hallway, a special place that enables them to travel through time and space. They must be well-versed in historical events and possess advanced technology to prevent paradoxes and other disruptions to the timeline.

Timekeeper: A serpent-shaped beastblood capable of time travel. They are omniscient and can control the fates of others with bloodlines traced back to Truebloods.

Time Prison: A highly-secure supernatural prison designed to hold dangerous beings. It's a place where inmates are isolated from the rest of the world and thrown in a different time period, making it nearly impossible for them to escape.

Trueblood: A magical humanoid being originating from the Veil. Truebloods identify themselves with human-categorized monsters such as angels, demons, vampires, shifters, and more. They are not affiliated with any religion. Truebloods can only open rifts from the Veil to the mortal realm but cannot close a rift if they are in the mortal realm. They migrated to the mortal realm during the 1800s. Truebloods possess magical abilities and often hold positions of power and influence in the Veil and mortal realm.

Veil: A mystical realm imbued with magic that is filled with unpredictable and often dangerous forces. It is the birthplace of all truebloods and beastbloods, and it is separated from the mortal realm by a thin barrier that can be traversed by opening a rift.

Wisdom Tree: A sentient and omniscient tree located in the Veil, guarded by three fierce warriors. Although the tree was once thought to be a mere rumor, the grove in which it resides is not difficult to find. However, once you leave the grove, your memories of the tree are erased, making it difficult to recall any information or knowledge gained from the tree.

www.ingramcontent.com/pod-product-compliance
Lightning Source LLC
Chambersburg PA
CBHW020510260626
47156CB00006B/1956

* 9 7 8 1 7 3 7 6 9 3 0 7 9 *